The Laws of Kings

Jennifer Loren

BOOKS BY JENNIFER LOREN

The Devil's Eyes Series

THE DEVIL'S EYES

THE DEVIL'S REVENGE

THE DEVIL'S SON

THE DEVIL'S MASQUERADE: THE POISON

THE DEVIL'S MASQUERADE: THE REMEDY

The Finding Ava Series

FINDING AVA

RECKLESS

THE LONG ROAD

Short Story

THE HAND THAT HOLDS MINE

www.jenniferloren.com

ACKNOWLEDGEMENTS

Copyediting: Erinn Giblin, Yours Truly, The Editor

http://www.yourstrulytheeditor.com/

Cover Design: Hang Le, By Hang Le

http://byhangle.com/

DEDICATION

This is dedicated to Riley, my beautiful sweet boy, you captured my heart from the first moment I saw your malnourished body and sad eyes plead for help. You were at my feet through every word written, supporting me the best way you knew how. My heart is still broken from your loss, but my head is still full of the loving memories I shared with you. You think I saved you, but in reality you saved me.

I will love you forever, Riley.

6/2005 – 4/16/2014

CONTENTS

CHAPTER I

Dace

My name is Dace Colletto. My family is known, understood, and feared. We have maintained a growing family business since my great, great grandfather. We have had, at times, other families attempt to remove us from power, remove my father from his high position in the world, but somehow, he has always managed to maneuver us around attackers, around controversy, and around anyone that might be a threat. My mother and father lived a relatively perfect life; they had two boys, Michael and Ettore. Michael is a born leader. He can navigate through any problem without a single drop of sweat from his brow, and his charming demeanor is only outdone by a smile that instantly puts you at ease. Everybody loves Michael, especially my father who is sure he will be the next JFK. Ettore, the second oldest, is a man about business. A savvy mind, he is always ten steps in front of everyone; his charm, however, is lacking. Ettore has never been one to care about making friends, but then again, he is a Colletto, and *friends* will always come to join his *crew*. With Michael, my father's clear favorite, there was never a doubt the family name would live on and escalate to higher social circles. With Ettore, my father was assured the family business would only grow stronger. There wasn't much need for any more children after them, but they came anyway and so did the heartbreak.

It was many years after the first two children were born before my mother, Raya, became pregnant again. She was hoping for a daughter; nevertheless, she had two more boys. We were the babies of the family, and with Michael and Ettore already of age to begin being groomed for the family business, our father had little time to deal with Antony and me, so my brother and I rarely left my mother's side. Our day to day lives were seen to and approved exclusively by her. While my father trained Michael and Ettore for their futures, my mother allowed Antony and me to live a somewhat normal childhood, away from the drama and the fears that my father's business caused—for a while at least. I don't remember the exact moment things changed, but at some point, my parents became distant from each other, and my mother became more on edge. She rarely slept. She always seemed to be watching us and never, ever, let any of my father's men be alone with us.

Her worry escalated, and one day, she took Antony and me to see a so-called family friend, only we weren't allowed to talk about him to anyone. "Boys this is John Scott, a friend of mine. He is going to spend some time with you."

"Hi boys, how are you today?" John asked us both. Antony simply looked up at the man silently while I did nothing more than shrug. John laughed. I really didn't understand the reason for us knowing this man, but our visits with him became more frequent and more fun. John taught us a lot of things that most fathers would teach their sons; it was a nice change from being with our mother all the time. When I became old enough, or what John deemed old enough, he took me to the side and showed me how to shoot a gun. I could barely hold it, but I enjoyed learning how to shoot it. Antony and I spent a lot of time with John, and the more we got to know him, the more we looked forward to seeing him. Our father barely paid attention to us; all we had for a father figure was John. On occasion, our two older brothers would take the time to play with us, Michael mostly, but for some reason, he was more interested in acting like he owned us, like we were his children. I always assumed it was because Michael was already feeling the pressure of being the next in line and felt the need to watch over everything and everyone about the family. It was John, though, that made everything fun and easy, something we never felt with our own father. Dominic Colletto was stiff and always about business, except when we got sick. He would drop everything to sit at our bedsides. No matter how busy he was or how serious he was about business, he wasn't going to let anything happen to his family. Nothing and no one would ever harm his children—not as long as he was still breathing. I think Antony would purposely get sick or hurt because he knew Father would be there for him. Although, I admit, I savored the moments as well.

No matter how gentle my father might have been in those

moments, it was clear at an early age how powerful he was and what *Colletto* really meant to people. My first real understanding was when I was ten and allowed to join a little league baseball team. I was late joining and worried that the cleats I wanted might sell out. I begged my mother constantly until she finally gave in and took me to the store. When we got to the local sporting goods store, I ran in knowing the ones I wanted, but sure enough, only one pair was left, and another kid was already trying them on. My emotions sank, but my mother tried to reassure me as she hunted down the manager. "Sir, would you be able to get my son some cleats ordered and in before Wednesday?"

The manager huffed, "No, we might be able to get some in by next month though. Let me get your name and phone number, and I will be happy to let you know when they come in."

My mother glances my way before looking back at the busy man that was barely paying attention to anything outside of her breasts. "The name is Colletto, Raya," she said with a cock of her head and concentrated frown toward the man who suddenly began to shake uncontrollably.

"Oh! Oh, Mrs. Colletto, I am so sorry. We have new people here, and they must have not realized that it was our last pair and it was surely promised to you ahead of time. Let me get this situation fixed for you quickly." The man rushed over and grabbed the box of cleats from the other mother with a whisper I couldn't hear and a callous concern for her vocal complaints. "Here you go, Mrs. Colletto, all wrapped up and we will throw in some extra socks and a new glove too. How about that son?" he said, handing me the glove with a nervous laugh.

"That sounds great. How much?" my mother asked.

"Oh no charge, our mistake. We shouldn't be rewarded for such stupidity."

"Maybe, but a Colletto never seeks handouts and will always pay their debts in full. We don't like to owe anyone favors." She took out her wallet, and the man apologized profusely as he rang up our purchases. As we walked out with my new desired cleats, I only glanced at the crying boy the shoes were taken from. I didn't fully understand why we were given such special treatment, but I understood the name Colletto means something to people. It means instant acknowledgment followed by respect—unwavering respect.

I am a Colletto, and even at ten, I was acknowledged and most assuredly respected.

I am not ten anymore, but I am still a Colletto. I have done my best to go to a place where my name means nothing. I lost interest in being a Colletto a long time ago, and except for my brother, Antony, my desire to separate myself from my family only grows with each passing day. I have been away from my so called home since my mother was killed. Antony and I were shipped off to our aunt's house soon after her death. Aunt Terri, as she was called, wasn't much of a mother. She despised children and only took us in because my father continuously sent money for our care, most of which she used for her own benefit. She was strict and didn't hold back on her punishments, except when Michael would come to check on us and then she was Mary-Fucking-Poppins. She had to act perfect after all of our complaining to our father about her; she had to prove we were little liars who were simply homesick. Antony and I hated her and begged to come home, but it was thought that we were better off there than in constant danger at home, so we were stuck with "Aunt Terrier". She sounded like a barking Yorkshire terrier whenever she was upset about something, so we, lovingly, named her as such. As I grew older, I would mock her dog like sound to piss her off. There was never a reason to stick around, and as soon as I was able to go to college, I moved out and took my little brother with me so neither of us would have to endure the witch any longer. Antony wanted to return to our father, but I wouldn't let him. He didn't want us when we needed him, so why should we ever go back there? I couldn't come up with one good reason, but Antony always tried to. I managed to put him off and redirect him for quite a while, but recently, he decided to try and reconnect with our father and older brothers. I have no idea why he picked now of all times to confess his secret. I love Antony, but his timing has never been very good. He misses our mother. Not that I don't, but Antony was devastated when she died and even more so by the way it happened. I have done my best to be at his side and help him get past it. The only problem with that is I am not so sure I have gotten past it myself.

That night changed me. It changed my life and the way I view family, especially *my* family.

That night, I slipped past my guard like I learned early on how to do, and Antony did the same after picking up on my techniques. We spent the night doing whatever we cared to do, which wasn't much of anything. We simply wanted to break free from our watchers. It happened once in a while when things would tense up around the house. Guard numbers would pick up around my father and two older brothers while Antony and I would be restricted to the grounds. We were young and didn't fully understand the ramifications of our actions. Outside of our mother and John, no one seemed to care about us anyway. It wasn't very hard to sneak out; when you're small, people overlook you. We would slip out the estate gates and into our favorite movie theatre, which just so happened to be down the street. When we grew tired, we would easily slink back through the security gates and wait for our mother to go to her room to read before sneaking into the house and up to bed. It was usually an uneventful process, but it wasn't that night. No, that night, instead of quietly slipping into her comfortable chair with her favorite book, in front of the fire, our mother was actually out of the house, frantically searching for us with minimal guards to protect her.

The lights are all still on within the main house, and our mother's bedroom light is still off.

"She should be going to her room by now. She never stays up this late. Do you think she is waiting up for Father?" Antony asks as we crouch down behind some bushes, waiting for guards to look the other way so we can get into the house undetected. The bastards keep walking past us and forcing us deeper into the cover of shrubbery. I keep pushing Antony back out of the way, knowing if either of us get caught, Father will have our heads and our guards

too, whom we have become fond of and would hate to see replaced with someone new. The house guards walk past us again, patrolling the area anxiously as they talk to each other. "Dace, what are we going to do?" Antony asks.

I turn to him and press my finger to my lip. "Shhh," I whisper softly. "Something is going on, and I don't think we want to get in the middle of it." As a guard comes near us again, he stops and listens, and I just know we have been caught. A light breeze blows through and chills the air, seeming to freeze my eyes wide open as the curious guard has his throat slit and is thrown to the ground in front of us. Masked men come running in from everywhere. As blood runs between our feet, we hear more scuffling develop into screams as our mother is dragged past us by her arms and one of her guards by a rope, tied around his neck.

"The police will be coming soon. The panic alarm was sent out," Tyson, my mother's guard, yells out.

"We are the police, you dead fuck," the man says, kicking Tyson in the head with his fancy, black, steel-toed boot. A deep, bloody wound appears on Tyson's face, the imprint of a skull and crossbones etched into his skin.

I grip Antony's hand as we both wait breathlessly, wondering if we are next. The screams become more intense, more excruciating to listen to. Antony pleads silently with me for us to run, but I am afraid we will be seen, and I have to protect him. I have to protect my brother and hope that my mother can somehow survive until our father can save her.

The wind blows against my face and pushes the curling ends of my hair into my eye as my mother pleads for her guard's life, but it isn't him that they want. "You want his life to be spared, then tell us where your two little ones are?" the man grinds out with a snarky laugh. There is a long pause. "It's you and your guards or your children, which will it be? Don't worry, we don't want to hurt them. We only want to ask them a question."

A rowdy brawl develops ... "Boys run, RUN!" my mother screams. "No!" she yells once before her tormenting cries are muffled. The sounds are confusing but still float through the air, forming a blade of agony that penetrates into my ears, shaking my body into a painful fear.

All I can do is hold my hand over my brother's mouth and try to calm his tears through my own fears. I don't even realize my own tears until my brother presses his hands to my face and wipes them away. My hands are trembling, and my head is spinning as I desperately try to block out the images *forming in my head. When the silence finally blows through, my stiff limbs are too heavy to move. The silence finally gives way to a door flapping in the wind and dogs barking in the distance. Can I move? I am not even sure that matters. The real question is, should I? With a slight twitch, I twist my head to one side to look around us before motioning for my brother to stay put. Pushing the lifeless body off our feet, I creep out of our cover and around the back of the house to the open, bloody door. I take a step inside and breathe. I take one more and breathe again. My next step creaks, and I swallow hard. Sliding to the edge of the opening of the next room, I wait and listen. Nothing. I twist my body carefully inside the room with my eyes facing the wall and slowly turn them to the depths of the destruction and to the bloody massacre that once was my mother.*

"Momma!" Antony screams out suddenly from behind me.

Before I can get a hold of him, he alerts the one man that stayed behind. The rapid footsteps coming for us only give me a few seconds to push my brother out of the way and dive towards the nearby table that holds one of my father's guns. I wait as the man rounds the corner with wild eyes ... and shoot.

It was hours later when I come back to reality. "Dace, give me the gun." Michael says to me as he pries the gun from my hand. "You're okay. You and Antony are both okay. Don't worry, Father is taking care of everything. We are going to get you and Antony out of here and somewhere safe. Okay?" I nod silently. My tall, older brother sighs and picks me up into his arms and wraps a blanket around me. As he carries me out of the house, I catch sight of my father buried deep into the palms of his hands over my mother's blood-soaked body.

Antony and I were carted off to Aunt Terri's house that night and left there as if we never existed. After I finished college, my father wanted me to go to work for a friend of his in London. I, wanting to defy my father anyway I could, demanded to find my own way, without my family's influence. My father didn't like it one bit, but I didn't give him a choice.

Antony was in college and enjoying life with new friends, so I packed a small bag and left on the first plane out. It didn't matter where it took me; anywhere was better than where I was supposed to be, or where he thought I should be. Since that first country, that first small town I stopped in, I haven't told anyone my last name. Hell, the places I've been, they didn't give a damn who I was. I was simply Dace, the smartass fuck that floated from one place to the next like a lost gypsy.

CHAPTER 2

Dace

Gypsy. That's the nickname people have given me because when they ask where I am from, I give them a random list of nowhere places. I grew my hair out and rarely shave. I have been anything and everything but a Colletto. It's easy to convince strangers that you're from nowhere in particular. It's impossible, however, to convince yourself, but I'll be damned if I won't keep trying.

Sitting in a bar with others who don't give a damn, I try to forget and look forward to filling my head with new memories to replace the old. This bar is a rundown place with what I wouldn't call the most upstanding patrons, but no one is making any trouble, and everyone is quiet, nearly silent actually. It's odd. I try to write it off and concentrate on looking straight ahead and ignoring all that is going on around me, but it's difficult. I have spent every day since my mother's death waiting for someone to come for me, so I have grown used to searching the shadows for trouble. *Let it go, Dace.* No matter how hard I try, I can't help but notice something odd about a man off in the corner. He makes eye contact with four other men surrounding the bar. All five men eye one man gambling at a nearby table. I wait until the stranger looks my way, and I instantly look towards the supposed leader of the group and back down at my drink. The stranger in trouble suddenly gets up and moves towards the broken down restrooms in the back of the bar. All of the men motion towards each other and start to follow the stranger. I am not sure how to help the clearly outnumbered man, but I devise a plan to try and even out the numbers a little.

Grabbing a bottle, I fling the alcohol across the floor, swipe a match against the counter, and toss it, lighting up a path in front of the back door and blocking the men from pursuing the strange gambler. I throw some money down on the counter and rush out of the bar to the back alley to see the stranger battling a man with a gun. When the gun gets knocked to the ground and kicked in my direction, I stare at it until a glimmer of light flashes across my eyes. I look up and spot the knife being pulled on the gambling stranger and take a quick step towards the gun. I grab it and shoot, sending a bullet through the hand and into the handle of the knife, ending the fight and giving me the opportunity to move on. I wipe the gun down and toss it in the trash before heading down the road.

The streets in this small city are lively, even this early into the morning. Whores and their Johns line the streets with their pimps hiding in the shadows, counting their money, just like any other city. The sound of water dripping down the rickety drain pipes is the only other sound you hear until the screams from a small doorway echo out into the street. The door slams open, and two men carry another out into the street and shoot him dead with his wife screaming in the background. I watch the wife's agony escalate into an uncontrollable rage. She rushes at the men that killed her husband with intent on justice, but her efforts are in vain. Out of the corner of my eye, I catch sight of a young girl crying for her mother, and I react without thinking. I go after them and pull the woman to safety before handling the two men best I can. I assume the police will come at some point. The commotion has to have alerted enough people to be of concern. However, outside of a single police car driving by down the street, no local police come anywhere near the fight. I am handling my own until a car pulls up and more attackers jump out to help their friends. I glance back as the lady I saved grabs her child, runs inside, and locks the door and windows behind her. *I guess it would be stupid to assume she is calling for help in there.* I look at the now ten men coming at me and take one step back and smile wide. "Oh hell! You're not Jack and Charlie, my bad. What do you say we just call this a case of mistaken identity and we go have a beer?" Their snarling figures don't seem to be a positive response. "I'll buy?" I ask with an optimistic tone but quickly realize running seems to be the better choice for me. I take off running from the angry crew and into another group of men. "Oh fucking shit." I stop dead in my tracks as the new group come at me with guns and promptly walk around my stiff posture and shoot the men at my back.

"Get in the car, Gypsy. We don't have all day," the gambling stranger I saved earlier says to me. I follow the men into a car and wonder where the hell they are taking me. "Never seen anyone get into so much trouble so quickly."

"You know I don't have that much money," I say, causing them all to laugh. "Actually, if you wouldn't mind, I would like to go to my hotel and get my stuff and get the fuck out of this city …"

"Don't worry about your shit, Gypsy. We already got it; you aren't going back there. You're a wanted man now." I am pushed out of the car and into a building where a well-armed group await me. I stop breathing for a second when I get a hard smack to my back, forcing the air from my lungs. "You can stop shaking now, Gypsy. You're amongst friends here. By the way, my name is Peter."

"Friends?" I ask, looking around for any face that might seem familiar other than the one.

"Yeah, that is if you want them? Otherwise, you're free to go on your own. I wouldn't recommend it, but we aren't going to stop you," Peter says.

"If I go …" I start to ask and am met with laughter before I can finish.

"Oh those men you were dealing with before will have the so-called 'law' here to arrest you, and then they will torture you until you pass out, and then they will wake you and torture you some more, and then hang you in the street as a reminder to not challenge the government here."

"And if I stay?"

"After knowing that, does it matter what happens if you stay?"

"Not really," I admit.

"Well, I'll tell you anyway. If you stay, then that's when the fun begins. We could use a guy like you to help us. We are preparing to help the locals take down their government and reinstate the old governing system."

"You work for the people?"

"We work for who we see fit."

"And who has the money to pay us!" a guy yells from the back of the room.

Peter laughs, "Well… yeah that helps."

"You're guns for hire?" I ask, knowing of men like these.

Peter, the tall rugged-looking fuck, stands and bows to me like a prince before introducing the rest of the men and some women in the room, all of which have their own look about them. You would never guess they all work in the same crew, yet each looks intimidating in his or her own way. "We are KRT, and we are at your service … for the right price. We are just like you, Gypsy— lost souls banning together to look out for the rest of the world in need."

"For the right price," I remind him.

"Well, we have to eat too."

"And drink!" someone yells out with laughter following.

"And Fuck!" another yells out from the back as the roar of laughter takes over the room.

Peter gets up and puts his arm around my shoulders. "Don't worry, Gypsy. We will teach you everything you need to know. Come on, join us. What else do you have to do? We're a family here …" he says, and I turn to look him over and the rest of the room. *Maybe it's about time I find my purpose in this world.*

"I guess I'm home," I say, receiving a welcome celebration like I have never seen.

At the end, they show me to my new room where I find all my things that they somehow managed to set up for me while others poured tequila down my throat. It's like they had this planned before they knew me. The bed is not the nicest in the world, but right now, I don't care. Swaying with the room around me, I begin trying to remove my clothes when a woman comes through the door.

The dark haired beauty shuts the door behind herself and smiles as she removes all of her clothes. "The better the fighter, the better in bed they are, so I'm curious … how good of a fighter are you?" She drops to her knees, releasing my pants to the floor, and finds my cock with no problem. I gasp as her tongue swirls the tip, but when a flash of metal catches my eye, I reach down and grab hold of her by the neck, pinning her down and releasing the knife she pulled from her pile of clothes. She lies underneath me, smiling.

"Who the fuck are you? What do you want? I don't have anything to do with my family anymore, so there is no need to come after me," I say, sobering up quickly.

"I don't know who your family is. I only wanted to see if you're as good of a rebel as Peter thinks you are."

"How would he know? I just met him today."

She laughs. "We have been following you for two weeks. We have watched you handle yourself a few times. What is really amazing is how alert you are, even when intoxicated. Who are you really? Ex-military, Navy Seal …" She releases one of her legs and fondles my balls with her foot and a desiring moan. "Or a man on the run?"

"None of your damn business, Puta," I say, grabbing her leg and pinning it back to her side.

"I'm Portuguese, not Spanish, and the name is Leandra … Babaca," she hisses back at me.

I look over the nude woman with my cock poking her in the stomach and don't bother saying another word. I lean down and bite her lip and lean back with a smile. "Did you come in here to test my fighting skills or did you want a fuck?" She grabs hold of me and spins me back on to the bed.

"Oh, I want to fuck," she says, jumping on me like she has been picturing doing so since she first saw me. The sex is dirty, emotionless, but enjoyable.

When I wake up the next day, my head is pounding. "Good morning, Gypsy. You better get up before the boys come in here to get you," Leandra says, climbing out of my bed still completely nude. "If you're hungry, there is plenty of food in the kitchen."

"You're not going to take care of my morning erection for me?" I ask, expecting to get what I want.

"Don't get cocky. You were good entertainment for the night, but don't expect to always get it from me," she says, dressing back into her black ninja gear and walking out.

The crew flowing in after her doesn't give me a chance to get dressed before they pick me up and carry me into a big empty warehouse.

"Nice of you to join us for training, Gypsy. Although, the outfit may not be best for what you are about to go through," Peter says, fighting a smile.

"I am happy to go back and change if you will allow me to," I say, adjusting my balls proudly for everyone.

"No time for that, and besides, you never know when you are going to be in a battle. Go!" he says, and suddenly, I am fighting with men from all sides. The beating I take first reminds me to always protect myself from every possible side, especially underneath. Thankfully, once I'm lying on the ground wreathing in pain, they stop the battle and allow me to get dressed before showing me techniques that I have never known before. "You have the awareness, Gypsy, and a good hand for your gun, but you have a lot to learn about fighting without weapons."

My intense training began that day and continued from one city to another. The group moves in, does what is needed, collects, and moves on to the next. With each new place, I learn a new skill and perfect the ones I already have. My ability to be aware of everything around me has heightened to the point that I have learned to sneak in and out of the most secure places with ease. There are no locks I can't get through, no guards I can't get past, and thanks to my technology training, there are no alarm systems I can't crack. I have become so good that my new friends changed my nickname from Gypsy to Ghost.

CHAPTER 3

Dace

We have a small break in between projects so Peter asks me, along with Leandra and Nate, to go with him on a fact finding mission about a possible new job. There is a possibility that the small group of us can handle this job on our own and quickly. A Mexican businessman has been stealing money from accounts of respectable small business owners. We have been asked to secure the accounts and get their money back. When we arrive, we are met by a woman named Nidia. The moment I lay eyes on the tall, angelic beauty, I have to remind myself we are here to work.

My wide smile must have given away my thoughts because Peter elbows me in the side. "Keep it in your pants, Ghost. We don't have time for your love adventures this trip."

Nidia guides us to an SUV that is waiting in a well-concealed area with what looks to be hired guns. An awkward exchange of looks are passed from Peter, to me, to Leandra, and finally to Nate. "I am getting the feeling this job isn't quite what we were told," I whisper to Peter.

"Please get in," Nidia says.

Peter holds us all back. "I don't think so. First, you talk to us about what you want."

"Welcome!" An older man jumps out of the van with open arms and a questionable smile. He shakes each of our hands with a vibrating excitement. "I am so happy to have you here. My name is Mateo Luis."

"Mateo, it's nice to meet you, but the situation you described doesn't seem to fit the picture we are getting here," Peter says with a guarded stance.

"Yes," Mateo says, taking Nidia's hand. "I was afraid you might not come if we told you everything." I roll my eyes, knowing

Peter is going to ask us to turnaround any second. "Please, this is my daughter, Nidia. She is all I have right now. Her sister was taken by a man named Vincent Guzman; he is the one that has been stealing from us, from everyone in our small town. A year ago, my wife was taken by the same man." The man looks down with a mournful expression. "She was returned after being raped and so severely beaten that she died only a few days later."

"Why? Why would he do this to you?" Peter asks.

"I know how to do things that most don't. I am a chemist, and I have the ability to make new drugs to sell that can be undetected when transporting across borders. He is trying to force me to do what I don't want to. I was hoping you could help me get my daughter back so we can leave here and get away from this man. We don't live here. We live in Canada now. We only came back for my father's funeral. Before we could return home, he showed up, threatened me to work for him, and we have been trying to leave ever since, but every time we try … I cannot leave my daughter —she is only fifteen. Please help me get my daughter back; that is all I ask from you." You can feel the man's heartbreak. It weighs heavy on us all, but this is not what we do. I am pretty sure Peter will deny him. For the safety of his crew, he must. He would never put any of us at risk for the sake of one, and he certainly wouldn't put us in the middle of unknown situation.

"I'll help you," I say on my own.

Leandra steps forward with a heavy sigh. "I'll help you, too."

Nate throws his hands up. "What the hell. We're here, aren't we? Might as well accomplish something."

I look back at Peter as he shakes his head at me. "Fine, we will check it out, but I can't make any promises."

Guzman's estate is more than just an estate, it is a military compound. Peter and I safely observe the comings and goings around the compound, and nothing makes us feel any better about the operation we are expected to perform.

"I don't know Ghost. This looks like a venture we should walk away from."

"Probably." I think on it again. "We definitely should walk away."

Peter punches the car and kicks the tires a few times, cursing loudly. "I hate being a nice guy, and if we get killed doing this, so help me I will make sure you live a miserable afterlife," he says, pointing at me.

I nod with a smile. "I am going to need to access some pretty heavy security systems to be able to see in there."

"There is a military base nearby. We can piggyback their system and dive in."

With the help of some old military connections we are able to look in on Guzman's house and get the full layout. We identify the heavily secured areas and where Mateo's daughter is being held. Nate and Leandra hook in some surveillance that gives us an opportunity to listen in on our target. We go through our plans over and over and then over again. I begin to think we are all trying to find a reason that this can't be done so we can feel better about walking away, but we know we can do this, and what's worse? We crave the challenge.

I get ready for bed by pacing. "Do you need a release?" Leandra asks. "It might be our last chance before we die."

"Is that supposed to be a joke because it's not funny," I say back to her.

She cozies up to me with a purr. "Come on, Dace. We're all

tense." One look into her eyes and I know she won't let it go until I give in to her. I grab the back of her head and pull her in, taking hold of her lips and undoing my belt at the same time. I boldly go in and give her everything she wants. Leandra twists into positions I wouldn't think possible as she tries desperately to hold onto me and keep me fucking her. When she finally lets go and gives me room to breathe, I explode and crash onto the bed next to her, feeling the tension release just as she promised it would.

Leandra, as always, falls asleep almost immediately. I, however, rarely can get to sleep so easily. I have to pace and wear myself out even more. Exhausted. I have to be as exhausted as I can be, then I will be able to sleep and maybe even without waking until morning. I walk outside to stare at the stars, thinking of making a wish upon the shooting star that flies by, but what I want can't be done now. I want my mother back. I want to feel her warmth, to feel the safety I felt within her arms again, comfort that will help me sleep soundly again.

"Can you not sleep?" Nidia asks as she steps outside.

"I am not much of a sleeper."

"Why is that?" she asks, cocking her head sweetly to one side and pacing towards me with one long step in front of the other.

"It's hard to explain. Why are you up?"

"I'm nervous. I'm afraid for my sister, for my father, and for myself even. I am afraid of what will happen if you don't succeed," Nidia confesses with tears suddenly in her eyes. I could imagine men from everywhere desiring this woman. I don't want to think about what Guzman would do to her if he ever got her. I am sure there is a reason he hasn't taken her yet, but I don't know what that reason is. I surprise myself and open my arms up to her. She falls right within them. She's soft and comforting to be around. "Please stay with me. I don't want to be alone tonight. I want to feel protected ... by you." She pulls me inside and tries to pull me into her bedroom, but I hold off, knowing this is not something I should do, not right now and not with her. "Let's just sit out here, and I will stay up with you all night if you want?"

She looks up at me in shock but nods with a sweet smile. It's nice, holding her. She needs me, and she's delicate, maybe a little too delicate. I fear for her. I don't know if she is strong enough to do what she needs to tomorrow. If we can't get out, she needs to run and leave here the fastest and best way possible. We have them set to leave on the first plane available; all they need to do is run and not look back. Nidia falls asleep in my arms while I enjoy watching her sleep peacefully. I manage a few hours of sleep before morning but not much more before Peter comes in and grunts at the sight of us curled up together.

"As long as I live, I will never understand the draw you have on women, but I will especially never understand the restraint you have."

"You were the one that warned me," I remind him.

"Yeah, but I didn't think you would listen," he says, shaking his head. "Idiot."

Everything is ready to go, and I arm myself with everything possible without weighing myself down too much. I volunteered to go in and get the girl while everyone else covers for me. We have a plan of sneaking in with the change of the guards. The shift change happens at a slow pace, which enables us to walk in casually and blend in with the many faces that this man has watching over him. I get so far and side step to a corner where there is a side door with an alarm on it. It's nothing I can't handle, but once in, I have to take a deep breath and steady my rapidly beating heart. I have never been on a mission where I feared death before, but suddenly, I feel something tugging at me to leave. I shake it off and move forward, watching every movement that crosses me. I only have to go by two doors to get to the room I need. I step by the first and immediately have someone walk out behind me. Before he can fully comprehend that there is a stranger in the house, I swing my elbow into his throat, silencing him. A quick slam of his head into my knee and he is out cold. I slide his body into a closet and move forward. I make it to the room and ease in, finding two men sitting and watching the multiple security cameras.

They turn around and stare at me while I try to keep the bill of my cap pulled down low. "¿Qué desea?" one asks, standing up and starting to take a defensive stance. "¿Qué desea?" he yells at me while I verify the surroundings and plan my next move.

A quick flick of my wrist and I grab my gun, shooting them both silent. The silencer thankfully works and allows me time to adjust the system and hopefully give us enough time to get away.

The next part that should be the easy part, is actually going to be the hard part. The girl is heavily guarded on the outside, so I take a different route. Going into the room next door, I cut a hole through the wall as quietly as possible. It's time consuming, way more than I would have liked it to be, but once through, I find the girl crumpled in a corner, bloody and disturbingly damaged. She can barely look up at me, forget walking. I pick her up and hold her against my chest, and she instantly lays her weak head on my shoulder. I have to maneuver her through the hole in the wall and then climb through myself. So far, so good—a little too good. Checking outside the window, I realize there is no way we can make it to where we need to be from this part of the house. I glance out the door and watch, waiting for an opportune moment to move. Running, that's my only choice right now. With the girl slumped over my shoulder, I do just that and run right into five armed guards. Diving behind a wall, I avoid the onslaught of bullets and alert Leandra to my whereabouts, but there isn't much they can do from the outside. I have to get out. Putting the girl down, I check the men trying to sneak up on me and shoot two. A third starts firing back at me, and I use the body of his friend to shield me before throwing the corpse on him. They fall to the floor, and I take my knife from my ankle and stab him in the neck. The other two come after me rapidly. Rolling to my side, I fire at them both and hold them off while I prepare a small distraction. Grabbing a nearby trashcan, I light it up and toss it in their corner, setting everything around them on fire. The distraction allows me enough time to get the girl out the window and meet up with my friends. I start to take a breath, but before I can, Guzman comes after us with a group of ten men with machine guns.

"Leave the girl and you can leave without trouble," he says, surprisingly in English. *He knew we were here.* My friends cover me while I run with the girl to our getaway car where Nidia awaits. She refused to stay behind. The moment I approach, she runs to her sister and takes hold of her. I rush back around and fight off the men coming after us when more come up from behind, and then from the left side, and then from the right.

"Get out of here, Nidia! Take the car and go! Go straight to the airport. Do not go home!" I scream at her while still fighting and trying to save myself. They get away, but I am forced to my knees and dragged to a secure room with my friends who, thankfully, are all still alive—for now.

"They're going to burn us alive in the town center," Peter says.

Leandra stands up, shaking her head with an attitude. "They are going to have to kill me before I get there because I am going to fight with everything I have."

I turn to them all and smile. "I discovered something while I was in the security room."

Peter starts to smile. "You better not be fucking with us," he says.

I shake my head and turn towards the sophisticated electrical system holding us in, a system I happened to have learned has a glitch. Peter catches on to my unspoken discovery and pulls a small, hidden knife from his ankle, sliding it over to me. I open up the wiring box and twist two of the wires together, confusing the system. I receive a small electrical shock touching the lock, but it doesn't deny me what I want. The lock releases, and I open the door, allowing us to sneak out a side exit and only take out two guards in the process. We steal their guns and flee.

We are all smiles on our way back, joking about each other's panicked expressions and thoughts of how we would say goodbye before our last few minutes alive. When we pull up to the safe house, our celebratory moods quickly turn more somber. Most of the place is tossed, and we find the young sister torn into pieces, left out for the animals to feed off of. Nidia is gone and so is her father, but his legs remain behind. They were supposed to run straight for the airport, not come back here. Guzman's men followed them, making it easy to take them and do what they wanted, without even a threat of witnesses. We may have technically accomplished our mission, but it was all for nothing.

Peter grabs my arm and pulls me back to the car. "We gotta go. Now!"

The flight back was silent, and we never discussed the mission again. I never wanted to think of it again, but for some reason it reminded me of my mother and the person that murdered her. The man with the engraved skull and crossbones on the steel of his boots, has never been found, but I have never forgotten him. I have been longing for the day that my father finds him, but I am beginning to think that day is never coming, not without my assistance at least.

CHAPTER 4

Dace

Lurking in the shadows, I wait for my moment and then slip through a slow closing door before making my way up a back stairway to the locked room. The room holds the computer system I need, to release the locks and shutdown the alarm system to the prison that holds the political leaders we are trying to put back in power. A few computer ruses here and there and ...*bam*, I'm in.

"Hey, how's it going? We are getting a little anxious over here." Peter's voice comes through my ear piece with an anxious tone.

"I'm in. Just give me a minute to crack this system."

"A whole minute? Damn you're getting old," he barks.

"Ha ha, I told you it was my birthday today only because you threatened to tell me the details about your night with Gina." I cringe, considering the possible images.

"Ahh... Gina. So first, she slid that tight fitting sweater off and released that dark, dingy, and tattered bra, and then ... ah damn those babies just fell to the floor and ..."

"Oh fuck! I'm hurrying! I'm hurrying!"

"Make it faster before I get to what else of hers fell to the floor when it was released."

"Done! Done! I'm done," I exclaim, stopping his story before it goes on any further.

"Thanks, and we are in. See you later."

I smile, rolling back in the chair with a few fist pumps in the air. My celebration is short lived though. Two guards come by before I can get out. Looking around the room, I quickly realize there are no windows and no way out of here other than the way I came in. I stand ready as they come in yelling at me. I don't speak the language, but I am pretty sure they are not happy to see me.

"Hey guys, I was just looking for the bathroom." They don't seem to believe me as they both come at me with intimidating knives. I dodge one as he flies over my right shoulder, but I take a hit on the left from the other. A quick dive to the floor and I cut his legs out from under him, forcing his head into the wall and knocking him out. Two hands wrap around my neck and drag me off the floor until I run up the wall and reverse the fuck's hold on me and drag him back down to the floor. A swift twist and slam of his body and he's out cold. "Nice to meet you gentlemen, but I have some birthday candles to blow out," I say, slipping out the door and back out to the alleyway where I run into Leandra. "What are you doing here?"

"Making sure you made it out okay," she says with her usual annoying attitude.

"I can take care of myself."

"Uh-huh. If it hadn't of been for me then you would have had more than two on your ass."

I look off to my side and notice a few bodies pushed off into the dark corner. "I could have handled that."

"Oh, you thought I meant them? No, I meant them …" she says, stopping me before we step out onto the street full of the army we are trying to take down. "Oh shit! What are they doing here?"

"Someone must have tipped them off. Lucky for you, I have found another way out of here. Follow me."

I follow her into a building and down, underground, into some dark tunnels. I pay attention to everything around us while she seems to think it's time to play with me. Grabbing my ass and rubbing the bulge in my pants, she moans as if she is having an orgasm from simply touching me. "Would you stop fucking with me and let's go?"

She climbs on me, running her hands through my hair. "Why, are you scared? Are you afraid the scary men will come after us right in the middle of us fucking?"

"If you want to fuck, let's do it when we don't have to worry about someone shooting us in the back," I say, pushing her off.

"You are such a prude sometimes."

"And you're such a lunatic sometimes."

She stops dead in her tracks and turns to me. "Wrong! I am a lunatic all the time, but that keeps me alive. You're too worried about dying, and *that* will only get you killed."

I ignore her bullshit and move forward until we make it back to the safe house and can enjoy a beer with the others. Leandra is fun at times. She breaks up the daily grind with smelly, abrasive men, and every once in a while, she acts like a woman and allows me to enjoy being a man with her. Most of the time though, she only likes to use me to relieve her own frustrations. We have both been with others, and jealousy has never been a problem, but lately, she has been clingy and needy, something I have never seen from her before. I am not sure what her issues are, but it's obvious we need to have a talk.

The mission is complete, and once we rejoin the others, we do our usual celebration. I sneak off to call my brother who is surely trying to get a hold of me for my birthday, only I can't find my phone. I dig through all my things over and over until Leandra comes in with a sheepish smile.

"Looking for something?"

"Give it back Lee!"

"Why? I thought you didn't have anyone—all alone, a reject, a loner like the rest of us?"

"Give me my phone back now," I repeat through my teeth.

"No. I think instead I will share it with everyone else." She runs out the door, and I chase after her, causing a cursed ruckus that forces everyone at the party to stop what they are doing and pay attention to us.

"What's going on between you two?" Peter asks, helping pull us apart.

"He's been hiding something from us, or someone rather," she announces, proudly holding up my phone to everyone.

"It's my phone and my business, no one else's. I have made sure it's secure. I haven't done anything to jeopardize any mission, and I certainly have not held back any. I have a right to have my private life stay private!" I yell at her and anyone else that might have a problem with it.

"Calm down, Ghost. We are not here to persecute you. You're right. You have a right to keep your personal life to yourself."

"Peter, you can't believe that he isn't hiding something important from us?" she yells at him.

"Shut up! Your jealousy nearly cost us tonight, and you know what I am talking about. That little stunt to impress him caused way more attention than we needed to deal with. Now, give him his property back and stay out of others' personal things or we will be forced to lock you down every night." Peter hands out his hand for her to give him my phone, which she does with a forceful plunge into his palm. Peter stares her down while reaching out to me with my phone.

I take my phone and rush off to be alone and make my call. I notice I have received many calls from Antony and messages saying, "I need you." No doubt, Leandra read all of them from the person I tagged as "A.C.". I take a deep breath and call Antony. "Hey, it's me, how are you?"

"Damn. I was beginning to think you were dead or something. Where have you been? I wanted to wish you a happy birthday. I was actually hoping to convince you to come home for your birthday and spend it with your favorite brother."

"That would have been nice, I'm sure, but I'm fine here. I have had a lot of work to do is all, Antony. No need to worry about me. What about you? Why do you sound so tense?"

"I decided to return to the family and work for our father."

"Ah fuck! I told you to move on, to find another life away from him."

"I tried, Dace! I tried, but I needed money and …"

"You don't need their money. I would have sent you money."

"I don't want your money. I don't want their money. I just want …"

I sit back sighing, knowing what he wants. "Their acceptance is not going to make the pain go away. Father's acknowledgment of what happened to Ma is not going to make everything okay again. They know you're gay, Antony. They are never going to allow you to be in a prime position in the family business. You're a liability as far as they are concerned."

"Dace, listen. I know I can prove to them I can do whatever they need me to; I just need a chance. If you would talk to them …"

"No! No, Antony. I don't want back into that mess."

"Dace, please. Please. You left. You ran away, and well, I don't want to runaway anymore. I want to face it, work it out, and be happy for once, and perhaps, get revenge for Ma. Michael wants the same. He is still a mess from Wendy being killed. I think he is ready to start kicking some ass too."

"And Ettore?" There is nothing but silence. "Antony?"

"Ettore is using his anguish and Father's aged mind to take over the family business. Michael is too busy trying to get elected to care. I mean, he cares about Ma, but he is busy."

"So, basically, you are the only one there that really cares about our mother. Let it go, Antony. Let it all go and move on with your life somewhere else."

"No, Dace! If you're not going to come back here and help me, then I'll do it myself. I'll get justice for our mother while you're finding it for strangers," he says before hanging up on me.

I go through a series of emotions, during the days since my conversation with Antony. Even though I travel to the next place with the crew, my head is with my brother. I try calling him over and over, but he won't answer. Antony has been getting into more and more trouble the last few years. The last trouble he met caused him to get into using drugs and other dumb shit that got him kicked out of school. I had to put him in a hospital to help him get over that asshole. I was hoping he would find his own way once he got out, and he seemed to be, but something drew him back to the family, or someone. I am assuming it is the same someone that has been leaving me messages to come back.

As I get ready to head out for the next information gathering mission, I am stopped by Peter. "You stay here and work out whatever is going through that head of yours. I need you to be focused, not thinking about whatever it is back home that has you distracted right now." He doesn't give me a chance to argue before seeing to it that I am blocked by others from leaving. Frustrated and unusually bored, I try my brother again and am surprised that he answers.

"Heyyy, Dace."

"Are you okay?" I ask, happy to hear his voice.

"I am fine. I am so fine that I am making myself even more fine. I have good news! I have met someone wonderful, and he and I are going to get married. I am going to talk to Father and ask for him to pay for the wedding. We can have a great, big, beautiful Italian wedding," Antony laughs. "It'll be the event of the century," he says as I hear another man's voice in sweet agreement.

"Antony, don't do anything stupid," I say.

"Stupid? How can being in love be stupid? Everything is perfect, Dace. Don't you worry; I got it handled." He puts down the phone, failing to hang up and allowing me to listen in as my brother discusses the lavish life they could have together once Antony secures his marriage trust fund, a fund set up for each child to help him get started with his new marriage, a fund I am sure my father never had in mind for my brother and his new partner that no one else has met.

My little brother is clearly in over his head and out of his damn mind. Antony was a good kid, but the older he got, the more it became clear that he was gay, and that made it even harder for him to be a Colletto. I tried to stay away. I tried to hope for the best, even tell myself that he didn't need me and he would figure it out. Every time I call, he sounds worse, more distant and even more lost than a wandering gypsy. It's time. I have to return home, no matter how much I hate to leave. I have made some great friends and become a part of something. It has been great with this crew. No one has asked or cares who I really am, who my family is. It's the greatest hiding place I could have ever hoped for; however, this wandering ghost gypsy needs to go home again and settle the past for good.

As I sit silently waiting in the dark, Peter comes in and sits down next to me with a deep sigh. "I'm not even going to ask, *why*, but instead, I will ask, are you sure?"

I nod. "My brother needs me."

"Brother. Well, that's better than the wife and kids Leandra has claimed." I roll my eyes. "You're the one that has been fucking her. You should have known she would become an issue for you."

"She came at me, and it never seemed to be anything but fucking."

"She's still a woman, and despite her hardened outer shell, she cares about you more than she says. Do me a favor and talk to her before you go. I don't need that crazy bitch making the rest of our lives unbearable because you left." I nod. "I wish you luck, and I hope it goes well. You know how to reach me if you ever decide to come back to us. You are certainly always welcome, my friend." I take his hand and silently say our goodbye before I head off to talk to Leandra.

I knock on her door and peek in, instantly seeing her scowl.

"Can we talk?"

"You're going to leave us, aren't you?" she asks, turning her back to me.

"I need to take care of some personal things."

"Are you coming back?"

"I hope to, but I don't know when."

"So who is she?"

"She is a he, and he is my brother," I force back in her face.

"Oh, well maybe you should bring him here."

"This is not the place for him."

"Maybe I can go with you and help you?" she offers shockingly.

"No, I need to do this on my own. What is this Leandra? What do you want from me?"

She gulps. "I love you." I step back, stunned. "I think. I don't know! I count on you to be here, and I depend on you to help me. What happens if I get into trouble? Who else is going to care if someone has a gun to my head?"

"Everyone here, and you know it. These guys will die for each other, and that includes you. You just have to trust them." I lean into her dropped chin and pick it up, looking into her eyes with a smile, "There are other women here too, and you should try and confide in them. Branch out of your hole and find comfort in being a human." She tries to push me away, but instead dives back into my chest, hiding tears I know are there but know better than to acknowledge. I wrap my arms around her, not completely understanding where the emotions are coming from.

"So when do you leave?" she asks.

"Tomorrow."

"Will you sleep in here tonight then?"

"As long as you don't tie me up and chain me to your bed in the middle of the night." She reluctantly agrees, so I allow her to strip my clothes off roughly. I lie back on her bed and she takes hold of my throbbing member that stands up proudly in front of her. She sits down on me, enveloping my dick fully within her pussy. She rides me hard and long until we both come, and then she takes in a deep breath and surprisingly makes her place for the night on my chest. Lee is not like most women. She challenges me and keeps me on my toes, and I care about her, but as much as I love her hard exterior and challenges, I miss the comfort of a woman who actually loves me, and Leandra doesn't. Leandra likes to control a man and have him chase her, and I have never been one to chase anyone. It drives her crazy. Maybe it is a good idea I get out of this crew for a while and give her a chance to realize her mistake.

CHAPTER 5

Dace

I fly into the city, and the first thing I do is buy myself some wheels so I can get around. Nothing too permanent, but something fast, something that makes it easy to get in and out of anywhere and something fun—a black Hayabusa. The salesman eyeballs me hard as if I am going to rob the place. I guess my look isn't exactly that of someone who could afford such wheels; however, he suddenly becomes my best friend when the bank transfers the money in full for my purchase. He even offers to take me out for a drink, but I decline his need for a new rich friend and move out through the streets like a bolt of lightning in the night.

Now to find my brother. The asshole hasn't settled in any one place. He has been living in hotels since he has been here. With Antony's security issues, he never stays in the same place for very long, which makes it impossible for me to track him down on my own. I try calling him a few times while looking through bar after bar, places I remember him mentioning to me. I have to fight off the advancement of other men in the process, but it doesn't bother me, especially if I can sweet talk them into helping me find Antony. Hell, if women can do it, then why can't I? A few claim to know my brother and his new man, Preston, so they point me to one person, and that person points me to the next until I finally get a strong lead on where he might be. The apartment number I was given is in an upscale building, and a highly secure one that, which makes me feel a little better about his judgment. The name on the call box says Miss Reed. Unless my brother has done some major life changing, I can't imagine that this is where he would be. Hopefully, this woman knows something more than the last few people. I am not sure who he is with or what trouble he might be in, so instead of asking to come in, I figure out a way around the security and slip inside the building undetected. I find the right apartment and knock on the door cautiously. Someone stares through the peephole at me before slowly opening the door a crack.

"Who are you and what do you want?" a woman says as I try to peek around the small door opening to see if I can see anything.

"I'm looking for Antony," I say.

"Why?" she says with a hardened tone.

"Listen, lady, I was told he was here. If he's not, just say so and tell me where he might be. I'm not looking to harm him."

"Dace?" I hear Antony say from the background before stepping out. "Son of a bitch! It is you!" Antony slams into me with open arms. "Oh my God I can't believe you are really here."

"Well, I was worried about you," I say, hugging my brother and feeling better than I thought I would seeing him again. I didn't realize how much I missed him.

"Come in and meet my friends." Antony drags me into the condo, and despite its modest furnishings, it's comforting and inviting, so maybe it's not that of lowlife criminals. "Dace this is my boyfriend, Preston." I look over the brightly smiling man and shake his hand, guarded. He's handsome, seemingly more together than my brother usually goes for. Hopefully Antony has matured enough to see through the bullshit and stop going for the assholes who only want to use him for his money. My brother is tall and has a contagious smile. He's innocent with a bad boy edge, of course. He is a Colletto. To look at him, you would never think of him as gay, but he doesn't try and deny it anymore. He is proud of who he is in that respect and will knock a fuck out if he has a problem with it.

Preston leans forward with a gushing display as he hugs my brother from behind and looks me over closely. "It is so nice to meet you. Antony doesn't talk much about his family, but I must say, handsome good looks do run in the family. A little rugged in your case, but I'm not complaining."

"Calm down, Baby. I don't share, especially not with my straight brother." Antony winks at me as I laugh at him. "Speaking of straight, Dace, this is Austin." I turn towards a woman as she stares hard at me through the blond tresses hanging down in front of her eyes. I look over her oddly masculine shoes, up her long muscular legs, and by the time I get past her curvaceous tits, I have a large smile to meet her perfectly, full-lipped scowl.

I hold out my hand to her. "Hello, Austin. Nice to meet you."

She gazes down at my hand before shaking it like she's trying to rip it off. "Hi, how did you get in here?"

"You opened the door for me. It just happened, right over there, remember?" I smile at her frustrated glare. "Are you not getting enough B vitamins in your diet? Memory starting to go?"

"I get plenty, thank you very much. No, how did you get in the building, and don't say security let you in because they wouldn't do that unless you know someone, and I doubt you know anyone in this building," she says, looking me over with judgment in her eyes.

"I might. You don't know."

"No, you snuck in somehow, and I want to know how?" *Who the hell is this woman? I am here five minutes, and she is already sizing me up to be some kind of a criminal?*

"Why would you think that?" I ask, paying a little more attention to her guarded stance.

"Because you are carrying a gun and what I suspect to be a small tool kit in your pocket, not exactly typical items everyday people would carry, and certainly not people that live in this building or friends of people in this building." I slide my hand in my pocket, feeling of my *access and means* kit with a bold smile. I look her over, careful to keep my hand safely still near the gun at my side. Her hand is just a little too close to a table drawer that I can only assume holds a weapon of some kind.

I pull out my kit from my pocket. "It's just a kit I use for my bike; it has problems once and a while, and I like to be able to take care of it quickly on my own." Lying without hesitation has become a little too easy for me since joining KRT, but it was necessary many times in order to survive.

The woman shakes her head in disbelief. "I am sure you do." Her focus on me is unbreakable and yet, arousing. "And the other item at your side?"

We eye each other pointedly for a time as if we both are waiting for the other one to make a move. I am just not sure what kind of move we are waiting on. Maybe I am too used to Leandra and her challenge-me-and-I-will-fuck-you-until-I-can't-move-any-longer attitude. "I have no idea what you're talking about, Sweetheart? Do you mean this bulge? It's nothing but my cell phone." I show her but hold up my hands above my head. "You're welcome to search me, make sure you do it thoroughly though. I would hate for you to miss something big. I should warn you however, that other bulge has a mind of its own. Don't get mad at me if it comes out swinging."

"Put your arms down," she says, stepping toe to toe with me and looking me in the eyes without fear. "You're his brother? I'm sorry, but we haven't heard anything about you before? Where have you been? You look like you just stepped out of the jungle. Don't they have razors where you came from?" I have to fight my desires as her blond hair sits down in between her breasts and her sweet feminine scent permeates up into my face. I feel my cock twitch in her direction, and I can do nothing more than smile at the impenetrable woman, wondering if she is going to cause me to bust a zipper. That might shut her up though.

Antony steps forward, putting his arm around my shoulders and laughs, breaking up the tension. "Don't mind him, Austin. He's been away in a cave for so long that he isn't used to being around actual people. They're a little scary to him."

She nods, drops her guard a little, and walks away from the table with the weapon. "A cave? Yeah I can believe that. You look like you just climbed out from under a rock. You better be careful. The rich people in this building may call the cops based on the sight of you alone." She laughs as my brother smacks my arm with a laugh, and his boyfriend laughs along with him.

"That's funny. Tell me something. How do you get your voice to do that? It's the best female voice I have ever heard a man impersonate. Did you have surgery or take some kind of supplements?" I ask her.

My brother falls back in silence, hiding his face as he laughs. She mumbles something harsh at me until I smile. "I am a woman."

"You are? Huh. So what's with the manly stance?" I smile innocently while pointing it out to her.

Antony quickly steps in between us. "Okay Dace, leave her alone." He walks over and puts his arm around her shoulders and kisses her cheek. "She has been really sweet to me, and I think of her as a great friend, so you be nice to her. Not to mention, this is Austin's place. She and Preston have been best friends for a long time, and he moved in here … what was it, a year ago Pres?" he asks the man, receiving a nod. "She has been kind enough to let me sleep over quite a bit lately."

"Austin works a lot at night, and I get lonely here all by myself," Preston says.

"Oh, late nights working at the steel mill, Mister … I mean Miss Reed?" I nod sympathetically towards her.

"I didn't tell you my last name. How did you know that? And you never answered my question. How did you get into the building? It's heavily secure to keep people … well, people like you, out," she responds with all kinds of feisty tension.

"People like me? You don't know me, lady. In fact, how do you live here? You obviously don't make the kind of money that most do in this building? Trying to be something you're not?"

"I have a roommate that helps with the bills, and I live here for the security of it, not the prestige. Now, you answer my questions, please. This is my home, and I have a right to know who is in it."

"I'm only here to check on my brother. If my presence makes you uncomfortable, I am happy to go. We can meet up tomorrow, Antony. I need to go find a place to sleep tonight anyway, unless I can crash …?"

"No," she says sternly.

"Alright, calm down, Mr. Lady. I'm going." I say goodbye to my brother who is shaking his head at me with a smile. "Call me tomorrow."

"Sure, try and stay out of trouble until I do. And maybe try and keep the gun better hidden from now on?" he whispers to me.

"Of course." I walk towards the door, and she follows seemingly to see to it that I leave. I walk out the door, and she continues to follow me. I look back and look her over with a smile. "Taking a late night stroll?"

"Just making sure you find your way out of my building."

I turn back towards her and line up right in front of her. "What is your problem? I didn't make you wear those manly shoes."

"What?! My shoes aren't manly. They are perfectly suited for... OH shut up! You show up here out of nowhere with questionable intentions. I don't care if you are Antony's burly brother; I don't appreciate you bringing a gun into my home."

"I am sorry; I forgot I had it, and if I had known ..." I look her over licking my lips, "that *you* would be on the other side of the door, then I would have approached the situation quite differently. I promise you."

She shakes her head while taking a step back from me. "What do you think, your brother is going to crawl into my friend's bed and you are going to crawl into mine?"

"Who said anything about your bed, Honey? How do you know I am not gay?"

"The way you look," she says with certainty

"Oh stereotyping. So you're one of those. You know, gays can come in all shapes and sizes. You shouldn't judge. It's just not right." I shake my finger at her until she grabs it and pushes it away. I look at her as I hold my finger with a pout.

"Oh please! I didn't hurt you. And I wasn't talking about how you look, but how you look at me. Your brother looked me in the eyes when he first met me. You looked me all over, as if you were stripping me naked."

My smile fights its way out, knowing exactly what she's talking about. "Or maybe you want me to picture you naked. Hey! You looked me over, were you picturing me naked?" I step back in shock. "Mr. Lady, I am not that kind of man... wait, actually I think am. What are we talking about here? Some oral trade off, or do you want to strip down completely and let me smack some ass?" She huffs, rolling her eyes away from me, giving me the opportunity to grab her waist and her arm, pinning her against the wall.

"Let go of me," she growls.

Nearing her lips with mine, I breathe in her suddenly rugged breath into my mouth. Her heart's rapid beating is so hard that I can feel it into the core of my own chest. "Admit it, you're attracted to me."

"I can't imagine any self-respecting woman attracted to... to you!"

"Admit it. You're thinking about me naked right now. Aren't you? I look good naked, even better than I do dressed." Her silence says it all. "Admit it," I whisper against her lips, causing her mouth to open in shock. I reach out with my tongue and touch the tip of hers. She stops breathing while I move in close to her body with a rough hand down her back and squeeze her ass into my hips. Just as she licks her lips, I take a quick step away from her. "Nah, I'm sorry, I am just not attracted to you. I tried, but you're going to have to seduce a different man into your bed tonight. Maybe try online dating, Sweetheart. Just make sure you use a picture without the shoes." I walk away feeling the daggers being dug into the back of my head. *She's mine now, and I can't wait.* On my way out, I catch sight of a realtor's sign, "Loft Available." I grab a card, glancing back at the focused blond. I smile and wave; she waves back, but with only one finger.

I found a nice hotel down the street from where my brother was staying and slept fairly well once I set up the simple security alarms within my room. It's a new day, and Antony is meeting me for lunch. *Little did I know, my father and brothers would be accompanying him.* I stand, meeting my father who snarls at me as he reaches out to hug me.

"Dace, my son, I am glad to see you are good, but I am not happy that you did not immediately come home to your family when you got into town."

"I was trying to be discreet because I didn't want any arguments when I left."

"Already thinking of leaving, Dace? You know I would really like to have my little brother around for a little while so I can enjoy picking on him some," Michael says with his usual, large, white smile and a tight hug.

I back off as Ettore squints his eyes at me before giving me the custom brotherly hug, not that he has ever been much for hugging, which is why we keep it short. "Dace," he says simply with his typical, rugged tone.

"What, no complaints about me being gone or thoughts of leaving again?" I ask him.

"I have never been one to tell someone to do something they don't want to do. It's your damn business. Deal with it. Just stay the fuck out of mine," Ettore says, sitting down, looking bored and put out already.

I nod, biting my tongue as my father growls his impatience. "Ettore!"

"Oh, I'm sorry, please, Dace, come home and be a part of this wonderful loving family. We miss you and very much want you to forget that we sent you away like an unwanted stepchild after our mother was butchered to death."

"Son of bitch, Ettore! Must you always be so crude?" my father says through his teeth, slamming his cane against the wooden floor with authority until Ettore sits down.

"Why would you ever want to leave this excitement?" Antony whispers to me.

I pull him back to me before he can get away. "I will get you back for this," I whisper through a tight smile.

"Sit down, Dace, and let's act like a family for once," my father says. I sit, and he nods towards me and calls the waiter over to take our orders. I take my time, knowing that, as soon as I finish, I am going to get an ear full about what I should do with my life, and sure enough, it comes instantly. "So Dace, I have checked your trust fund, and it hasn't been touched in quite some time. How have you been living all this time?"

"I have been doing contract work, Father. I learned some new skills to go along with my degree and the combination has helped me advance quickly," I say, causing his eyebrows to rise. My silence on the details lets him know enough. He is smart enough not to ask much else. That's the way it is in this family—don't ask the questions you don't want to be responsible for once you learn the answers.

"Did Antony tell you, Dace, that I am running for governor?" Michael asks.

"No shit." I sit back, shaking my head. "Trying to finally earn that nickname Father gave you, Michael? I don't believe JFK was a governor though."

"Well, I like to be an individual who does things my own way," Michael laughs. "Either way, I could really use some help. If you're interested, I could see to it you are a part of my campaign team? Antony has already been a big help for me." I look at Antony as he widens his eyes with a forced smile. *Yeah... he looks excited about it too.* I do nothing more than take a deep breath and stay silent. "Come on, Dace, you have to come home eventually and settle down? Don't you want a family?"

Ettore growls his impatience. "Or you can say to hell with that political bullshit and come work with me and be an honest crook and not a smooth talking piece of shit," Ettore says unapologetically. I laugh along with Antony even though we are both hushed by our father.

"Either way, both are better places for you, son. You should be with family. Family will always be there for you. This is your home, your heritage; you should be here to help oversee it."

"What am I? A prince to a kingdom? I am the son of an organized crime family, not exactly overseeing a long line of traditional, royal values," I say, shaking my head. "I can see it now. I will be dubbed Prince Dace of Holland Hills, given my family engraved Glock, and crowned with a fedora, add a feather just for style," I say sarcastically, surprisingly causing Ettore to lose his typical above average self-control and laugh out load.

"I see your sense of humor hasn't changed much, unfortunately. Maybe you should work with Ettore. You two could go out on the road and do standup together," my father says with a frown. "Dace, you belong here, and your family needs you."

"Needs me for what? What am I going to do here?"

Michael sits forward. "Calm down and listen before you dismiss your own family. We love you, Dace, and we will support you in anything you decide to do, but we would appreciate your help. I need help with my campaign efforts, and Ettore needs help transitioning into a lead role in the family business. Father, as you know, isn't getting any younger, and our enemies are determined to prove he can't handle himself anymore. The same people that killed Wendy and my son are the ones aiming for Father's head. It's not been easy the last year, Dace. I think the one thing we have all learned is that we need to stick together in order to get through it." Michael, the constant politician, works the dead wife and unborn son angle on me. "We know about the skills you have learned with your new ... 'friends' and we would very much like to use them to our advantage."

I laugh, shaking my head. "You just couldn't let me go. You had to question Antony to death to find out what I was doing. And don't say you didn't because there is only one way you could have found out about what I was doing. Cause there is no way any of your people could have found me. I made sure of it."

"You're my son, and I will not apologize for watching over you, no matter how far you run from me." My father and I have butted heads since I was a kid. I have always wanted to do things my way, and it drives him crazy. *You're too much like your mother! Why do you have to be so stubborn? Just let me help you.* He would always say. Despite it all, I love my father, and for some reason, even after everything he has done, I believe he loves me. My father has, for a long time, been the most feared and revered man around, but even after being gone for as long as I have, I can tell something is not right with him. "We … I would like for you to stay at least a little while longer," he says solemnly before concentrating on his food, not that he is eating much. I watch him as sadness exudes from his whole being. My frustration and anger suddenly turn to concern, another trait of my mother's I could never break from—caring about others even when I don't have a reason to.

"Dace, we are only asking that you…" Michael begins again.

"I'll stay," I say, causing them all to look up at me with wide eyes, but I lock eyes with my father. "I'll stay, just tell me what you need me to do to help." My father fights his smile for as long as he can before looking away with a tear in his eyes.

Chapter 6

Austin

I remember that moment perfectly, the exact moment my mother's expression changed and my life changed forever with it. That moment when my mother walked into the house and seemed noticeably troubled. It happened so sudden, as if she ran into an invisible wall. I wasn't sure what it was at the time, but now, I understand. It was the day I recognized the sixth sense, the one that tells you something is wrong, that something terrible is about to happen. The memories of that day haunt me, but I manage to evade their painful grip by working hard and keeping my mind as occupied as possible. It's when I go to sleep that the memories are too hard to fight off. I do my best to relax and think about better things—how I am alive, how I survived, even though my mother didn't.

She did her best to protect me against the masked strangers. I could barely see through my tears as they raped her, but I saw, clearly, her subtle nod towards the open door. I ran as she wanted me to and ignored the men screaming threats at me if I didn't come back. I ran until I could safely call for help. It didn't come soon enough for my mother, but the police arrived in time to save me. Picking me up from a dark corner of my father's office and wrapping me in a blanket, they carted me away so I couldn't see my mother as they carried me out of the house.

There were three men. Two were arrested, but the third got away somehow, and I am determined to find him. I have looked at the crime scene photos a million times and my twin brother, Aaron, has done the same. Neither of us can figure out what we are missing. We have finally given up on my father giving us information that will help; he is still bitter about finding out she hired an attorney to file for divorce against him a week prior to her death. Since we are on our own, I decide to take what little free time I have and search the old newspaper files to see what coverage they have of the incident. The local paper only uploaded partial information from their story and stored the rest of the information in their basement library where they allow access, for a price. I pay the guy what he wants and work my way through their horrible filing system to find the right timeframe and, then, the right date. I take out the notes made and read through, finding nothing new. The only thing left are the rolls of film taken at the scene. Grabbing a seat at one of the old film viewers, I begin looking through and make note of some interesting people standing by and watching the crime scene be investigated. One man looks particularly interesting as he talks to a cop from the other side of the crime scene tape. He's well-dressed and a known criminal. I haven't seen or heard about him in years, but I remember his picture in my father's office as one of the many high profile criminals he was able to put in jail. I make note of the pictures I need and look for someone to help me print them.

"Excuse me, can you help me find someone to print these for me?" I ask a man sitting and viewing film himself.

He turns around, and I roll my eyes with a hard sigh. "Ah shit, and I was having such a good day too. What are you doing here?" Dace asks me.

"I could ask you the same thing."

"If you want something printed, ask Shelly over there. She is good at getting things blown up or printed out as detailed as you want them," he says, hiding his screen from me as I try to sneak a peek.

"You always got something to hide, don't you?"

"I'm not hiding anything more than you are …" He looks me over as if he can see through my clothes. "Austin."

I eye him harshly only to receive a mocking glare back from him. He's not worth my trouble. I leave to find Shelly who happens to be in the corner fantasizing about Dace and twirling the flower he brought for her. *I bet he didn't have to pay a thing to get in here.* He looks back over his shoulder at me and smiles, as if he knows what I am thinking.

The man in the picture has been dead for years; he hung himself in jail, soon after he managed to stab and kill Rupert Wallis, one of the men arrested for my mother's murder. His connection to them was obvious, but who was connected to him? I have to know, and apparently, the only man left that might know anything about the man is his son who owns a nightclub in town. Tyson Wallis is not much better than his father. He runs drugs in and out of his club, operates a prostitution ring, and in his spare time, he seeks out women for his own sick desires. My best chance to get close to him and find out all I can is to get him interested in me. I borrow a dress and heels, slowly make my way into the club, and quickly finding a bar seat before I fall on my face in these ridiculous high heels. These types of outfits are not my usual, but I cross my legs and make myself available to the man I spot laughing with some associates across the room.

"Can I buy you a drink?"

"No, thanks. I'm not interested," I say to the man who sits down next to me.

"Oh, I know that. You have made that clear more than once." I slowly look over, and Dace smiles wide at me. "You look nice. Who are you trying to impress?"

"Certainly not you," I say, causing him to laugh. I shake off the nuisance and go back to working my womanly assets to get Tyson's attention.

"What the hell are you doing?" Dace asks.

"Would you stop bothering me?! I am interested in someone else."

"Well, you aren't going to get his attention doing that."

"And how would you know?"

"I am a man." Dace looks over his shoulder at Tyson and shakes his head at me. "Are you after him? Seriously? You need to stay away from him; he's not your type."

"I don't need your advice, thank you very much. I know what I am doing," I say, looking back at Tyson who suddenly is watching me. Hmmm.

"He's watching you, isn't he?" Dace says proudly as he tosses a few peanuts into his mouth. "Men want what they can't have. If he thinks I am about to score with you, then he, of course, suddenly becomes more interested in you." I smile, turn my whole body towards Dace, and begin flirting openly with him. "Oh my God, please stop."

"Come on, I know you want me, Dace."

"I what? No. No, please stop doing whatever that is you're doing."

I move in closer and nearly trip over my heels but manage to get a hold of the bar to steady myself. "Come on, Dace. I could make you feel so good if you would just let me …" I push into him, losing my grip on the bar and falling into his lap.

He sits me back up on my stool. "You are so bad at this. I mean, I have seen some horrible flirting before, but *you*, you are the worst. You need to just sit there and cross your pretty legs, smile, and don't move, that's your best bet at this point."

"If it wasn't for these shoes, I would be just fine."

Dace looks down at my shoes and back up again. "Oh yeah, clearly they're the problem," he says sarcastically. "Although, they are women's shoes," he laughs, looking away from me. I ball my hand up in a fist, punch him off his stool, and smile with pride when he nearly stumbles to the floor. "Watch it, Blondie, or I will take that stool you're resting on and force you to walk in those shoes," he huffs, sitting back on his stool. I kick his seat and nearly send him tumbling again.

"Oh don't be mad. I was only teasing. Isn't that what women do … tease men?"

"Not the way you do it, Mister." I steady myself to punch him, but he catches my fist and knocks my stool out from under me. I stumble around, trying to reclaim my perch, but I can't get my balance enough to fight for it back. Dace laughs until two bodyguards come up. "Oh, it's okay gentlemen. We are only teasing each other," Dace says while placing my stool back down in front of me.

"It looks like more than teasing. We are going to have to ask you both to leave," the bigger of the two men says, helping me up and nodding towards Dace to move forward. Dace tosses some money at the bartender and helps me walk out of the stupid club.

I curse under my breath until we reach my car, and I jerk my arm away from him and lean against the car to take my stupid shoes off. "What were you doing here anyway?"

"Not that it is any of your business, but I was meeting someone for a drink. Now I have to find a way back to my bike, and since you caused me to get kicked out, you can take me."

"Why me?"

"Because my bike is at your building anyway. And before you ask, I left it there when I went to meet up with Antony this morning." He takes my keys and opens the car door, sliding into the passenger seat.

"You have got to be fucking kidding me!" I yell.

He shamelessly starts my car and rolls down the window. "Can you curse the world later? I have places to be."

After some harsh words exchanged between the two of us, I drive the dumbass back to my place and believe our night together to be over, except he keeps following me. "Why are you following me?"

"Antony is here, and he said Preston is having a party that he wants me to come to," Dace says, fighting his smile, knowing I am not at all happy about the idea.

"Come on," I growl at him. I walk into my place and find a group of Preston's friends having a good time and welcoming Dace right into my home.

"Oh Austin! I thought you said you would be out late, so I …" Preston begins apologizing as soon as he sees me.

"It's fine. I'm going to go to bed anyway." I sigh deeply, walking into my room and freeing myself from the constricting dress I will never borrow again. After a hot shower, I climb into bed ready to pass out and have no trouble doing so, despite the music and the boisterous conversations people are having outside my door. It's been a long day, and I hope I can get plenty of sleep before I have to be at work tomorrow.

I sleep well until someone wakes me taking a shower at … 3:33 in the morning! You have got to be kidding me. Preston is taking a shower at this hour? Why is he using the guest bath to shower? He knows that it is horribly annoying when the water hits that rickety old shower door. I get out of bed determined to remind him that it is a week night and I have to be at work in the morning. I knock hard on the door, "Pres, come on, I was sound asleep."

The door opens, and Dace pops his wet head out with a small town wrapped around his waist. "Sorry, I didn't know your shower door was loose. I'm done now."

"Why …" I clear my throat, trying to avoid looking down. "Why are you here … wet and … here?"

"The party ran late, and Preston said I could crash until morning. You don't mind, do you? I promise I won't shoot or steal from anyone … while they sleep anyway." He smiles, looking me over. "You sleep in that? Nice," he says, reminding me of the tank top and panty outfit I settled on when I could find nothing else better clean.

"It was clean, and …" I glance down to catch my breath and see what I had been trying to avoid. Wow, the outline in his towel has my head spinning with curiosity.

"Excuse me, are we done here? I would like to dry off and get to sleep. Unless you would like to continue staring at me?"

I snap my head up, "I am not staring I am thinking about

whether it's the best idea that you sleep here. You really should find your own place and sleep there." He rolls his eyes. "Don't rolls your eyes at me. This is my place, and I have a right to decide who sleeps where."

He steps out and towards me until he backs me up against a wall. He leans into me with the water dripping off his skin and onto my chest, tickling as it runs down in between my breasts. I take a quick breath and look up into his eyes.

"Hi?" he says as if I just noticed him.

"Hi."

He nods with a smile. "Austin?"

"Yeah?" I breathe.

"Where would you like for me to sleep?" he asks, playing with my hair.

I am pretty sure my heart is going to race right out of my body, but I can't seem to catch my breath enough to slow it down. However, I am stronger than he thinks. "The sofa will be fine," I say, ducking under his arm, running back to my bed, and pulling the covers over my head before exhaling. "Wow."

CHAPTER 7

Dace

She said get my own place, so I will get my own place, in her building. The dweeb realtor seems less nervous today as he shows me around. Maybe it's because I shaved or maybe because he has checked in with my bank. The penthouse is wide open, not much in it other than a newly remodeled kitchen. That should probably deter me, but I like the idea of being able to make the place my own, plus the ability to tap into the security cameras easily saves me a lot of time and money. Sure, some of the building residents are "added benefits" shall I say. Unlike my brother, I prefer a place to settle down in and make my own. It's been so long since I have had an actual home that I am damn well going to take advantage of my forced time here and have one. "I like it. When I can move in?" I ask the dweeb who instantly fidgets with his iPad.

"Oh yes, here it is. It looks as though we can schedule everything to be transferred over by the fifteenth," he says with excitement.

"Make it the first."

"But that's in two days." He holds out his hands as if I should understand the ridiculousness of it.

"I know that. I want to move in on the first. I have a lot to do to get this place ready, and I need to do it as soon as possible."

"While that's understandable, we still have to meet the schedule of others in order to get all the paperwork handled properly. I can't possibly arrange …"

"Who do I need to talk to in order to get this done?"

"Excuse me?" he asks.

"Who do I need to talk to in order to get this done by the first?" I say clearly and with a tone that he will understand.

61

"Hamilton Rich." He hands me the man's number.

I nod and make a call. "Hi, Hamilton Rich? This is Dace Colletto. Your man Sterling says that you can help me get moved in by the first rather than the fifteenth?" I listen with a smile as the man on the other end seems to understand my needs. "I thought you might be able to. Thank you." I hang up with the man. "I'm moving in on the first. Make sure to have everything ready before I get here." He nods and runs out of the place ahead of me. Not surprisingly, they have me ready to move in a day before the first. Sometimes, it serves you well to be a Colletto.

My new place is nearly set up the way I want it. Once I got the security issues worked out, I furnished the rest of the place minimally for my comfort. Concentrating on the bed area and making sure it has its own privacy from the rest of the space, add a secure room for me to keep my computer and security links in, and the place is perfect. It was a late night securing my new home, so of course, my first visitors decide to show up a little earlier than I intended to get up. I check my cameras and allow them up before opening the door to two smiling faces. "Do you know how early it is?" I ask.

"Early? Damn, little brother, you need to get your schedule straight. Things get going around here at the crack of dawn, and you better be ready before it does," Michael says as he admires my new loft.

"I'm ready, I am always ready. I don't have to be awake to be prepared. For instance, I know you had men trying to sneak in a few hours ago." I glance over at Michael as he looks at me in shock. "Next time, tell them to turn their cell phones off. My system tracked them as soon as they got within a hundred feet." I laugh, remembering the dumbasses jumping around as their phones began malfunctioning.

"Damn it, Dace! They are some of my best men, and you …"

"Oh stop whining. They'll be okay. A little minor electrocution never hurt anyone." My brother rolls his eyes while Antony crashes into my sofa, laughing.

"Don't encourage him, Antony. I swear I am not excited about you two being back together causing trouble. Aunt Terri told me all about the trouble you two would get into."

"Aunt Terri was a bitch. We snuck out to get away from her," Antony says, walking over to the bar and grabbing an apple with a wink in my direction.

"She was a sweet lady. You two never appreciated what she had to give up to take care of you."

"Give up? What could she have possibly given up? She never went anywhere, never cooked. She never cleaned; thankfully, she paid someone to do that. She slept with any man that would have her, whether we were there or not, and she never missed one of her shows on her favorite big screen TV. *Shut up kids! I'm watching my program!*" I mock her.

"Don't forget the money," Antony reminds me.

"Oh yeah! She had to give up that shit job and crappy apartment to move into that brand new home that Father bought for her and get paid how many thousands a month to take care of us? Oh yeah, she really suffered."

Michael sighs deeply. "Two peas in a pod as always. I'm not going to bother trying to defend family, but she did develop some kind of bad cancer after you two left. I thought maybe one of you would go back to …" Michael exhales harshly as we both laugh so hard tears come to our eyes. "*Anyway,* I need you two to check out this business for me," he says, handing me a piece of paper with a name and address on it. "I think they are a front for the Aksakovs. Ettore is concerned about them."

"The Aksakovs?"

"Yeah, a new Russian alliance that has moved in the last few years. We are afraid they are aligning with the Robiks, but for now, they seem to be acting on their own. Once you get that done, you can go meet with Ettore and let him know the details. I have to distance myself a little from him and this Aksakovs mess now that this campaign is starting to pick up. If I try to tell Ettore to keep a low profile, he will do the opposite and do whatever he can to tell me to fuck off."

"So you two still get along like oil and water?" I ask. The two have fought since I can remember. They supposedly got a long when they were kids, but at some point, their relationship became tense, I assume because of our father.

"You know I love him and have tried everything to get closer to him, but I'm afraid this political career I have chosen has pushed him that much farther from the family. The other day at lunch, with you, was the first time we have sat down together in months."

"And even longer since they both have been in the same room without screaming at each other," Antony adds.

"Don't ask why. I surely don't know," Michael says as if he really doesn't know. Michael has been Father's favorite since he was born, and Ettore has been the forever-forgotten middle child. Michael is the smart one, the handsome one; he's compassionate and adored by everyone who meets him. He even has my mother's blond hair, setting him apart from the rest of us. It was like the heavens decided the light should shine down on his head and for the rest of us to live in the shadows of his glowing halo. He was the perfect prince to inherit the kingdom, and Ettore was the perfect background jester. Outside of his bad luck with being born into this family, which has cursed anyone who gets near him, Michael lives a charmed life. He glances at his phone as it beeps. "Damn, this day is getting away from me already. I need to go. I have a lunch meeting on the other side of town with the chief of police. Call me if you find out anything unusual." Michael oddly rushes out of the loft with nothing more than a hand wave goodbye.

"What the hell was that about? He's meeting with the cops now? Since when does anyone in our family seek out cops?" I ask Antony.

"I don't know. He's been acting weird for the last few

months, but at least he isn't sulking anymore. I swear, after Wendy died, he was so depressing to be around that I almost wanted to slit my own wrists. Have you even seen Sage since you have been back?" I shake my head. "You really need to. She's absolutely adorable. She's in desperate need of a mother, attention of any kind that isn't from a nanny. Michael is a really good father. He would give his life for that little girl, but he should be around for her more. He's too much like Father. I think that's why he is trying to do this whole politician thing and make a clean living for her."

"I could see him being a good father. He always handled us like we were his kids rather than brothers."

Antony nods, "Mom used to tell me that he would come into our rooms when we were babies to look after us and make sure we were okay. She caught him, one day, taking me out of my crib and calming me down before putting me back to bed. Yeah, he's a strange one. Hell, outside of Sage, I don't think I can get near a child without breaking out in hives. They're scary little creatures," Antony says as I laugh.

"Oh yeah, kids, they are real scary." I shuffle his hair laughing. "Come on little brother. Let's get to work."

"Before we do that, tell me something ... why did you pick here of all places to move into? It wouldn't happen to be because of a pretty blond you met, would it?" he asks, thinking he knows a secret of mine. "You know she doesn't like you."

"I don't know what you mean. I like the neighborhood is all, and the building security is amazing."

"Yeah, secure from everyone but you."

"No place can be perfect." I smile.

"Next time, call me rather than walking into a poor unsuspecting woman's home with a gun and scaring her to death."

"She wasn't scared. She should have been, considering she knew I had a gun, but she wasn't. She is rather... interesting for a woman. She sized me up and knew everything about me within seconds. What does she do?"

"I don't know much other than she works for the city. Preston says she works a lot, real dedicated to her job apparently, and doesn't get out much."

"A hottie like that, and she isn't getting laid constantly? That's a shame."

"Uh – huh, a real shame," he says, shaking his head at me.

"Don't worry, I am only curious."

"If I know you, it is more than curiosity. Hey, how about once we are done we go get a drink and satisfy some of that curiosity with someone other than my boyfriend's roommate?" I cock my head, giving him an awkward look. "It doesn't have to be a gay bar, but you know you would get a lot of play in that arena. Tall, dark, and mysterious is like a gay magnet. Not to mention that wavy hair and sensitive eyes, whew baby!"

"Oh yeah, is that how you work it?"

"Hell Baby, I am in a committed relationship now."

"And I am sure you had him checked out before you spent countless nights with him alone?"

"Why are you so distrusting of everyone? You need to learn to trust your heart, Dace," he says, smacking my face. "And it wouldn't hurt to shave once in a while."

I rub my face. "You think if I do Austin will like me more?"

"No, but I will. You're bringing down my status with that crazy Grizzly Adams look."

"Well we can't have that," I laugh, going to the bathroom to do as asked.

CHAPTER 8

Austin

The day is just beginning, and already, I can hear my brother through my ear piece telling another one of his ridiculous stories. With all the trouble that boy gets into, I am shocked he has made it this far in life. Then again, I have been right behind him ever since we were born, keeping him from jumping into any major trouble, at least until we went into the military and were separated for our own good. Aaron wouldn't allow anyone to get out of line with me, and being one of the few women on base and the only blond, I got a lot of hell from the other men, and Aaron got into a lot of fights because of it. They sent him away, and I stayed behind, learning to fight my own battles for once. With the help of an understanding Major, I learned a new way to fight to make sure any trouble I would encounter would end quickly. *For our own good*, we learned to survive without each other, but it didn't keep us from joining the force together or the same station.

Aaron continues his story with amusement. "So there I was, no shirt, no shoes, no pants, and my top hat … and that damn rabbit, trying to get a cab."

"I can't believe any cab in the city would ever pick your dumbass up," Billy, his best friend and partner since they both graduated from the academy, says with a laugh and surely shaking his head as he always does at my idiot brother.

"Her name was Sylvia Crawley, and she was an illegal immigrant running from an arranged marriage. She was a former beauty queen with a sex addiction. I am telling you, she was drop dead gorgeous and the only ride available. I didn't have any money to pay for the cab, obviously, and she refused to drive me anywhere until I paid for the ride somehow … so there I was, sitting in the backseat with my rabbit and my top hat ready and willing to do whatever I needed to get back home. It was clearly time to do my magic, so I put my rabbit to the side and put my top hat on my head and … abracadabra Ms. Crawley."

"Oh shut up!" Billy yells at him. "You are so full of shit! A rabbit and a top hat!? I swear, I will never understand where you come up with that bullshit." Jamee and I sit next to each other laughing. "When is this son of a bitch going to show up anyway? I can't take much more of this. It's been two days, and if I hear another Aaron Reed fantasy story I am going to go insane."

"I thought you liked my stories?" Aaron asks.

"And I thought the Reed twins were two girls when I agreed to be your partner; otherwise, I would have chosen Austin."

"That hurts. I look much better in heels than Austin."

"You look better and can walk better too," Jamee, my partner, chimes in.

"Hey! I may not be able to walk in heels, but I can certainly look better in them than him."

"Hold up, people. There he is," Aaron says. "Alright, Austin, you and Jamee take the south side entrance, and Billy and I will go in through the north side."

Easing out of the car, Jamee and I creep in and block the exit while my brother and Billy flush the murderer, Masterson, out of his hideout. We have been looking for him for three months and finally got a lead from his scared shitless mother. I guess she got tired of worrying if her son would come and put her home at risk of being raided.

These are the moments that drive me, the moments that get my heart going and my blood pumping, waiting for the unknown. I pride myself on thinking like a criminal, figuring out how I would escape and going there to wait for them. Then, I hear it, the yelling, the gunshots, and the shuffling of feet running towards us. I move fast and wait, watching for him until he steps around the corner, looking for us. He shoots everywhere, trying to get out the door before we can get to him, only he misses the one place I knew he would. He gets by Jamee with no problem, and she gives up the chase when he turns to shoot her. He gets past the stairs and runs right into my path at the door. I take him down and wrestle him to the ground, fighting for his gun.

"You got one choice. Surrender now or take your chances on getting out of here alive? And you know damn well you don't stand a chance to make it to your car from here before I shoot you. Trust me, I have no problem shooting a coward like you in the head," I reason with the man who killed his own child and ex-girlfriend before killing her new husband.

"Fuck you!" he yells, punching me in the ribs and pushing me away. He makes it to his feet and runs. I take out my gun and shoot him in the leg, bringing him down wailing about the pain.

I tie his hands and smile. "No, fuck you! Now you have pissed me off. No easy death for you. Instead, you can enjoy the confines of your cell for years thinking about the needle that will be coming for you. You're under arrest, you son of a bitch." Not giving a shit about my prisoner's bleeding leg, I shove him in front of me and walk him to the front of the building. My brother fist pumps before high-fiving me.

"Well done, Sis. Damn! My sister is a badass!" Aaron exclaims.

Masterson is surely locked safely away until his death. After a long three days searching for that murderous bastard, I am in the mood to celebrate tonight, but Preston is already out celebrating by the time I get home, so I guess it is going to be just me tonight. I get into my comfortable sweats and begin making dinner, but I have a craving for some wine, which we don't have. *No problem. I will simply run down to the market, and maybe I can find a movie to rent while I am out.* With my hair tied up on my head, I throw on some shoes and a coat and walk down to the nearby market. I pick up some wine and some chocolate, too, before searching for a movie at the rental box.

"That online dating thing not working out, huh?" Even

though I am afraid to look off to my side, I do so anyway and see him smiling at me and looking way better than I remember. "Nice outfit, and oh, with your man shoes too? Always a classic."

"What are you doing here, Dace? Following me?"

"No. Why would I do that? I am getting some wine for my date," he says as a beautiful woman, looking over my questionable attire with a scrunch of her nose, walks up to his side. I fidget my outfit into some kind of respectable order while trying to hide underneath the hood of my coat. "Honey, this is a neighbor of mine, Austin."

"Neighbor?" I ask.

"How do you do?" the woman says, nodding towards me.

"Neighbor? You live in my building now? But you can't."

Dace smiles wide. "You said it yourself, it's worth spending the money for such a secure building. Thanks for the advice. I'll see you later. Enjoy your movie and wine, and try not to get into too much trouble."

"No. Nooo. Oh no," I say repeatedly as he walks away with a smile. "Oh damn, there goes my celebratory mood. Now I need the wine for a whole new reason."

This morning, I wake up and go through my usual routine before running into *him* on the elevator, again. I swear, this is becoming too much. I think I am going to have to move. It's like he knows whenever I am coming and going. What did he do? Tap into the building security cameras or something?

"Morning," he says, happily, in his incredibly fitted jeans, richly tailored biker jacket, and smelling like a man, a well-cared for man. He may be a criminal, but there's no harm in admiring him from afar for now. I take him in, close my eyes, and then open them back again to see his amorous blue eyes watching me. "Enjoying yourself?"

"What? No, I am just thinking about ... pushing you off the building," I say proudly.

"Ah, that's sweet."

"That's an expensive jacket."

"I wouldn't know. I found it."

"Liar. How do you afford such things?" I ask as the elevator doors open.

"I sell my body to rich, horny women. What can I say, business is good," he says, arrogantly walking away. *The asshole probably does ... trick rich, old women into giving him money.*

I watch him get on his bike, put on his helmet, and take off, and I swear he winks at me as he flies by. I wonder what he does all day. It certainly isn't selling his body ... *I don't think.* I need to find out. As soon as I get to work, I search everything to find him, but there is no record of him anywhere. Now I am even more curious about him. What kind of man has a name that doesn't exist? A criminal, for sure. I'm just not sure what kind.

"Austin, come on, we have a call to get to," Jamee yells. I grab my coat, and we run out the door to check out a double murder.

The scene is gruesome, a robbery gone wrong it would seem, but I don't believe it. Somebody did this to this couple to prove something, to send a message. Aaron walks in, looking over my shoulder while I check out the woman's hands. "The best we can tell is the husband was a campaign manager for Michael Colletto. I assume he wouldn't kill his own manager."

"Why would anyone do this to a man who seemingly has nothing to do with organized crime?"

"This man might not, but Colletto does," Aaron reminds me.

"They tortured the man and made his wife watch; they must have wanted him to tell them something. Why do this for no reason?" I ask, looking at the ultrasound picture the woman was clutching in her hand before she hemorrhaged to death. While I am knelt down at the woman's side, I see something under a nearby table. "What's that?" Reaching under the table, I find an English book.

"What is it?" Jamee asks.

"It's a text book, a teacher's edition with notes in it." I look up at Aaron. "She was tutoring someone. The notes are dated for yesterday." I scramble to my feet and begin searching for her cell phone.

"What are you looking for?"

"Her phone."

"Billy! Billy found it," Aaron says, racing to the stairs to wait for him.

Billy walks down the stairs with his eyebrows raised. "Yeah?"

"What did you do with her phone?" Aaron asks.

"I bagged it and put it with the rest of the evidence. Why?"

"How did you find it?" I ask.

"It was beeping and vibrating from a corner upstairs. Someone was texting her that he was going to be late for class," he says. I look at Aaron, and he smiles back at me. "What? What's happening?"

"I think we have a witness," I say happily.

"A live one at that," Aaron follows.

"You know I hate this twin bullshit. I never know what's going on. Maybe one of you could fill me in."

We explain to Billy, as well as Jamee, about our suspicions, and sure enough, they are correct. Mrs. Martin was set to tutor Nelson Boone near the same time they were killed. Now, we just have to find him. Unfortunately, Nelson is a known runaway and has only recently been getting back on track with the help of the Martins. The chances of us finding him are not good, but the good news is no one else will be able to find him easily either.

It's been an exhausting day, and by the time I get home, the market is packed, and I have to make a decision on whether it's worth waiting in line for soup or surrender to the canned soup I have in the apartment. Then, *he* walks in. I stand up a little straighter and watch him casually wander the store, picking up fresh vegetables and spices as if he knows what to do with them. He doesn't notice me until he gets in line. I quickly turn away to let him know I am not the least bit interested in talking to him. I race back to the building and try to get to the elevator before he gets in, but I don't manage to get the elevator doors closed before he gets on with a new girl. She is all over him, biting his lip and moaning at his every touch of her body. I can barely find a place to look without noticing them. By the time we get to my floor, I can't get around them before the doors shut again. It's like he does these things on purpose. We ride all the way to the top, a penthouse loft. *He's in the penthouse?* When the doors open, I sit back against the wall. He doesn't say a word as he glances my way and walks out of the elevator with the latest casualty to women's lib. Whispering in her ear and rubbing his hand over her body, he escorts her into his lair with no apologies. And here I am ... wondering how it feels to be *her.*

CHAPTER 9

Austin

Trying to find a runaway in this city is impossible. I might as well be trying to find a needle in a haystack. The only lead I can find on this kid is that he used to buy drugs from Merlin. Merlin is a small time drug dealer we have arrested a few times, but it rarely sticks since he usually gives up someone else to save his own neck.

"There's the loser now." Jamee points out Merlin rounding the corner. We both jump out of the car, and immediately, he takes off running. *He really needs to stop smoking.* We jog to keep up with him and wait until he hits the fence that we know he will never make it over.

Jamee and I both stand at the bottom, waiting for him to finally fall back to the ground. "Give up, Merlin. You're never going to make it. Besides, we only want to talk."

"Talk, my ass! Last time you two wanted to talk I had to hide out for three months." He grunts and groans as he tries to pull himself over the seven foot fence. Jamee shakes her head at me. "Alright we don't have all day." I grab his leg and pull him to the ground. "Help! Help! Police brutality! Help they are hurting me, hurting me bad. Oh so bad," he cries, flopping around on the ground.

"Oh shut up. We haven't touched you, but I swear I will if you don't quit," Jamee says.

I grab his collar, pick him up off the ground, and put him back on his feet to his shock. "If you try running again I will shoot you in the foot," I say to him.

"Don't worry. I think I busted a lung on that last run," he says, taking out a pack of smokes. "So what do the queens of the police force want today?" I take out Nelson's picture and show it to him. "Oh Nelson, yeah what about him? I haven't seen him in a while."

"Do you know him well enough to know where he might hide out?" I ask.

"Nope. All I know about him is that he likes comic books and weed. If you want to know more, I would checkout runaway row, down at 9th and Ponce. Those kids know every runaway there is, but I doubt they talk to you two."

"Can you talk to them for us Merlin? It's really important. This kid possibly witnessed a murder, and we need to find him before the wrong people do."

Merlin nods. "He's a good kid. Helped me out a few times. I'll see what I can do, but I can't make any promises."

"That's all we ask. Thanks Merlin," I say, punching his arm playfully as Jamee does the same.

"Owe! Damn it! If I bruise, I'm suing!" he yells as we leave him be.

When we get back to the station, our shift is technically over, so I try to sneak in some work to try and locate this kid before it is too late.

"Reed! What are you doing?" my captain asks as he catches me hiding behind my computer screen.

"I was just finishing up some paperwork."

"Well finish up your paperwork and take a couple of days off before getting back to work. You are over your hours already," he yells. "I don't need your father on my ass any more than he already is about budgets."

The paperwork has never bothered me, but the idea of a few days off, with no clue of what to do with my free time … "Oh, sir, I am happy to come in and help out with filing or …"

"Reed, no. Go home. Do whatever it is you do when you're not here and enjoy it."

"I swear, Austin, you have got to be the lamest partner ever." Jamee crashes into her seat looking me over. "Why don't you go out, go get laid or something, anything to loosen up that tight ass of yours? I mean, I love you and all, but I can't take much more of your overenthusiastic love for your job. It's a job, one that I thought would be exciting but most of the time it turns out to be nothing but paperwork. And the pay is for shit. I really need to find a rich husband. I would quit this in a heartbeat if I did."

"I think you would be back. You know you'd miss this place," I say to her.

"I most certainly would not! I can adapt very easily to being taken care of and living the high life." She puts her feet up on her desk, checking her email and shopping for new clothes while I fill out our reports.

I roll my eyes. "If you have some place better to be, feel free to go."

"Are you sure? I would hate to put you out, keep you from … Oh what am I talking about?! You never go anywhere interesting, and you certainly don't have anyone to go home to. Thanks. See ya," she says, grabbing her coat and running out the door before I can even think of changing my mind.

When I finish my paperwork, I think of asking my brother and Billy if they have plans tonight, but they are already gone too. I head home and hope that Preston may be home and available to go see a movie or something. I really should stop being a homebody and get out and … most certainly get laid. It's been since … since, I don't even remember. *Oh shit.*

I get a sudden rush of excitement when I do indeed find Preston at home making himself something to eat. "Hey, you are home. You would not believe my day. How about before you take that bite of food we go out to dinner and then maybe a movie. We can catch up on each other's week?"

"Breathe girl. Don't worry. I won't rush out the door and

76

leave you here alone. I think dinner sounds good ..." he tosses his food in the trash after taking one bite, "Because these leftovers are awful. However, no movie."

"Why not?"

"Because sitting in the dark is depressing; we might as well sit here and ... no, we are not doing that either. We are going to get dressed up and go out and have fun." My shoulders sink as I sigh. "No pouting. Surely we can find something in your closet that isn't so manly."

"I'm not manly."

"No, you just tend to dress like one. If I didn't know better, I would think you were gay."

"Maybe I am," I say causing him to laugh. "What?"

"Nothing, but I have never known a gay woman get all nuts over a man before."

"What man have I gone nuts for ... ever?"

"Hmmm ... I don't know." He hums wandering into my room and opening up my closet. I chase after him and stomp my foot with crossed arms, waiting for him to explain. He sorts through my closet, trying to ignore me. "You can stand there all day pretending you don't know who I am talking about, but you were dreaming about him the other night, and it sounded like it was a hot and heavy dream." I step back in shock. *Oh shit! I didn't realize that dream had gotten so vocal.* "So you have been dreaming about him. I knew it!"

"You liar! I haven't been dreaming about anyone."

"Oh Dace, ohhhh, touch me there, and ohhh I love when you ..." I throw a pillow at him as I crash onto my bed, wanting to deny it. I don't know why I can't get that distasteful piece of shit out of my head. "I still can't believe you let him put his tongue in your mouth."

"I didn't let him. He caught me off guard."

"You?! Ha, I don't think so. I think you would have fucked

him right there if he had asked. I don't blame you, he is ...."

"Disgusting. A beastly ..."

"Hunk of a man! Those deep blue eyes and that dark wavy hair, I could run my fingers through it all day long. And did you see how tight his undershirt was on his chest. I saw him drive up on that motorcycle the other day. Damn that man is ... well all man and more."

"Aren't you seeing someone, like his brother?"

"Oh, don't get me wrong, Antony is amazing, a great body albeit thinner than his brother's and he has that bad boy persona that makes my knees weak, but he doesn't have Dace's piercing eyes and confidence. If I were you, I would play a little hard to get before you fuck him."

"I am not going to fuck him. What good would that do?"

"What good would it do? Oh my, it has been awhile for you, so long, you have surely forgotten what sex feels like." I huff at him. "Don't get upset just put this on."

"What's this?"

"It's called a dress and high heels. I was surprised too that you would have such a thing." I hold it up to me, and we both snarl at it. "It's not sexy at all, but I can fix that." He runs out of the room, yelling at me to stay away until he's done. He comes back and has done some horrible things to a dress that once was modest and somewhat fit me.

"I don't think this is going to fit me now."

"Sure it will. It will fit better than anything you own, trust me. Now get dressed while I go do what little I need to in order to look Ahhh-mazing myself."

I managed to get the awkward dress on, and after a lot of coaxing, I even take my coat off before sitting down to dinner. "So I am all dressed up. Where exactly are we going after dinner? Dancing? To see a band? Or watch a movie?" I murmur the later quietly to Preston as he quickly stops texting and shoves his phone into his pocket. I narrow my eyes at him, but he ignores my obvious distrust of his actions and begins talking about something else. "Preston! Who were you talking to?" I ask him over and over again all the way through dinner before he finally gives.

"Oh my god! You are insanely persistent. Fine, I was texting Antony. He wants to meet up."

"Don't you ditch me! This is our time; you promised!"

"I would never do that. I wouldn't even think of it."

I watch him closely as he looks everywhere but at me. "You're going to make me the third wheel then?" He shakes his head and smiles. "Oh no, no Preston. Who is it? Who are you forcing me to deal with all night while you canoodle with your boyfriend?"

"Canoodle? Really?" He snickers at me.

"Stop stalling and tell me ..." I say as Antony walks into the room with some flowers. *Oh boy.*

He leans over Preston and kisses his cheek respectively as he hands him the flawless display of flora. "Hello, Handsome. How was your day?" Antony says smoothly, causing me to get a little excited, and it causes Preston to actually giggle like a school girl as his love sits down next to him and takes his hand. Oh wow. He is head over heels for this guy. I can't say that I blame him; Antony is one tall, good-looking man. *I wish he wasn't gay, but they are kind of cute together.* I shake my head smiling as I turn up my drink and look down the glass at stormy blue eyes.

"Hello again," Dace says to me, and instantly my heart

flutters. I hate that he can do that to me.

"Hi," I say, looking around him and toward the people dancing. I don't like him, and he is not at all good looking … not even a little bit. I glance at him, and his cocky smirk forms. *Oh wow.* I haven't been able to sleep without dreaming about him or work without thinking about him. His confidence is attractive, but his bad boy outer layer seems to hide a layer of a man that would hold me all night to protect me from my nightmares. He's strong and obviously intelligent, and he watches me when he thinks I don't realize it. There is something about him, and I hate that I am so good at seeing through a person because I really want to dislike him right now.

"Nice dress," he says with a deep hum in his voice while looking over my body with a slow wandering eye. By the time he looks back up into my eyes, my tongue is quivering. "Did you wear that for me?" I shake my head, unable to speak. "Is that silk? I love how silk feels." He reaches over and rubs his hand along the fabric up my leg.

"Um, no. I think it's a poly blend … I think," I say, feeling a tingle along my skin with his touch.

He laughs. "Okay."

I look up at him, and suddenly, I feel like an idiot. Taking a deep breath, I sit up straight and cross my legs to the opposite side, causing my dress to push up my thigh. Dace instantly takes notice, giving me my confidence back. "So did you wear that for me?" I ask him, looking him over with a bite of my lip.

"Actually, I didn't know you were going to be here until we walked in," he says with a cool attitude.

I huff softly to myself as he, seemingly bored with the evening, looks away. Determined, I scoot closer to him and rub my hand up his leg as he did mine, which seemed like a good idea in my head but, in reality, doesn't work out quite the same. "So is this silk?" I mumble awkwardly, sitting in front of him with my hand on his thigh and staring right into his confused expression.

Before I can pull away, he grabs my hand and leans in close.

"Is there something you need, Sweetheart?" I shake my head and pull away, mortified.

I look over at Preston and his wide eyes as he mouths, "What the fuck are you doing?"

"Um, I think I need to go …" I get up and quickly try to grab my purse as the three men scramble to stand and help me up, only causing more confusion. I am not sure which direction to go to leave, and I end up rushing away from Dace and right into a waiter who accidently knocks me backwards and into Dace's lap. Thankfully, he looks as shocked as I do. I try to get back up, but he blocks me. "No, I really want to go home."

I jump up, and he hovers around me, trying to wrap his coat around me. "I think you should take my coat; it's longer on you," he says as I look down at my dress that is coming apart at the seams. The moment I stand up fully, the dress comes apart. Dace buttons his coat around me, and I stand silently, looking at this man that is trying to protect me from complete humiliation, but for some reason, I am disappointed that he is so quick to cover me up and dress me. I would have thought he would enjoy seeing something of me, if even for a split second.

"Thank you," I say with my hand over my face. "I … I have to go." I rush out of the restaurant, forgetting my own coat at the coat check, and catch a cab ride home. As soon as I get through the door, I, still wrapped in his coat, crawl into bed and bury my face in my pillow. For once, I wish I could be one of those perfect girly girls and be able to seduce a man, make him want me. I have never been good at being a seductive woman. I prefer wrestling men to the ground and holding them there while I tie their hands and arrest them. I like control more than bending over and letting them have what they want. I prefer my sneakers over heels, my weapon more than a purse, and I would never ask a man for permission to do anything. Needless to say, I haven't gone on many dates; I'm a little too hard and manly, I guess. The only dates I do go on are ones with fellow cops because, for some reason, when I am on the job, all my awkwardness and social ineptness disappears, and I seem… no, I feel normal, like I belong. I still can't believe I said that to him and touched him like I was at all sexy in that moment. "Stupid! Stupid! You should have just said, 'If you like the dress so much then you should see what's underneath, if you're man enough that is'." *Oh! That's pretty good.*

"I did like the dress and what was underneath, not that I was expecting to see both in such a short period of time, but I'm not complaining," Dace says, leaning against the door frame of my room.

"Oh no, please go away and leave me alone."

"I can't. You have my coat and my phone too." I look down and push my hand into his pocket, pulling out his phone and a couple of pieces of paper with female numbers on them.

"Oh, sorry." I look down at his phone as a woman's name appears. "Scarlett wants to know how much longer you are going to be. She misses your big … wow, and she wants to do some pretty dirty things to you." I hand him the phone. "You better hurry before she explodes as she says she will surely do."

"I still need my coat, too," he says as his tongue moves across the edges of his teeth, reminding me of its touch against mine and the trembling it caused within my body.

My desires suddenly give way to anger. I don't know why, but I am pissed that he was supposed to be my date for the night and he was planning on ditching me the whole time. It didn't matter what I said or did. He really was going to write me off for Horny Scarlett. "You know what? You're an asshole!" His cocky expression quickly changes to a puzzled one. "You know you are. How dare you make plans with another woman when you were supposed to be out with me."

"Excuse me? When were we on a date?"

"At the restaurant. You showed up so I wouldn't be the third wheel. I know Preston and Antony are trying to get us together. Why? I have no idea. We have absolutely nothing in common." I babble on while he stares at me blankly. "The proper thing to do Dace … is to give a woman a chance, treat her with respect. Not every woman is smooth, with a sharp witted comment for every situation, but that doesn't mean they aren't just as wonderful as any of the rest. What is it about Scarlett that makes her better to spend time with over me? Huh? What?"

"Do you need medication of some kind?" he asks.

"No, I don't need medication! What I need, Dace, is some respect. You want your coat back so you can go see Scarlett, well here." I take off his coat and toss it to him. I stand up straight and proud in nothing but my underwear. "Enjoy your night since apparently this isn't good enough for you." I walk away only to turn back with another point that comes to mind. "And another thing …," I stop as he tosses the coat and begins walking towards me. "What are you doing?" He doesn't answer; he only continues to look me over before walking right up on me.

"Let me tell you something, Austin. I think you're one of the most beautiful women I have ever seen. You are certainly the most fascinating I have ever met, and I have known a lot of women around the world, but not one has ever criticized me for asking for my coat back. There was no plan to set us up. I was simply planning on dropping Antony off and borrowing his car to take Scarlett out on a date. She complains when I pick her up on my motorcycle, but she was running late, so I came into the restaurant to have a drink while I waited to hear from her. I saw you and thought maybe we could try again, since we haven't seemed to have gotten along so well, thus far."

"You stuck your tongue in my mouth."

"Yeah, I do that sometimes."

"What do you mean you do that sometimes? Who does that?"

"I wanted to see how you would react." He moves in closer, backing me up against a wall. "See, like now. I try to get closer to you, and you back away. I need the help of walls to keep you near me." He runs his fingers through my hair, sliding them down my face. "Do you want to be near me Austin? Do you want anything from me?" He leans in and kisses my neck softly; I feel a twinge of excitement race down between my breasts, causing my nipples to harden. "If you want me to stay, then ask me. If you want a date, then encourage me to ask you."

"Stay if you want, but I won't be manipulated into begging for you, and I am certainly not going to ask for a date when it should be offered with respect." He looks at me in shock. "Now, if you don't mind, I'm going to get dressed and sit down and enjoy a movie. You are welcome to join me if you'd like, but don't expect much more from me." I walk away from him with a sway of my hips and a bite of my bottom lip as I slide on some pants and a shirt. He starts to say many things, but somehow, I captured his tongue, and he's speechless. I push him to the living room and show him where to sit. We don't say much, and he really doesn't say anything at all as he watches me from the corner of his eyes. I trade glances with him throughout the movie, but I'm careful not to scare him away with too many words. All this time all I had to do was treat a man like he was a suspect, and I could gain the control I want. I only need to be patient. "I just ordered some new movies, and I have margarita mix. We could play a game together, a board game or something…" I am not going to have sex with him, I'm not. Preston was right; he wouldn't respect someone like that.

"Movies and board games?" he asks.

I nod. "I understand if you would rather go be with that other woman, but I am sorry. Despite my appearance, I am not going to do those same things she has planned for you. So, Dace, it's your choice. Scarlett and all her new fantasy ideas and toys or stay here and try to be my friend, get to know me a little, and watch a movie." I go into the kitchen, waiting for the front door to shut, which it does. I sigh, not surprised but still, I have to admit I am a little disappointed. I grab my drink and a blanket and curl up on the sofa, preparing to watch the scary movie by myself. When the door opens again, I sit up with a wide smile. *Oh wow, it worked.*

Dace tosses Preston's keys on the side table with a frustrated sigh. "Stop smiling at me. What's this damn movie we are watching? It better be good if I am not going to get laid tonight. He curses himself as he crashes next to me on the sofa. He eyes me harshly as I hide my smile. "My coat smells like you now. She would have cut my balls off if I showed up with your scent all over me. And Antony took Preston to my loft, so I have nowhere else to go, thank you very much."

"You can stay here. You can even sleep on the couch if you like."

We eye each other with a humored smile. "Thank you, I will. I do sleep in the nude though, so try not to sneak in a peak while I sleep."

"Oh I wouldn't even consider it." I breathe slowly.

CHAPTER 10

Dace

I'm on the fucking couch. I am actually being forced to sleep on the fucking couch. I sat here all night watching her stupid movies and playing her stupid games, and yet, I am still on this fucking couch. I am starting to despise this woman.

When I open my eyes the next morning, I see Antony sitting across from me, clearly humored by the situation. "Sleep well Dace?"

"Fuck you," I say, slowly getting out of my awkward position. "Are you done with my place? Can I go back home now?"

"Oh, yeah. I was done last night. We came back here and slept."

"What? Why didn't you tell me that?"

"Because you looked so peaceful. I don't think I have ever seen you sleep so soundly and without the protection of all your high-tech security even."

"I was tired—more than usual I'm sure," I say, grabbing my things and leaving so we don't have to discuss me being comfortable in what is still a stranger's home.

I can't get her out of my head. All day I try to figure out what happened. I had control. I had her. I should have been waking up in her bed this morning with her naked body stretched out over mine. I must have done something wrong, looked her way too much or something. I need to be indifferent and uninterested. I step into the building as she is getting her mail. I don't even give her a second glance as I walk by, and when she steps onto the elevator, I look straight ahead, and when she sweeps her hair behind her shoulder and it floats her invigorating scent across my face I ... I turn and face her with anger.

"Yes?" she says, which really pisses me off.

"Would you like to have dinner with me?" I ask.

"I would love to," she says sweetly.

"Alright then. I will see you ... later?" I say, still unsure of what just happened.

"I'll be ready by eight."

"Okay", I reply to the air as she walks out the elevator and to her place. "What the fuck just happened? I'm not even hungry."

I show up at her door promptly at eight, still cursing myself for ending up in this mess. I should leave, show her that she can't trick me into doing what she wants. I can still get control back by leaving her waiting. I smile and step back from the door and start to walk away when the door opens. Austin steps out from behind it looking...

"Speechless, are you? Then I guess you like my new outfit? I'm not used to such things, but I thought I would try something new for one night." I know she is talking, but every curve of her body shows within her tight sweater and even tighter pants and those fuck me boots are enough to send me kneeling at her feet. She suddenly throws on a biker jacket and grabs a helmet.

"Got your own helmet do you?"

"I thought it best, that way I can make sure of its safety. I don't know you well enough yet to trust your judgment on such matters." She smiles, shutting the door and walking ahead of me. I follow after that amazing ass happily. She follows me to my motorcycle while I wait for her to change her mind, but she never does. She puts her helmet on and climbs on back with me and feels her way around my back to my chest and then she says, "Go."

I rev it up and go like the lady asked me to, driving around the streets finding the best roads to take her on. The more I feel her enjoyment of it, the longer I go, the faster I go, and the more fun I have. "Are you hungry or are you having too much fun?" I ask her.

"Just a few moments longer and then you better buy me the best meal I have ever had."

I rub my hand down her thigh. "Deal." We ride into the next city, and I stop at an old pizza parlor that my mother used to bring me to. I take her hand as we walk in and find my favorite place to sit, a nice quiet place in the back.

"This is the best meal I could possibly have?" she asks.

"Oh, yes it is. I promise you," I say, enjoying her happiness. "You aren't that scary."

"Who said I was scary?"

"Well, you come off a little hard, and you don't seem to like people much."

"I don't. People only cause pain, and they rarely can be trusted to do otherwise—even when they say they love you," she says honestly, and I begin to understand her a little bit more.

"I agree." She doesn't say much while we eat; she simply enjoys the meal with a few sweet glances my way that make me a little crazy. I am so distracted watching her swirl that cheese around her tongue I miss my own mouth. She laughs grabbing a napkin and wiping my face for me, looking into my eyes the whole time. Before she can pull her hand away, I take hold of it and kiss the palm of her hand, getting a nice whiff of her perfume she sprayed on her wrist. "That's a nice perfume."

Austin smiles warmly running her fingers along my face and removing some strands of hair from my eyes. "You have warm eyes, I like it better when I can see them." My heart flutters and I am not sure why.

When we finish eating she follows me right back onto my bike. We ride for a couple of more hours before I take her home. I walk her to her door, and that is as far as she willing to let me go. "You're not going to let me in to watch a movie?"

"No, I'm tired now and need to get some sleep before work tomorrow."

"Can I not even have a kiss? I did buy you dinner."

"And gave me a nice ride too."

"Let me in and I could give you a much better one."

"Hmmm, as tempting as that sounds, I think I would prefer sleep tonight. But I will do one thing for you."

"And what's that?" I ask as she leans in and touches my lips with hers so softly I barely feel them. "Is that all I get?"

"For now," she says, looking into my eyes as if she is searching for something.

"What do you want from me, Austin?"

"What do you want from me, Dace? After all, you asked me out." She kisses my cheek and leaves me at her door, confused and with a bulge in my pants that is anxious to get out. Unfortunately, I have no place for it to go.

Another date with Austin, and I still don't make it inside afterwards. We had a great night at the movie theatre; she held my hand and let me sneak in a quick kiss here and there but never much more. I have never been more frustrated. If that's the way it's going to be, then I'm not going to ask her out again. I'll wait for her to ask me, which I'm sure will happen.

Days later, she hasn't even texted me. I end up going to bed early since I can get nothing else done. I wake up in the middle of the night sensing something is wrong. I'm not sure why. Even after I check the security cameras, I can't shake the feeling. I call Antony, and after he chews me out for waking him up, I assume he's okay and hang up. Michael and Ettore should be fine with all their bodyguards and my father the same, so what is it? I pace around, take a drink, and decide to check on her. I knock on her door and then think about running until she opens the door in a towel. "Ummm, hey. What are you doing up?"

"What are you doing at my door so late?"

"I ... I don't know. I was having trouble sleeping and was wondering if I could borrow that pillow I used when I slept here. It was really comfortable." I know it sounds completely ridiculous, but I was desperate, and she's distracting me with all her wetness.

"I guess I can understand that. I have trouble sleeping too sometimes. I haven't found a pillow that helps though. The only thing I found that helps at all is ..." She grabs her towel. "Is a hot bath."

"Why can't you sleep, Austin?"

"A lot on my mind I guess. Let me go get that pillow for you." She comes back with the damn pillow and hands it to me. "It's not a very expensive pillow, but you are welcome to keep it if it helps you that much."

"Thanks, I owe you one. You know, I have a great recipe for a drink that will help you sleep."

"It's not that I can't get to sleep it's ..." She sighs and smiles. "I think I'm okay now."

She doesn't look fine. "Since you're up, how about going for a ride with me, maybe the night air will help relieve your stress a little bit." She looks at me and laughs as if I'm crazy. "Come on, can't hurt. Maybe it will help us both." She thinks about it for a minute before surprisingly agreeing.

The good thing about Austin is she doesn't take any time to get ready to go anywhere. We are on my bike and driving down the road within fifteen minutes. The streets are quiet this late at night, and it is certainly cold. I can feel her shivering against my back. I start to say something, but she tightens her embrace around me, and it feels too good to stop. I put a hand on hers and hold it and go around a few more times before driving back and getting her into the warm building.

"I wish we could stay out there longer, maybe drive and never come back."

"You're shivering. You need a warm bed and possibly some hot chocolate. Let me make you some. I make the best hot chocolate around." I don't give her a chance to say no. I take her hand and escort her to my place. I can't get rid of my smile as she comes in and waits for me to make her the best hot chocolate she's ever had.

"Wow, this is really good."

"Told you," I say, sitting down next to her. "Are you still cold?" I scoot closer to her and pull a blanket onto both of us. She watches my every move but avoids looking into my eyes. "Austin …" She looks up at me and I take advantage. Taking hold of her lips, I savor each one fully and encourage her mouth open so I can tease her tongue. The kiss feels so good, I want more. She relaxes, grasping my face and turning her body towards me. I pull her into my lap and situate her perfectly when my cell goes off. *You have got to be fucking kidding me!* I try to ignore it and enjoy the moment I have been waiting for.

"You should probably get that," she says, moving away from me. "People who call this late are usually in trouble."

If they aren't, I'll make sure they are. "Okay, stay right there though. Don't move." I get my phone and answer it. "What?!"

"Don't yell at me. I'm just checking on you," Antony says sarcastically. "Payback is a bitch, and I haven't been able to get back to sleep since you woke me up asshole."

"Drink some hot chocolate, Antony, and call me tomorrow, late tomorrow. I'm hanging up now." I hang up and turn off my ringer so he doesn't interrupt me again. I rush out to Austin who is sound asleep on my sofa. *Damn.* I take the blanket, cover her up completely, and give her the pillow she gave me to sleep with before going to bed myself. I, somehow, fall back to sleep and have the best sleep I have had since my evening on her couch. She's gone by the time I wake up, but she left the pillow with a note pinned to it.

Thank you for a great night. I have never slept so well. — Austin

I can't find anything on a John Scott that matches the man Antony and I once knew. My system seems to be working fine, but I am still having trouble getting it to find what I need it to. I'm not sure why. I can't seem to get anything to work right these days. I stand up, kick a chair, and fist my hair in frustration with a roar.

"Problem?" Antony asks, looking up from his magazine.

"Why are you here?"

"To help."

"Help with what? All you do is sit there and read."

"No, I don't. I went and got lunch for us both."

"Thanks." I shake my head, punching one of my boxing bags. "You know, you should let me teach you some fighting techniques since you're here."

"Will that help with all your pent-up sexual frustration?"

"I don't have pent-up sexual frustration. Now, come on. I need a good workout so I can clear my head."

"You need a good fuck," he murmurs.

"What did you say?"

"Nothing, just excited to get our fight on," he says sarcastically. "What? I am. I really am."

I roll my eyes and point him to an area of the room that is clear for us to fight. Antony is okay to win a regular bar brawl, but to deal with real killers, he is nowhere near ready. I prepare him so well he sheds his shirt, wipes his brow, and stares back at me with intensity. "You almost look as if you want to kill me."

"You're pissing me off!" he snaps much the same way I did when Peter was teaching me.

"Good," I laugh and begin again. When we finish, I feel refreshed and able to think again, so much so that I devise a plan to take back control over that woman.

CHAPTER II

Austin

It's been a long day searching for a runaway in between doing more "important work" as my captain calls it. I am so tense and ready to relax that I can hardly wait to jump into a hot bath. Preston is out, and the place is quiet except for some great relaxing music, a hot bubble bath, and then … there's a knock at the door. I peak through the peep hole and see Dace. I argue with myself, trying to decide if I should let him in or not. I am liable to give in to him tonight. I'm too tired to be hard to get, and I really want to kiss him again. I open the door a crack. "Hey Dace."

"Are you going to let me in?"

"I don't know," I say a little too honestly.

He laughs. "You don't know? Why is that?" I shake my head and open the door, motioning for him to come in. "I only wanted to see if you would like to go get something to eat or go for a ride?"

"I had a rough day and really wanted to have a quiet night here."

"Does that mean you want me to go?" he asks, looking oh so good.

"No, of course not. If you want to stay here and be really bored, then you can."

"I doubt I'd be bored unless we play another one of those horrible board games," he laughs. "We can stay here together and watch a movie if you want?"

"Okay and maybe we can talk and get to know each other better. We really haven't done a lot of that yet."

"Yeah… I was kind of enjoying the no talking thing," I sigh, and he laughs. "Okay fine, we can talk."

He makes himself at home while I make us some popcorn for the movie he selected. I do my best innocent look before offering him some popcorn, and he takes some, seeming impressed with the snack. "Did you make this or was this out of a microwave."

"Microwave, but I add my own special ingredients that my mother taught me about."

"It's pretty good."

"Better than sex good?" I laugh, but he doesn't. It's been a long time since I liked a man so much that I would give up my peaceful night alone. My last boyfriend was wonderful, until I caught him in bed with another woman. Being a cop doesn't always make things easier, especially when you get an unexpected night off and decide to surprise your boyfriend by tracking him all the way to another woman's house. I look Dace over and shake my head, thinking he would be the type to do the same thing, only I doubt he would bother to even chase after me to apologize. I shouldn't get involved with him. Why do I keep letting him in? "So, Dace Coleman, you don't look Irish."

He looks over at me oddly, "What?"

"Dace Coleman; that is your name, isn't it? I assume your last name is the same as Antony's, right?"

"Oh, um, yeah, our … father is a mix of many things."

Nodding, I try to think of something else to ask him, anything to get him talking and, hopefully, giving up enough information so I can find out who he is and why I can't locate him on any database. "So, what do you do?"

"I work in the family business, handling the company's technology framework and making sure we are keeping up with our competitors. And you?"

"Oh, um …" I never know what to say to this question. Being a cop, a detective even, usually scares people, especially men with a suspicious background. I need him to feel comfortable with me so he will keep talking, "… I basically do a lot of filing and paperwork for the city."

"Hmmm, exciting," he says cynically, pissing me off.

"It is actually. I learn a lot about what's going on in the city, and I am usually the first to know." He nods, sighing as if I am bothering him with conversation. "I know a lot about computers too. I have a double degree in computer science and criminology."

"Oh yeah, criminology," he laughs.

"That's funny?"

"Um no, not really. Interesting that we have similar degrees though."

"You went to college?" I ask in shock.

He sits back and turns completely towards me. "Yeah, I went to college, a big one with books and everything."

"Good for you ... jackass," I say to his amusement. I try to think of something else to ask, something simple, and he answers simply, so I ask another question and another until he sits back, sighing.

"I feel like I am being interrogated," he says, causing me to laugh.

"Sorry. I just thought since you're here we could get to know each other better. I know you're not really interested in this movie."

"No, I would prefer to be enjoying getting to know you in a different way, but you keep putting me off, playing hard to get. So, if we aren't going to make out or have sex, then I guess I am stuck playing twenty questions with you, or rather a thousand questions, considering we passed twenty a while ago. I could be going out with Scarlett, you know, and having sex with a hot model, but I chose to be here." He winks at me, reminding me of our previous argument.

"Oh, so she's a model? And where did you meet her?"

He throws up his hands, exasperated. "Again with the questions?"

"Okay. If you won't answer that question, then answer this—

why did you do what you did to me after we first met?"

"Do what to you?" he asks as if he has no idea what I am talking about.

"You know, with your hands and tongue … all over me. You know what I am talking about."

He smiles, shaking his head. "I was only trying to get you riled up, and I guess it worked if you are still stewing over it."

"I am not stewing. I just don't understand why anyone would do that?"

"You obviously liked it," he retorts, knowing it to be true whether I admit it or not. I scoot away from the obnoxious ego. "Why are you scooting away from me? You keep moving away. Did I bite you and not realize it? I don't usually bite, although sometimes, if I have the right ass in front of me, I do like to take a little taste and move from there to …" he looks me over with a smile. "Turn around let me see your ass. Maybe I left a mark." He pulls me up before I have a chance to realize what he is doing.

I smack his hands away. "Don't look at my ass!"

He holds his hands out as if he is confused by my actions. "How else am I to know if I bit your ass or not?"

"You didn't bite my ass or any other part of me, I know it."

"Oh, do you want me to? Is that why you are throwing such a fuss?"

"I'm not throwing a fuss."

"Oh, I think you are. You are standing up and all flustered and upset. Your nipples are even poking out of your shirt. Look." I look down and quickly cross my arms in front of my breasts.

"You're a jackass. Have you ever had a girlfriend? And before you point out all the girls you have been with, I mean an actual girlfriend, someone you have been with for longer than one night."

"Do I need one for longer than one night?" he asks, unashamed.

"Wow, so you're not able to keep a woman. That says a lot," I say, returning the frustration back to him.

"I can keep a woman, if I want to. Trust me. I have no problem with that. In fact, I have a hard time getting rid of them. Women always want to be clingy and know everything I am doing. I prefer to come and go as I please."

"Lonely are you?" I say with a sympathetic tone.

"I am not fucking lonely. I just told you I don't like to be tied down is all."

"That's what lonely people say." I bite my lip, trying not to laugh at his frustrated sighs.

"Are you enjoying yourself?" I nod happily. "Oh, well good for you. You pissed me off. Now I know why you're single."

"I am single because I work a lot and don't have a lot of free time to date."

"Uh-huh, spending a lot of late nights filing and wearing men's shoes. I am sure men all over the city are crying about their loss."

"My shoes are perfectly suited for the job duties I have to perform."

"My shoes are perfectly suited," he mocks me, "… who the hell talks like that?"

"I do, and I am good with my life. At least I have relationships for more than one night."

"Oh yeah, where is he?" He stands up, looking around.

"I told you, I work a lot."

He crashes back down next to me. "Bullshit! You're too much of a tight ass to get a man. I seriously doubt you can hold onto one, if you do manage to stumble into one," he says, getting ready to stuff some popcorn into his mouth while I steam. I reach over and knock the popcorn out of his hand. "Hey!" he yells before I slug him in the mouth. "Motherfucker!" he growls with tense lips. I become determined to take him down and force him to apologize, but my intentions suddenly turn into a wrestling match. My military training has always served me well, but he is, for some reason, not easy to take down. "What the fuck is your problem woman?"

"I am going to make you apologize," I say, taking my socks off and getting down to my bare feet, readying myself to take him on.

"Oh this is way better than board games," he laughs just before he dodges my right hook. He strips down to his bare feet and prepares himself to clash with me. "You want to do this? Let's do it then, Baby."

"Where did you learn how to fight?" I ask, fascinated by his moves.

"Where did you? I thought you were a filing clerk for the city?" I fall to the floor and sweep his leg, and he follows by flipping backwards and pinning me to a wall. I break free from him and smack him in his face, really pissing him off. We push the furniture out of the way, roll up our sleeves, and I tie my hair up. "Come here, Sweetheart. I have something I want to show you." He grabs me and forces me on the ground, hovering over top of me and feeling very proud of himself until I twist and break free of him again.

"Sorry, I don't need anything you have. Maybe you should try online dating. I hear it works well for repeat lonely daters."

"Ha ha, now come here." Dace chases me while I grab the tieback from the draperies. He grabs me, and I wrap his wrist and spin around him, taking his other and pushing him up against the wall, face forward.

My smile is so wide it's glowing. "You owe me an apology."

"I apologize. Now that I have gotten to know you better, I am sure you tie up men all the time and keep them in your bedroom. Am I next? You going to take advantage of me?" He grimaces.

"Please, you would love every second with me, so much so that you would never want to leave me."

He spins around, ties up my wrists, and holds me against the wall. "Oh yeah? Prove it," he says with his blue eyes beaming. His heart is pounding in rhythm with mine; his manly essence wraps around me, and I begin to realize why I can't get him out of my head. He lets me go and holds his hands out from his side. "I apologize and surrender."

Taking a deep breath, I drop the tieback and race into his arms, taking hold of his lips with pleasure. His kiss is so powerful and strong and with the softest lips I have ever known. My head begins to float as I step back to think.

"Anyone ever tell you that you think too much Austin?" he questions.

"I …" I don't get another word out before he picks me up and carries me to my room. I am in my bed, grasping his shirt tight as he holds my body oh so close to his. His lips along my neck, his hands moving down my pants and gripping my bare ass.

He stops just long enough to pull his shirt off. "I am pretty sure you don't need yours either." He watches me as I raise my arms above my head. He kisses along my side and up my ribs, pulling my shirt off, and within a single breath, his face is buried in between my breasts. I look down on him, watching him, running my fingers through his waves of dark hair and fisting it when I feel his hand slip down from my ass and in between my legs. He doesn't hold back when he touches me and seeks out what he wants from me. His lips move to mine, maneuvering with such skill that my breathing becomes difficult. "You're so wet …" he says with a kiss and a sweep of his tongue, "… I love when it's wet," he continues, licking his finger with a smile. He sits up and rips my pants off to the floor. He smiles suddenly, and I become nervous. He spins me over and pulls down my panties to show my bare ass. "Nope, no bite mark here." He turns me back over, removing my panties and pushing my legs apart as he leans down in between them. "How about a mark here instead…" He kisses my inner thigh and feels inside of me with fingers that are clearly made from the devil's hands because nothing else could feel so good. Dace sucks on my skin with a bite and a teasing trail of his tongue. He slides one hand under my ass and lifts me up to his mouth. I cry out, fisting his hair and begging for control, but the tip of his tongue knows no bounds. I am so hungry for him that I begin to whimper. He sits up, grasping my breast as he leans down to kiss my lips. "That's it. You're mine now. You're marked with my mouth." I nod for some reason; I don't know why, maybe because I want to believe that I am only his and he's only mine. Vulnerable, I lie, completely exposed, in front of him, unable to deny him as I watch him undo his pants and pull out his already brimming cock. I take hold of it, rubbing my hand all over it as he moans against my neck. I want it. I have never craved anything more in my life, and when he finally looks me in the eyes and adjusts his throbbing erection against my pussy, I gasp, feeling the hardened pressure against me. Then, he thrusts, and he thrusts again. I beg out loud for more, so he thrusts again, forcing himself deep inside me. Every motion, every touch, is a pointed fire rushing through my veins to the stirring inferno at my core. He never lets me go, holding my legs around him, caressing my lips with his. My body begins to tremble, and I can hold on no longer. Dace hovers over me, watching attentively. I drop my head back and only regain my composure when he leans in to kiss my lips.

"You are really beautiful. Do you know that? I will admit to you that I have wanted you since you first challenged me, but I be damned if I knew you would feel this goooood." He comes with a roar, and all I can do is hold on as his hips swing down and in, over and over again. I am not sure if I passed out from the pleasure of it all or from exhaustion, but I wake up in the middle of the night cradled in his arms and fall back asleep peacefully.

CHAPTER 12

Dace

"Dace, where have you been?" Ettore asks as I step into his office.

"Working, like you asked. I got all the information you needed, even set up bugs in your enemy's house," I say, falling into a chair.

"Oh yeah? And how did you do that without being caught, or without any assistance from anyone?" Ettore asks in disbelief.

I laugh, throw a speaker onto his desk, and turn it on. Instantly, he begins to hear every movement within the house, "You can switch the channels to change rooms." He does so and sits back in amazement when he hears Aksakov discussing business.

Ettore stiffens as he listens in. "What was it that your friends called you?"

"Ghost," I say proudly.

Ettore nods. "Yes, that's it."

The Aksakovs have a problem with some of their own, a small outfit of drug dealers they are trying to rid themselves of. They are constantly causing more chaos than they are worth. The Aksakovs plan to finish them off today. Ettore wants me and Antony to go and watch how they work. We need not get involved, only watch. It is easy and simple to do. The lowlifes hangout at a corner market, and we sit and wait down the street for the melee to begin. As we wait though, Austin walks up out of nowhere and begins talking to one of the lowlifes.

"What the hell is she doing here?" Antony asks.

"I have no idea, but she is going to get herself killed," I say as she walks inside. Antony looks at me as I quickly try to think of what to do. "Meet me on the other side of the building." I get out of the car and walk up to the market, meeting instant disapproval. None of them scare me; I have battled much worse. Their attacks on me barely knock me off my direct path as I walk right in and find her. I grab her, throw her over my shoulder, and walk out the back, straight to where Antony is waiting for me. I put her in the car and drive away as the market is attacked from all sides. The place is leveled, a complete blood bath, and Austin is pissed off. She screams at me the whole way back home, and I say nothing even though I have a million questions for her.

I escort her back to her place to make sure she stays put, hoping the Aksakovs don't know she was there. She pushes me back from her still steaming figure as soon as we step inside. "What were you doing there? Why did you carry me out of there? Who are you? Who do you work for?"

"I didn't have anything to do with that, Austin. I only knew about it and saw you walking in. All you need to know is that I risked my job for you." She focuses on me. "I was not supposed to get involved at all, but I messed up and got involved to get you out. Now a family that was going to cleanly wipe out those men had issues because those men were on alert and were ready to do battle. There were more lives lost than necessary all because I refused to let you die." She doesn't say a word. "Now, tell me, what were you doing there?"

"I have my reasons just like you have yours. I was looking for someone that they know, and that's all you need to know."

She is so frustrating! "Damn it, Austin! Who does that? I know you think you are a badass, but you shouldn't be walking up on a known drug house."

"I was only looking to buy a soda, Dace," she says calmly, turning her back to me.

"Don't walk away from me. I have a million questions for you." I grab her arm, forgetting her skills for a second.

She throws me to the ground and holds me there. "Leave before you get hurt," she says.

I flip her on her back and hover over her. "No, I'm not leaving you until I know for sure they aren't looking for you."

She squirms out and lands on top of me in a very erotic position. "I can take care of myself. I don't need you. I don't need anyone to take care of me."

I grab her face and pull her in close. "You are so much trouble. Just a sexy, beautiful bundle of trouble." She relaxes some, and I kiss her. "You can't keep me from looking out for you, no matter how hard you try to push me away, Trouble."

"I can push pretty hard."

"And I am pretty strong, so you're going to have to do a whole hell of a lot of pushing." She stares at me with a heavy exhale, and I slowly lean up and take in her lips again, lift her shirt off over her head, and undo her bra, enjoying her breasts bouncing in my face. Austin cradles my head to her breasts and then allows me to roll her over and slide her pants off. We are both naked in an instant and fucking each other hard in the middle of her living room floor. It all feels so good until we hear a noise. Someone lurks outside her door, and we both scramble towards our guns and wait as they fumble with the lock. When Preston walks through, he immediately stops breathing.

"Preston, you're home early," Austin snaps at him.

"Um… yeah, I wasn't feeling well, and … why are you both pointing guns at me? I'm not really enjoying that."

We lower our guns and relax. "Sorry, are you going to be okay?" I ask him. He breathes deeply and then looks me over, before stopping at my still hard cock. "Oh we were …"

"Uh-huh, I got it. Thanks for that at least," he says, walking to his bedroom and shutting the door behind him.

I look at Austin holding a gun completely naked and smile. "I knew you had a gun in that drawer." She smiles, and I walk towards her. "Now, what else are you hiding?"

"Nothing, can't you see?"

"No, let me get a closer look." I pick her up, take her to her room, and forget about the rest of my day.

Her bed is comfortable; her body, stretched out naked against me, is warm and incredibly sexy. I am not sure what woke me up until I see Antony poking his head into the doorway. We forgot to shut her bedroom door after we ate. I carefully squeeze out from under her and pull on my pants before walking out into their living room. "When did you get here?" I ask.

"A few hours ago, in time to hear all the heavy breathing and the … Oh Dace, Dace Oh, Ohhhh," he moans into a dramatic presentation.

"Shut up. Now what's the word?"

"Things happened so fast that no one recognized either of you coming or going. Anyone that did, died, so I think you're both in the clear for now, unless Ettore finds out. Now, can I ask a question? Because you two looked like you were ready to kill each other when I dropped you off, and she was determined to get you to tell her everything. So how did you two go from being pissed off as hell at each other to fucking all day and night? You obviously didn't tell her who you really are."

"We fought it out, and after wrestling around with our issues, we realized we both are just two very private, sexy people who have a lot of questions for each other. Now, if you don't mind, I am going back to bed."

"Make sure you answer every question thoroughly or she might punish you."

I look back at my brother's overly smiling face. "Hm, maybe I won't answer them at all then. I kind of like her rough touch." I slide back into her bedroom, shutting the door behind me.

"I thought you left," she says, sitting up in bed, holding the blankets over her naked body.

After unzipping my pants, I ease back into bed with her, kissing up her arm and neck before enjoying her lips fully. "No, why would I do that when there is so much here I would miss if I left?"

She lies back, opening her entire naked body up to my lips and wandering hands. I move slowly, teasing her and enjoying her fondling of my ass. "You like my ass, do you?"

"Among other things."

I push my hips a little further into her. "Yeah, like what other things?"

"Your gun," she laughs.

I nod, laughing. She's so much sweeter in this light, but I am still completely confused by this woman. Who is she? And what is she about? I don't know why I care, but I want to know more about her. "Why are you so scared, Austin? Why did you move into a building like this, lock every door, and watch every move every person makes around you? Did someone hurt you? Is that why you were there today—looking for someone who hurt you?" I ask, kissing her and caressing her body to try and make her feel comfortable enough to confide in me. I hear a slight whimper, and I raise up to look at her suddenly shy eyes. "Is it that bad, Trouble? You don't have to tell me. I just don't like to think of you scared of anything."

Her focus changes to her fingers, tracing circles on my chest. I suddenly feel as if I have gone too far. There is more to this than her simply hiding something. She's protecting herself from someone, and that, I feel, is none of my damn business. I start to shake it off when she begins to speak. "It was my mother." Her sad eyes pull at me as she fights to explain something obviously painful. "We were out shopping, picking up the usual things for dinner. It was a normal, happy day with my mother, one I didn't have to share with my brother for once. When we got home, these men came out of nowhere and forced their way inside. My father and brother were out together somewhere. I don't even remember where, so there was no one there to protect us. They …" She pauses, and I gulp, kissing her forehead and wishing I had kept my mouth shut. "They raped her, beat her, and made me sit there and wait my turn. The first chance I got to sneak out of their sight, I took it and called 911 … those men were so mad. They were searching for me and screaming for me, threatening to kill my mother if I didn't come out. I knew they were going to kill me if I did. Before they could get to me, the police came, and the men ran off. They caught all but one; they saved my life and nearly my mother's, but her injuries were too great. She died a few days later. They were wearing masks, so I couldn't identify anyone. Plus, I was too scared to look at them anyway." She takes a deep breath. "I'm sorry I was so distrusting of you, but … I know someone ordered her death, and I am determined to find out who."

"No! No, it's okay. I completely understand why you would be." She doesn't shed a tear; she gives me a soft smile, seemingly hardened and unaffected by her story, but I know her pain all too well. No one gets over something like that; they bury it deep inside and hide it from the world or talk about it enough that it becomes a story, a story to tell as if it isn't even your story, simply a story to tell. "You are pretty impressive. Even as a child you managed to think clearly enough in the face of danger to get away and save your own life. That's amazing. I don't know too many people that could do that, let alone a child being able to."

She smiles up at me. "Maybe, but I would have never survived without the police coming as quickly as they did. They were my life savers."

I shake my head with a roll of my eyes. "You got lucky with them one night. I wouldn't put too much stock into their abilities to help you or their concern for you."

She suddenly sits up and stares at me. "No, you're wrong. They saved me! I would be dead right now if it wasn't for those men. Why are you so against the police?" I hesitate, trying to think of a reason to tell her anything. I don't need to explain myself to this woman. I sit up, turning away from her and wondering if it's time to go. I have really enjoyed our time together; I wasn't expecting to be done with her so soon. "Dace?" she says softly. "What happened?" She pushes her fingers into my hair, rubbing the back of my neck, trying to persuade me to look at her. And for some reason, I do. At first, I am angry that she was able to get me to turn at all. *What the fuck does she care about me?* She resituates her body directly in front of me and takes hold of my face. "You don't have to tell me. You don't have to tell me anything." She wraps her arms around my neck, her legs around my waist, and sits in my lap with her head on my shoulder. "Is this okay?" she asks. "I know we still don't know each other that well, but I need this, and for some reason, I think you do too."

I feel along her legs, up her back, and around her body, pulling her in close to my chest. The soothing sounds of her soft breaths and the soft thumping of her heart against my chest ease my anger and cause me to exhale deep into her hair. "They killed my mother," I whisper, feeling a painful weight lifted from my soul. I translate my pain into a sensual embrace, lay her back into the bed, and give her every reason to be glad she survived. In the end, I feel surprisingly comforted, and as before, I sleep perfectly sound.

My brother is going through all the information I gathered from his competitor, cursing under his breath as usual. He grunts every other page which is beginning to annoy the fuck out of me. "Is this not what you asked for?"

"What's wrong with you?" Ettore asks me.

"I do have other things I would like to be doing. You know… something other than sitting here listening to you complain about nothing."

"This isn't nothing. I am actually quite impressed with what you were able to get, much more comprehensive than what my own people have been able to get, and they have been working on this for over a year." Ettore looks towards Father who sits back, nodding with a smile. I don't know why it makes me happy that I please him; I have never cared before.

"I told you, Ettore, I told you that you could use him. I was right," my father says proudly.

Ettore glances my way as if to remind me not to say anything about my ability to sneak in and out of places undetected. He had a long talk with me about our spying on the Aksakovs; he doesn't want anyone else to know for some reason. I'm fine not talking about it. I really don't care to discuss my abilities with too many people anyway, even with my family. Ettore looks away and nods.

"Yes, yes, you are always right, aren't you? Dace did fine this time, but how much more can he do?" Ettore says, leaning back in his chair with a cocked eyebrow in my direction.

"Not right now. You need to learn to be patient," our father says.

"Why be patient when you can act when they are least expecting it? I guarantee you they are not overlooking us at the moment. They may be distracted but not foolish."

"They are nothing to be of concern right now, and I don't want anything jeopardizing my campaign right now," Michael adds, evoking an instant growl from Ettore.

"How long are we going to sit around and twiddle our thumbs?!" Ettore yells back at him.

"Until I say so!" Michael retaliates strong. I have never seen him like that before. My father places a hand on him, and he calms. There is something going on between them all that I am missing.

"I think you're purposely holding off for all the wrong reasons."

"I don't care what you think." My father and Ettore glare at each other. "Have a good night, Dace. We will see you in the morning as usual, and make sure Antony comes with you this time," my father says to me without breaking his focus from Ettore.

I exit as quickly as possible. Their arguments have only escalated since I have been back. If I thought it was because of me, I would be happy to leave town, but I have a feeling it has to do with Michael and Ettore's escalating battle to be the one to have complete control of the family.

I head home and pull up to my building as Austin walks up from the other direction. The smile that overtakes my face is annoying as hell. I feel like a foolish schoolboy with a crush. She's fun and exciting and, at the same time, soft and comforting. Yet, I still feel like she is a complete mystery. I walk in at her side, and that damn annoying smile reappears as soon as she looks my way. I get in the elevator with her, push the button to my loft, and then lean back against the wall, waiting for her to look up at me. She tries to avoid doing so, but as soon as she does, I wink at her, causing her to smile. "Come here, Trouble." I reach out for her hand. She barely takes another breath before taking it and letting me pull her into my arms. Her lips taste so good. "How was your day, Baby?"

"It was good. I got a lot done."

"Oh yeah, did the filing gods smile down on you today?"

She laughs, taking the initiative to take hold of my shirt and pull me back to her lips. "So how was your day, Sunshine?"

"Sunshine?"

"Yeah you are always so bright and pleasurable to be around." she says sarcastically.

"Don't act like that's not true." The elevator doors open to her floor, and I shut them back. She looks surprised when I pick her up and wrap her legs around my waist. "You know damn well I can pleasure you all night long. I am very pleasurable."

"Dace, I should go home. I haven't been …" She gasps as my erection rises up against her. "Oh! Dace I really shouldn't." As soon as the doors open, I move us both out into the hallway to my front door. We don't make it through my door before clothes begin coming off. We both laugh as we stumble over things to get to each other and pull off that last shoe while attempting to clumsily reach my bedroom. Opening the door was an obstacle in and of itself, but my bed is much bigger than hers and a lot more fun to maneuver around on, so I want her here.

Kissing down her chest, I hear her stomach growl. "Are you hungry?" I ask as she grabs her stomach, blushing. I laugh at her. "If you're hungry, just say so."

"I haven't had a chance to eat since early this morning. That's why I wanted to go to my place."

"I have food. What do you want?"

"No, I can't ask you to do that. I can go home and eat and see you later."

"No, you stay right where you are. I can cook. Let me show you." She wants to argue with me; I can see it in her eyes. "Listen, you stay right there, naked, and in my bed, and I will bring you a full meal. You like red or white wine?" I ask as I slide some pants on.

"I like both, but I am in the mood for red."

"Perfect." I leave her hiding behind the translucent room dividers so I can make us dinner and watch her figure stretch out around my bed checking out everything that she possibly can without being obvious. I laugh to myself watching the sly Trouble work her body into the oddest of moves. "What are you doing?" I yell out, startling her and almost causing her to fall out of bed. I hold my mouth closed to keep from laughing out loud.

"Me? Nothing, just stretching out the knots from the long day."

As I finish up dinner, one of my alarms go off, and soon after, someone is buzzing my place to come in. I take a quick look at the camera and instantly curse under my breath. "Fuck. You couldn't have picked a worse time to visit me, Father." I allow him in and then quickly pull draperies and dividers around the bedroom. "Hey Trouble, do me a favor and stay put for a few minutes. A family friend is stopping by, and he likes to get into my business and never leave. So please stay in here and make it so I have a reason to kick him out nicely." I kiss her on the head and give her a plate of food and drink before closing her off from the rest of the loft. *Please stay put.*

I rush to open the door for my father as he gets off the elevator. "Hi. What are you doing here? Slumming?" I ask as he gives me his usual smirk.

"Always with the smartass comments, although yours tend to be funnier than Ettore's lately. I wanted to come see your new place and talk to you about some upcoming business that I want you alone to handle. I don't want you to talk about it with your brothers." He walks in further, looking around at the tall ceilings and rustic modern environment. He stops gazing the moment he catches sight of Austin's image sitting up in bed and seemingly trying to listen without being noticeable. I shake my head with a smile as my father slowly turns towards me. "I see this is not the best time to talk about business?"

I shake my head. "No. I'm sorry. If I had known you were coming, I wouldn't have made plans."

"Hm… your plans got busy quickly. You couldn't have been home long to do much more than have open the door and rush right into it," he teases.

"Well, we didn't quite make it through the door," I say, and he pats me on the back.

"Ah… I am glad to see you're enjoying yourself too while you are home."

"Yes sir," I say, looking back at Austin and her determination to know. "How about breakfast tomorrow? We can meet at our favorite spot," I say, turning towards him as he looks over the clothes on the floor suspiciously. "Father?"

"Hm? Oh yeah that sounds great." I walk him to the elevator and kiss his cheek, but the expression on his face as he looks at me is odd. He saw something that bothered him, but even as I go back in to clean it up, I can't figure out what it might have been.

I return back to Austin who instantly tries to act innocent. "Don't even try to act like you weren't doing everything possible to listen in. It wasn't anyone you would care about. I promise you."

"If it's no one then tell me who it was," she gently argues. Of course she wants to know. It is in her nature, apparently, to ask every question she can to find as many answers as she can.

I crawl into bed with her. "I'll tell you everything you want to know if you tell me everything I want to know about you." She instantly shies away. "I guess that's a no?" I look over her defensive figure and realize I was right. There is still so much more about her I don't know. I lean in next to her. "Don't worry, I'll tell you who it was. It was my pimp, you know, checking on me and making sure I am not cheating him out of his share. So, if you don't mind, can you leave my payment on the table before you go? Oh, and by the way, tips are appreciated."

"It should be more like you paying me."

"Oh! Suddenly you're the badass?"

She pushes everything out of the way and then pushes me onto my back. "You want to see a badass? I'll show you how badass I can be," she says, straddling me and releasing her hair down over her shoulders and working her hips against my cock until it stands up straight and is able to disappear perfectly inside of her. She overpowers me, holding me down and forcing me to watch her sway her hips and fondle her own breasts as she moans and looks down at me through her fallen hair. Fuck me. I sit up and grab the back of her head and pull her to my lips, my actions cause her to stop moving.

"What are you doing? Don't stop fucking me. I'm loving watching you move." I help her sit back up into position, lift my hips up into her, and enjoy watching her beautiful body sway and rise along the shaft of my hardened cock. This beautiful woman is amazing, and she has me completely rapt.

CHAPTER 13

Austin

"You're late," Jamee says with my brother eyeballing me from across the room.

"I'm sorry. I overslept."

"You? Miss-By-The-Book?" Jamee says in disbelief.

"Yes. Now can we move past it and get to work?"

"Maybe you can, but the way you have been smiling lately and now … oversleeping? Who is he?"

"Who is who?" My brother asks, looking at me like I am a wounded animal.

"No one. Now let's go," I say.

"Austin?"

"Aaron? I'm fine. Now stop worrying about me," I say with a reassuring smile and a grasp of his hand before leaving with Jamee to go checkout a lead we got about our runaway, Nelson.

One of the kids he has been known to hang out with was found beaten to death in a back alley. We didn't have much to go on from the victim until I noticed his hoodie zipper was a small key. I asked around, questioning some of the kids on the corner, and one noted it was similar to his locker key from the youth center. That was helpful, but not enough to tell us which locker might be his, so we spend most of the day trying every locker. The kid's bag of clothes, personal items, and a sketch book were all in there, and within his sketchbook, we found an old business card.

The old, long ago closed up auto body shop is nothing special and doesn't seem to be worth checking out. Maybe I was too hopeful, but I search the outside, trying to find access without actually breaking anything.

"Oh come on. Just break through the door already. No one is going to care. No one has cared about this place in decades it seems," Jamee says exhaustively.

"Why are you so quick to forget the law that you chose to represent?"

"I only got into this career because I like telling people what to do. I am short and Asian. I don't exactly look intimidating, but with my badge, I not only have the right, but the ability to scare the shit out of people, and I like that – a lot." She smiles wide while I give her a disapproving glare—not that it does any good. She kicks open the door and walks right in. "Wow, that door just fell open. Did you see that? Someone must have been beating up on it before we got here."

Rolling my eyes, I follow her in, ignoring the fallen door as I look around. There isn't much here worth being concerned about, but there is a strange break within the dust on the ground. Something was dragged all the way … to a back wall, to what seems to be opposite a storage room.

"Find something?"

"I thought so, but it dies right into a wall, and then nothing." Jamee searches around the corner to look into the storage room. "I don't see anything in here, so it doesn't seem to be a magic disappearing and reappearing wall. So unless whatever it was flew out of here, I don't know."

I look up, searching through the rafters until I find what I was missing—a pulley system. That's what they did. They came in through the roof and dragged whatever it was with the pulley system. But what was it? I jump on some shelving units, climb up to the roof hatch, and pull myself through and up onto the roof.

"I hope you don't expect me to follow you? I just had my nails done yesterday," Jamee yells out. "I understand no one cares what you look like, but there are many watching me."

I want to say something to her, but I have gotten so used to the bullshit that comes out of her mouth that it doesn't faze me anymore. "Fine. Stay down there and check out the rest of the area for me." The roof has definitely been well-accessed. I immediately catch sight of a tent and supplies, clearly what was dragged up from the floor. I don't see anyone in the tent, but the loose vent cover on one of the rooftop units is interesting. It's been removed and replaced with one corner of the cover broken off. I pull out a knife from my jacket side pocket and pull out the other three screws. The cover is rusted out and cracks at the edges as I place it off to the side. It makes me weary about sticking my hand down into the dark hole. I wrap my hand up with my jacket and feel around for anything odd. Feeling something, I reach in further and take hold of it. It doesn't come out easily. Finding leverage, I pull hard, jerking the object from the safety of its protective tube. Once I have it, I realize it's a notebook full of numbers and indications of names via initials and nicknames. The book looks like any other school notebook, but this one is clearly written by someone much older and about something other than high school homework. I bet this is what they were looking for. Nelson must have had it the whole time. *Now, where is Nelson?* A sudden noise on the other side of the roof startles me, and I take out my gun and walk slowly towards it.

"I'm detective Reed, and I need for you to come out slowly with your hands up." I pace myself a little closer and a little closer until I am sure someone, if not two someones, are there. "Come out now or I will be calling an entire squad of cops up here to surround you and drag you out." I prepare my stance and then kick the mechanical unit they are hiding behind. Two kids jump up with blackened, wild eyes, ready to strike me with the rebar in one of their hands and a bat in the other's.

"Nelson? It is you, isn't it? I'm here to help you. I know what happened, and I only want to protect you. Calm down and put the weapons down. Everything is going to be okay. Don't run, you don't want to make it worse on yourself."

"It doesn't matter. I am the last one left. They're all after me, so you might as well be the one to kill me first," Nelson says, shaking his bat in the air.

"Who's after you? Tell me who it is and maybe I can help get you some protection."

He laughs, shaking his head with a neurotic twitching while his smaller buddy has lost his ability to comprehend what's in front of him, except for the invisible flies that keep chasing him. I slowly call for backup while talking to them gently and being as reassuring as possible. The more they begin to twitch, the more worried I get about their emotional stability.

"I have to go before they find me, and I need that. That's mine!" he yells at me while pointing at the notebook I pulled out.

"It's not yours though, is it? Where did you get it?"

He calms and steps back. "I thought it was mine. It looks just like mine, and I was going to give it back the next time I saw her but ..."

"But people were there, weren't they?" He nods. Did they see you?" He shakes his head. "Did you see what happened?" He nods. "Okay, why don't we get you into a warm car and talk about it? Come on, let's at least get off this roof and then we go get some coffee, some waffles?"

"I love waffles," he says, stepping forward.

"Well then, let's go. I know I'm hungry, too. Put down the weapons and let's get the hell out of here." It's a slow process, but eventually, they seem to trust me and do as I ask them to. Nelson's friend goes down and is subdued before being put in the back of our car. However, Nelson is hesitating for some reason. "Go ahead, it's fine. Use the ladder and then cross over to the point there and then jump down. It's easy."

"Well, I don't like heights, so you go first," he says.

"No, I need you to go first." He shakes his head, and my patience is wearing thin. "How about we go down together?" He seems to be okay with that, so we both move down through the hatch. When we get half way there, he pushes me off the ladder, sending me flying towards the ground until I can grab a rafter and hold on long enough to swing my feet up and hold on securely with them. The jackass takes off down the ladder and then runs out the door. Thankfully, I kept the notebook with me.

Jamee comes walking in under my dangling body. "My guy is

secure. What happened to yours?"

"Oh he left. He had somewhere to be apparently."

"And so you decided to do some acrobatics while we are here?" Jamee asks.

"Can you just get something to help me down please?" Cursing and shaking her head, she finds a box for me to jump down to and off, onto the ground. I instantly grab my arm and notice my shirt is ripped open, showing a deep gash in my arm.

"Alright, let's drop this guy off for someone else to deal with and get you some stitches. It's always interesting working with you, Reed," she says.

We finish up at the hospital, and they find that I also pulled a muscle. They prescribe some pain meds that don't seem necessary until I try to sit up and feel the pain in my shoulder. Due to my drugged state, Jamee drives me home and pulls up to my building as Dace pulls up on his bike. He looks concerned, but I am afraid for him to talk to Jamee and her big mouth, so I rush to him and nearly fall over once I get to him.

He grabs hold of me as he slides off his bike. "Are you okay, Trouble?"

"I hurt myself climbing up some filing ... um thingys. They're really tall, and I ...fell off ... of them." He doesn't say anything, which worries me.

"Hello, and you are?" Jamee asks with her hand out and eyes all over him.

"Dace, and you are?"

"She's my co-worker, just a co-worker that brought me home because I don't feel so well. And because I fell up ... off ... the files."

"Austin did some acrobatics today that weren't quite flawless, so I took her to get some stitches and some pain meds for her pulled muscle."

"Filing is sure a rough business," Dace says.

"Filing?" Jamee asks

"She's my co-worker," I say, falling into his chest. He smiles down on me, wrapping his arm around my waist. "She's just my co-worker."

"I got that, Trouble. Now, do you need some help getting upstairs?"

"Yeah, that would be great. Wait, do you mean your help? I am so dizzy." Burying my face into his coat, I hold onto him and close my eyes.

"So you're him?" Jamee asks with a knowing tone.

"I am going to take her upstairs and get her into bed," Dace says.

"Oh, I am sure you are. If you need anyone that's actually awake to tuck into bed, I am available," she says as I lift my heavy face off his chest and stare at her harshly. She shrugs with a laugh, enjoying herself too much. If I could stand up straight, and if I could figure out which one of her is actually her, I would hit her.

"Okay, well it was nice to meet you," Dace says as he lifts me up into his arms, holding me against his taut chest. "Do you have your key or do you want to sleep in my bed?"

"Oh, your bed is so comfortable, and you're there. I really like when you're there, especially when you're naked. But don't tell you that I said that okay?" I say, feeling good about my secret when he agrees with a smiling nod. He places me in his bed and begins helping me get my clothes off. I smile. "Are we having sex?" I ask.

He laughs, "No, I don't think that would be a good idea."

"Oh come on. Don't you find me sexy?" I ask as I fall into the pillow unable to lift my head up.

"Usually, but not so much right now." My heavy head floats onto his pillow, and I grasp his hands as he caresses my body. Forcing my eyes open, I look up at him with what I think is a smile. "Don't worry, I won't take advantage of you. You can close your eyes and go to sleep, and no one will harm you here, not while I am watching over you."

Holding his hand, I cradle it to my face with a rush of warmth coming over me. "Dace?"

"Yeah?"

"I think I could fall madly in love with you if you're not careful."

"And what if I want you to?" he says with a deep hum against my cheek. I smile, rolling into the pillow, crushing my face against it. Dace runs his fingers down my back, and with a kiss to my head, he whispers, "I wish you would let me know who you really are." I drift off to his delicate touch and calming voice.

The darkness I wake up to is confusing. I jump up, trying to understand where I am, when he reaches out from his side of the bed and pulls me to him. "You alright?" he says with a raspy voice.

"I wasn't sure where I was for a moment," I reply, feeling his lips against my head and a slide of his warm hand down my back. I don't know why, but when I am in his arms, I feel at home, and everything feels right. This is something new for me, something new and wonderful.

The moment I walk back into work, Jamee is there, waiting

for me. She is never here on time, and suddenly, today, she is anxious to get going? I can only imagine the questions coming my way. I sit down at my desk, and she leans forward as if she has already asked me a question she is waiting to receive an answer for. "I don't know what you are waiting for, but you can stop staring at me that way," I say to her forcefully.

"You know damn well what I am waiting for. Who is he? What does he do? Are you in love? How long has it been going on? Although I could probably make a pretty good guess at the latter. He seems to have money too. Does he have any friends or a brother that I could meet?"

With a deep sigh, I decide to give her something, without giving her too much. "His name is Dace."

"Oooh... Dace, I like that. And that fits his bad boy persona. He has all kinds of sexy badness about him—the height, eyes, that just out of place wavy hair of his with enough facial hair to say he doesn't give a shit about what you think." She moans into her chair as if she is picturing herself with him, which pisses me off. "Wait, didn't we arrest him once?"

"No! And stop!" I yell, snapping her out of her dream state. "He's taken, by the way."

"Oh he is, is he? Does he know that?" she asks, pissing me off even more.

"Don't you have work to do Jamee?" She moves into her desk seemingly to be working, but I know better.

Jamee jabs me with comments throughout the entire day about Dace, even asking about the size of his penis at one point. I can't wait to get away from her. We have been friends for a long time, but I have never been so irritated or bothered by her before, of course I have never had anything she ever wanted before. She's the one that's always had the rich boyfriends, thanks in part to her rich mother making sure she is always taken care of. I am not even sure why she works; her mother gives her everything she wants. I think I enjoyed being the friend she dismissed as anything important rather than the one she is suddenly curious about or rather the one with the man she is curious about. Thank goodness we get a call to help bring down a known drug house and we have to stop talking altogether.

I dress in my secure uniform and get into my assigned position, waiting for the go ahead. We sit for hours, waiting, and all I can do is think, of course, about him. I am in the midst of a wonderful daydream before I get the go ahead to move in. The distraction was nice, but it causes me to miss my mark, and I let three men sneak out the side and get away. I chase after them, and yell for them to stop, but one turns and shoots at me, forcing me to fire back and kill him instantly. The other two stop and surrender, but my fate has already been sealed. I have used my gun, and now there is going to have to be an investigation.

"Austin! What the fuck is wrong with you?" Aaron yells at me, angrier than I have ever seen him. "Where is your head?! This is not like you at all."

"I know, I'm sorry. I am not sure what happened."

"You're not sure?" he asks, flailing his arms around like a wild man.

"Aaron, calm down, buddy. She's having an off day. We have all had them," Billy says, pulling Aaron back out of my face.

"No, this is my sister, and I want to know what's wrong with her. If she's not able to do her job then I want to know before she gets herself killed."

"Aaron, please. It's bad enough I killed someone. I know I let you down, but I don't need this right now," I plead with him. He settles down some but still has to walk away from me. Jamee raises her eyebrows and smirks at me before following after him. She has always had a crush on him and will take any opportunity she can to get close to him. She is too materialistic, though, and I wish she would get it through her thick skull that my brother is too good for her.

"Austin, you need to go to the station and file your report." Billy grabs my hand and kisses my cheek. "Don't worry, Sweetheart. It's only one day—one, single, bad day out of many great ones. No one is flawless, and you did what you needed to.

Okay?" I nod, trying to believe in his words. "Okay. Now, have a stiff drink tonight, and if you need someone to talk to, don't hesitate to call me. You know I'll be there for you in a heartbeat, especially if you want to talk shit about your brother. I need an outlet for that motherfucker," Billy says with an encouraging smile before sending me on my way.

They took my gun and suspended me until they can verify all the details of my story. The next day, I am out wandering the neighborhood in the middle of the afternoon. I need something to occupy my time. I have done all the research I can on my mother's murder, and the only person I need to talk to is in jail. They won't let me talk to him without my badge, so I go talk to a woman that was supposedly his girlfriend at the time, Brandi Davis. She isn't exactly receptive to seeing me but lets me in when I explain my mother was murdered in front of me and her ex knows who ordered it.

"I don't know what I can tell you. I mean, I'm sorry about your mother and all, but Manny was not exactly a talker."

"I understand. He's no different than most men. I was only wondering if you ever noticed anyone of significance meeting with him or his brother?"

"His brother? Victor? What does Victor have to do with this? He died years ago."

"He was the one that raped and killed her." She looks down at her feet as if she is remembering something. "What is it? Someone you saw with him? Something Victor might have mentioned?" She stays silent. "Were you sleeping with Victor, too?"

"No! No I didn't want to; he didn't give me much of a choice."

"So you're the reason the brothers had a falling out."

"Yeah. Manny came home and found me in a bloody mess and his brother passed out on our couch, drunk. I thought he was going to kill him, but Victor managed to get away. The next day, a man came by and beat the shit out of Manny and threatened us both that, if we said anything, we would be killed and our bodies never found. I have never been so scared in my life. I don't know who that man was. I was never told his name; all I remember was those steel toed boots he kept kicking Manny with. They had a red stripe down one side, like a stain almost, a bloody red stain. Oh and that horrible engraving; it left the skull and crossbones imprint on Manny's skin for weeks. I was afraid it would never go away." She shakes her head with a sarcastic laugh, "I'm sure it was to intimidate people, let them know he had killed before. You know, I don't care anymore. I'm old, and it's not like my life is all that great. Fuck him. He's had us both running scared for a long time, having people come by here and force us to do things for him since Victor is gone. I don't care anymore. I was diagnosed yesterday with lung cancer, so I don't have much time left anyway. Thank God," she says with a look that exudes pain and suffering. Life has beaten her down and worn her out. She doesn't have any fight left in her, and I think, in this case, she believes God is doing her a long overdue favor. She gave me a few more details about the man, but nothing really stands out except for the boots.

I leave and return home, wandering around the area, thinking about what I can do to waste some more time until Preston gets home. I'm bored, and I need someone to talk to. I don't know what to do with myself, and then he drives up on his motorcycle.

"Hey, Trouble. What are you doing out here? Shouldn't you be working?" he asks, fingering the curl of his hair back into place.

"I got into trouble at work, so they asked me to take a few days off," I confess to him.

"You look so sad. I don't like that."

"I'll be fine. I need to go find a hobby for a few days is all until they let me come back."

"Or maybe you need to take a little trip with me?" he says.

"A trip to where?"

"Do you have to know every detail before you say 'yes'? Can't you simply be excited about the unknown and the idea of a surprise? Trust me."

"Trust you? I don't know if I can trust someone I am still getting to know."

"You mean you're sleeping with a person you don't trust?" I laugh, shaking my head. "Come with me and let me surprise you; let me show you another side of me."

"And what side is that?"

"That's the surprise," he says with a wink. "I have to go take care of some business, but I'll be back in an hour. Pack a small bag, and I'll text you when I'm pulling around the corner to pick you up." I try to get more information out of him, but he gears up his motorcycle and turns around to take off again. "A small bag," he yells out to me.

I can't believe I am doing this, but I rush up to my condo and pack the bare minimum of what I need and wait anxiously for him. When I get his text, I leave a quick note for Preston and rush out the door. The moment I see him coming, I smile so wide it hurts.

"Hey, Trouble, you ready to go?" I nod, and he slides my helmet over my head and adjusts it perfectly before helping me onto the back of his bike with him. With my backpack on my back, I take hold of his body and lay my head against his back with no regrets.

CHAPTER 14

Dace

The timing couldn't have been better. Ettore needs me to keep an eye on one of his competitors, Rory Aksakov, who happens to be going to a resort for a sudden vacation that we suspect is a cover to meet up with one of our *loyal* family friends, Scott Ellington. The man doesn't know me; he hasn't seen me since I was a kid, so spying on him should be easy, especially with Austin at my side. I can blend in as another tourist with his girlfriend.

Driving up to the resort is amazing. Austin feels good against my back. This doesn't seem like work at all. I'm excited to spend time with her without worrying about interruptions, and possibly finding out more about her is intriguing to me. But most of all, I want to find out why, when she said she thinks she could love me, that I suddenly became excited about the possibility. We arrive at the resort with little baggage, but I do not expect to need much, especially since Antony has already been here, setting up bugs and wires for me to spy on our old friend. Austin and I walk into our luxury cabin and find a bouquet of roses.

Austin gushes and smiles, assuming I did it. "Oh my gosh, I can't believe you did this and on such short timing. You're amazing," she says, kissing me and whispering in my ear how appreciative she is. I need to remember to thank Antony later. The cabin is fully stocked with food, and an amazing view of the mountains rests beyond the large windows, including a nice line of sight to the cabin across the way where Aksakov is staying. I walk out onto our deck and take notice of the hot tub. "Going to need to use that while we are here."

"This is beautiful, Dace. I have never seen anything like it. I thought you said a cabin, but this is a lot bigger than the cabin I used to go to as a kid," Austin says, walking out and burying herself into my arms so I can keep her warm. "I love it. I could get used to this … as long as it's legal."

"You still don't trust me. I really need to fix that. Don't worry, it's a family place, but I'm glad you like it."

"Your family must do well in order for you to afford a place like this."

"Is that another question?" I laugh at her. "Yes, they do well, and I have done well enough. I don't rob banks or anyone's homes to get it. I do work for it." She seems to feel better about my answer. I move my hands underneath her coat and get in close to get personal with her. "What do you say we get this hot tub going and enjoy ourselves?"

"I didn't bring a bikini or a swimsuit of any kind."

"Who said you needed one?" She fights me on the idea for a while, but a little kiss here, a removal of this and that with another kiss, a persuasive feel of her body against mine, and I am able to lift her out of the cabin and out into the steaming, bubbling water. She claims not to be an exhibitionist, but the moment my dick slides into her, she rises up and leans back with her breasts bouncing in the cool night air. Her nipples go hard and call out to me. The steam from the water rises and envelopes our nude bodies, heating up our already wet skin. Wrapping her long legs around me, I lift her up out of the water and hold her against the side. She lies back onto the seat of the tub, and I begin to get a craving. "Turn around for me," I whisper, giving her the choice. Austin kisses my lips, turns, leans down, and sticks her ass out at me with a bite of her bottom lip. I feel up the back of her legs and down in between them, spreading her just like I want her. Taking hold of her hips, my perfectly erect tool dives in against the bare cheeks of her ass and into her pussy with throbbing pleasure. I nearly explode but, instead, grab her ass and smack it hard to give her encouragement to push back onto me.

Austin looks back at me with her pouty lips, "Dace." She moans.

I lean down over her back, feel up her breasts, taking those beautiful lips in and then lick the water off of her neck with a deep push of my cock inside of her. She moans, and I feel her tighten.

"Let me help you come." I slide my hand down, tickling her clit with my finger. "Come Baby, I want a feel you come hard." She gasps as her body begins to shudder. She becomes so wet that I crave having my own release even more. With her bent over, I hold her hips still and fuck her so hard that she screams her pleasure into the night with wild abandon, causing us to gain some attention. Our sudden audience doesn't force me to stop; I come proudly. Rory Aksakov, I'm sure, can't make us out fully with the surrounding steam, but he certainly can make out the smile on my bright face.

Once Austin is sound asleep, I sneak out of bed and meet up with Antony who has been staying in the nanny suite attached to the back of the house. He has been listening in on Aksakov and waiting for our friend to show. "Any sign of him?"

"Sounds like something is going to happen tomorrow night; he is expecting a dinner guest," Antony says, handing me some headphones to hear what he is referring to.

"I will have everything ready by seven. We can meet after that. Just make sure you have my payment," Scott says.

"I'll have it. I will even provide dinner, but if you bring me shit, then I will make sure your dinner is poisoned," Rory says.

I take the headphones off and hand them back to Antony. "So maybe I need to borrow some spices for dinner?"

"From what I am hearing through the walls, you have got enough spice. You need some cold water and cool your dick off. I am not sure how you can concentrate on work."

"Don't worry, little brother. I'm concentrating just fine ... on everyone."

"Okay, but how about we take the easy route and cut Scott off before he gets to the house full of armed guards?"

"You always want to take the easy route," I laugh, agreeing to his plan.

Austin is happily playing with me as I take a shower, and I am rather enjoying her teasing, but I have to be careful not to get too excited. I need to make an excuse here soon and leave for a little while, and I'd prefer to do it without a hard on. "Hey, watch the hands. I am trying to clean up nice for you."

"Why bother? Let's have fun."

I wrap my arms around her and kiss her lips gently. "I want to make a nice dinner for you, and I need to go out and get a few things to do that." I kiss her forehead and step back. "So, I need to calm down in order to fit into my pants. They prefer you dressed when you're in public around here."

She sighs, relinquishing her pursuit of me. "Oh, actually, I could use a few things too. We can both go and maybe do a little shopping in town?"

"Oh. Well... I was really hoping to go and get back as soon as possible. We could go shopping tomorrow if you like? Yeah, it will be better tomorrow. The afternoon is when all the stores are open. Most of the ones you want will be closing by the time we get there now."

"They close early here, huh?"

"Yeah, most tourists don't spend the nights shopping here." I nudge her. Cornering her, I hover around her. "Stay here, relax, and enjoy the quiet because when I get back ..." I lean into her ear. "We are going to be busy making a lot of noise," I whisper to her instant smile.

Austin isn't easy to say goodbye to, but I somehow manage to get away and meet up with Antony. There is one road into this area, and thankfully, we know the time Scott will be coming down it. Antony waits with the hood of his car up and parked in the middle of the road to make sure the asshole has no choice but to stop and help him. The plan seems simple, but Scott is no ordinary passerby. He would rather kill you than bother with helping you do anything. To prevent anything from going wrong, I wait nearby but out of sight.

"Antony, the signal from Scott's phone has him heading this way. He should be coming over that hill any minute now. Are you sure you are okay to do this?"

"Yeah, I'm fine, Dace. Stop worrying about me," he says, already acting out his fussing over his car and in good time. Scott heads his way and slows down with some obvious cursing. He is not one to help out of the goodness of his heart, but in this case, he has no choice.

He slams his fist against his steering wheel and gets out. "What the fuck are you doing in the middle of the road, you stupid fuck? Pull the damn car over to the side."

"I'm sorry. I would, but I can't do it by myself." Antony amps up his inner gay and plays helpless.

"A motherfucking fag! Awesome." Scott slams his car door shut, walks over to Antony, and pushes him out of the way. "Move Peter-Puffer!" Scott gets in and puts the car into neutral before getting out and shoving Antony in the car. "Now drive the fuck over there while I push." Antony does so, but as soon as Scott starts to push, Antony starts the car and backs up into the ass.

I run out, exasperated, and make sure to hold my gun on Scott who is lying on the ground, screaming in pain.

"You dumbass! What the fuck is wrong with you!?" he yells until he sees me.

Antony gets out of his car, comes over, and kicks the shit out of Scott. "Want to call me a name, asshole?! Go ahead, call me a few other things! Go ahead!" Antony enjoys himself for a while before I pull him back. "What are you stopping me for?!"

"Because we need him to tell us a few things."

"I ain't telling you fucks nothing," Scott spits out with the blood in his mouth.

"Oh I think you are. Otherwise, my brother is going to do some really nasty things to you and your son, Sam, is it? I hear he is now getting his business going too."

Scott jumps up in anger. "Don't talk about my son. I'll kill you both, rip your bodies into a million pieces, and feed them to my pet rat. Who the fuck do you think you are?"

I step into his face. "My name is Dace Colletto."

Scott steps back with wide eyes. "Dace?" He looks over at Antony.

"Yeah, dumb fuck, I'm Antony Colletto."

Scott falls to his knees in front of us. "I thought you both were dead. Your father said you died with your mother."

"What are you giving Aksakov, Scott?"

He holds his head down. "They are paying me for the key codes to enter Michael's headquarters and homes. They want to destroy his campaign before he becomes any more popular."

Scott makes an odd movement and suddenly he pulls a gun from his ankle. Before I can pull the trigger, Antony pulls his and kills him instantly.

"Well that felt good," he says.

"Good, now you can help me put him in his trunk and leave his car for Ettore's men to come get him?" I say to him. "I have a dinner date I have to get back to, and did you get the items I asked for?"

"Yes, and yes. I found all the items on the list even though I didn't know what half of them were. Thankfully, this very sweet man helped me find what I needed. I had to flirt a little bit, but I am sure you will repay the favor. Right?"

"Sure." I smile happily, patting him on the back

"Dace, that 'sure' didn't sound too sincere," he teases as I grab my bag from his car and jump on my bike to go back to the cabin.

I open up the door and am greeted with a huge hug. Suddenly, I feel at home, and it has nothing to do with the cabin. "Hi Beautiful, miss me?" I ask, tossing my bag of groceries to the side for later.

"I did. Now let's play."

"What would you like to play, Trouble?"

"The one who pins the other one gets to decide who does the dishes."

"Oh but Sweetheart, there's a maid for that."

"Hm, then let's just fight for … clothes." She punches me in the gut and runs off with my belt.

"Quick hands, but mine are quicker." I chase after her, laughing along with her as we play. She's fun and comforting. Even through dinner we enjoy pretending, pretending we are other people—without secrets.

The beauty around us is serene and placid, but as great as it is, having Austin in my arms with her bare breasts pressed against my chest and her perfectly rounded ass out for me to admire, is the ideal moment—the moment I never thought would happen to me. Though she lies here with me, I crave more. I crave her eyes and her lips, and the feeling of her legs wrapped around my waist, but mostly, I crave her arms and the heaven that I find within them. No one has made me feel so at peace as she. She suddenly moves and wakes up to smile up at me.

"Hi," I say simply, playing with her long blond hair that flows down her back.

"Hi. I missed you."

I laugh, "You missed me? When? I've been right here."

"No, in my dreams. You weren't in them, and I missed you, so I woke up to find you again."

Her sweet words cause the blood from around my heart to flow with a greater warmth than I ever thought possible. I lift her face up to mine and kiss her. "I'm sorry. I will never be absent from your life or your dreams again. I will follow you everywhere, even into the clouds of your fantasies." I reach over to my bag and pull out a leather necklace with a carved wooden elephant attached and put it around her neck. "Keep this near your heart, and I will be able to find you wherever you go."

She lifts it to admire. "It's beautiful. Where did you get it?"

"A place I visited once. A woman gave it to me to thank me for saving her husband. She said it would bring warriors, knights you could say, on white elephants to protect me from all evil. I liked it so much I had a replica tattooed to my chest."

She leans forward, tracing the image. "Oh yeah, you have so many tattoos it kind of gets lost in them, like a hidden treasure." She smiles.

I lean in, kissing her face and down her neck. "And now you have a treasure, to bring me back to you, to protect you in reality and in your dreams."

"To be my white knight on a white elephant. I never knew I needed one, but I am not opposed to the idea as long as it is you," I hear her whisper as I take hold of her hands and fall back into bed with her.

CHAPTER 15

Dace

"So your trip was successful?" Ettore asks me.

"Yeah, he was up there the whole time, and Antony and I were able to listen in on his every conversation. He's not that smart or very organized, Ettore. Why are we so concerned with this family?"

"Why indeed?" Michael asks. "We need to let this go. Once I move into office, I will have the power to go after him properly, leaving you to focus on business."

"Shut up, Michael. I am going after him. He may not be well organized now, but that is no reason to sit back and wait for him to get organized," Ettore fires back.

"No. No you won't. You will allow your brother to finish his campaign and then we will reevaluate our competition and discuss as a family. We have put a damper on his plans to attack Michael; I doubt he has much power to do so before the election," My father says with a finality.

"That's the wrong decision. If we wait, it may be too late. It will be too hard to take care of him and his cronies," Ettore stresses, standing up instantly to my father.

Michael gets in between them. "Back off Ettore. The decision has been made. We discussed it and checked it out as you wanted, and there is still nothing to worry about, especially now that Dace and Antony have put a stop to the leak," Michael says, pushing back on Ettore's chest. "You even had Antony follow his wife. You think I wouldn't find out about that? Stop being so paranoid and listen to reason." I look over towards Antony who seems to feel as uncomfortable as I do. "And why Antony? Why not Dace? You afraid Dace would end up fucking her? Give away your precious secrets in the heat of passion?" Michael laughs, but it doesn't seem like a laughable moment to the rest of us. "Hell, maybe he would impregnate her and we could infiltrate the enemy from the inside out."

"I want to go after him now when he least expects it—before he becomes more powerful than he already is. Before he has a chance to become a friend to another enemy," Ettore fights back.

"Antony and Dace, step outside and wait," my father demands. We get up instantly and rush out the door.

Antony and I sit outside until Michael walks out. "Don't worry about it guys. We fight like this all the time. Ettore will get over it like he always does. He's just being stubbornly overprotective of us all right now." He smiles his typical without-a-care-in-the-world smile. "Hey, could you guys do me a favor and see to this group that has been causing some major issues for Ettore? I feel I need to give him a peace offering. They are a part of the Robiks crew, not much to worry about, but Ettore seems to think they are aligning with the Aksakovs. So to prevent that, let's blow their cover and lead the police to them. No one wants to deal with a group who has the cops all over them. Here's the address." Michael hands me the address, and Antony and I take off out the door as quickly as we can. The sooner we get out of here, the less brotherly drama we have to deal with.

"Okay, all I need to do is go in and mess with their alarm system so the police can get in undetected and catch them before they can get rid of the evidence. You stay here and wait for me to let you know where to pick me up. I'll be in and out in no time," I tell Antony, leaving out the one other thing Michael called and asked me to do so as not to worry him.

"Be careful. I know you have done this a thousand times, but I have a bad feeling about this," Antony says. I nod and get out of the car with the same bad feeling. *Listen to your gut*, Peter would say. It is nothing for me to sneak in and mess with the alarm system; I am in and finished in no time.

It's that extra part of the job Michael requested late that bothers me, *"Download all their information so we know their contacts."*

"Why is this even important, Michael?" I asked.

"To see who of the Aksakovs they are meeting with, of course."

"I doubt they would keep that on their system, Michael."

"Maybe not, but look anyway. It can't hurt, can it?"

"I guess not."

I gave in knowing I can get the information easily, but now, I am regretting agreeing to it. I have to get to a whole other room in order to access it all. Once there, I run into a couple of guards and put them down for the time being, giving me only seconds to get what I need. Their system is antiquated and easy to deal with but also slow as hell.

"Dace, the cops just drove by. You need to get out of there now," Antony texts me.

"Fuck, they're early." I get what I need and jump up, searching for the way out. I locate the back stairs and run up to the roof, quickly vaulting to the roof of the building next door. Running for the roof top hatch, I snatch it open and climb through. The building is dead silent. I make it to the last door and wait, listening. The cops are everywhere, and I have to wonder how many are smart enough to come to this building too. I ease open the door and step through. Someone is here. I know it.

I spin around, pulling my gun on them as they put theirs in my face. My heart beats rapidly, and still, I breathe out slowly, blowing her blond tresses from her eyes. "Austin?"

"What are you doing here, Dace?" she asks with her gun still raised. I glance down at her badge, continuing to hold my gun on her.

"You're a cop?"

"And you're clearly a criminal."

We pace around each other without blinking and without

releasing our hold on our weapons. "Let me go, Austin."

"No," she says, beginning to shake with anger.

"Are you going to shoot me if I run?"

"Yes."

"No you won't."

"You have your gun in my face. Are you going to shoot me to get away?" she asks as I feel a tug at my heart.

"No, now let me go."

"Do you work for the Robiks? Are you one of their drug smugglers?"

"No. I have nothing to do with them, except my family wants them taken care of before they align themselves with an enemy of ours."

She shakes her head. "I don't know your family. They can't be very big. Why worry about a family that is beyond their reach?"

"Because my family *is* beyond their reach." I stare into her pained eyes and am crushed and angry all at the same time. Maybe I want to hurt her, make her feel the betrayal that I feel right now knowing that the woman I love … is a cop. She's a fucking cop. How dare she hide that from me, knowing how I feel. I lean my head in. "I'm a Colletto, Austin. My name is actually Dace Colletto. Yes, I lied to you … too." Her eyes widen, and the pain I inflicted on her becomes clear, but I feel no better about revealing my revengeful secret.

She shakes her head, still holding her gun on me. "No, you can't be. There are only two brothers."

"Antony and I are the ones that were thought dead. We were sent away when we were young."

"Oh," she says as if it is hard for her to admit it out loud.

"Let me go, Austin. You know damn well if you arrest me, I will be out before you know it. You won't be able to hold me on anything."

"Dace?" she says, and I think for a second that she is going to cry. Her expression is pained, but instead, she punches me and knocks my gun away. She takes a step back and kicks me to the ground. I grab her leg and throw her down with me. "I can't believe this!"

"Are you really trying to fight me right now, you crazy ass woman?"

"Damn right. I want nothing more than to hit you." She swings her fist into my jaw, and I have to slam her against the wall to keep from receiving another blow.

"Stop and let me go before it's too late," I say, looking deep into her eyes and wishing like hell we were not who we are. "I never meant to hurt you, Austin. I …" I inhale deeply and shove her to the floor, grabbing my gun and reaching for the door. I want to leave without thinking, but instead, I glance back at her to see if she will follow me only to feel guilty for leaving her tangled in some decades old debris so I can get away. As I walk out, I hear another man and then another coming in, screaming and fighting with her. I stop, regretting what I am about to do already. "Fuck," I huff, running back in and helping Austin battle a group that did the exact same thing I did to get away, and she is their last barrier. They don't care whether she lives or dies, but I do. She has two on her with two more filing in to kill her, and I step in. I down two in an instant and pull one off of her and knock him out. She handles the other one with ease as several cops come busting through and throw me against a wall with the rest.

I am handcuffed and escorted out past her without either of us saying a word.

Michael actually shows up with Antony to get me out. I guess he is so sure of his prestige that he doesn't believe a lawyer is necessary. Apparently, he is that important. Not only does he get me out, but they drop the charges.

I walk out to Antony's semi-smile and Michael shaking his head. "I guess you're not as good as you think you are."

"Thanks for getting me out," I say, ignoring his snide comment.

"I had to pull a lot of strings to get you out without suspicion being put on your shoulders too. You owe me big time," Michael says, turning away and leading us further into the police station. "I need to talk to a few people before we go."

We step into a room full of cops, and Michael stops to talk to one man dressed in a stiff, cheap suit. I wait impatiently as Antony sighs next to me. "Oh no. Now I know why you got caught." I look up and see Austin walking towards us.

"Austin," Michael says gleefully, surprisingly hugging her as if they are friends. "A big bust for you guys today, huh? I'm sorry my brother was caught up in the middle, but I promise he won't be of any trouble again."

"He was no problem. I was surprised to hear that you have … two other brothers, Michael," Austin says, glancing our way.

"Yes, they only recently returned. We sent them away when they were young to protect them, but now they are big boys …" Michael wraps his arms around Antony and my shoulders and squeezes with a kiss to the sides of our heads, annoying the shit out of both of us. "They hate when I do that. These two aren't much to look at now, but they were adorable when they were little."

Antony looks at him with a scowl. "Excuse me? I am the best looking one in the family."

Austin continues to stare at us in shock. "You really are related? You don't look that much alike?"

"Do you think I would lie about being related to someone so ugly?" Michael laughs, not understanding the situation at all.

A man walks up on Austin and puts his arm around her shoulders, as if he has no boundaries with her, giving me a reason to look him over more closely. "Austin, we need your input on this

... oh, hi Michael," he says with a sigh. He clearly is not too fond of my brother.

"Hi, Aaron. Great to see you again. I really enjoyed our talk at dinner the other night. Please tell your father that, next time, we should all get together at my place."

"Uh-huh, sure," Aaron says with little enthusiasm.

"Oh, and these are my brothers, Antony and Dace," Michael says, motioning to each of us. "Aaron is Austin's twin brother, guys."

"There are more of you?" he asks, clearly irritated by the idea. "Oh wonderful. Austin, can you help me or are you too busy flirting?" Aaron asks while I catch Antony looking him over with interest. I give him an evil glare, and the asshole shrugs.

"I'm not flirting," she snaps at him. "And I will be there in a second." Aaron walks off with a slight nod to each of us.

"You can flirt with me anytime you want, Austin." Michael flashes his political white teeth at her. I stare at him in disbelief. *Oh my God. This is not happening.*

"Thanks, but um ..." She looks my way and sighs. "I have to go. See you later."

"Count on it," Michael says as she walks away. "That woman, boys, is going to be the next Mrs. Colletto if I have anything to say about it."

"You want to marry her?!" I yell at him. Antony stands behind him, shaking his head frantically and motioning for me to calm down. "I mean she's a cop."

"I know, and her father's the chief of police." *Oh this is just getting worse and worse.* "Don't worry little brother, I know what I am doing. Their family has been leaders in law enforcement for generations and probably one of the most respected families in the city. What better way to clean our family's reputation than to join with that of a long-adored family of the city? Not to mention, the chief's daughter is the epitome of a politician's wife. Smart, beautiful, and damn the things I would do to see her naked. Hell, the things I have thought about doing to her naked."

"Wow, well that is way more than I wanted to know," Antony says, stepping in front of me, shaking his head with a dramatic laugh.

Michael laughs, "I get it. You are not interested in women, but I am sure Dace agrees with me. You think she's hot, don't you Dace?"

I open my mouth to talk, but nothing will come out.

"Him? Hell no, she's too clean for him. You know Dace. He likes them rough and dirty," Antony says, causing Michael to laugh harder and me to sigh with relief.

The moment I shut the door behind me, I breathe a little freer. This is unbelievable. She lied to me. Successfully lied to … me! And I fucking believed her! And my brother! Of all people, my brother is chasing after her. My brother—the guy who never gave up on us, who held me to his chest, and was the only one that could calm me after our mother's death. He said he wished he could have been the one to have killed that guy instead of me and put all my pain on his shoulders. *Argghhhh!* I slam my fist through a wall as Antony comes in.

"Oh good, you've calm down," he says sarcastically.

"You! This is your fault." He points to himself in shock. "Don't act like you're innocent. You introduced me to her. If not for you, I would be fine. I thought you checked them out before you got too involved?"

"I did. Well, I checked him out. Good news. Preston isn't a cop." I stare holes through him. "Yep, he's a hotel manager. A nice one."

"Oh yeah? Which one?"

"Huh?" he says, clearly not knowing.

"Unbelievable, Antony!"

"I know, I'm sorry. You know me, though. I meet someone, I get so excited I don't think about much else. Besides, I wasn't ever planning on dating her." I crash into a chair, fisting my hair. "What are you going to do? And damn Michael is in love with your girl—that's fucked up."

"She's not my girl. Not anymore anyway."

"You're going to break up with her?"

I look up at him in disbelief. "Antony? Really?"

"Well you just seem to really be … falling in love."

"Doesn't matter what my feelings are. I'll get over it. What I won't get over is her being a cop."

"Okay… if you say so."

"Yes, I say so. When I set my mind to something, then that's what will happen. All I have to do is break the habit."

It's been a week since I found out about Austin, and she has been blowing up my phone ever since. She is even trying to chase me down at home and everywhere else. I had to literally run out of our building this morning to get away from her. I think I am going to have to move. *Damn.*

"Mr. Colletto, where do you want me to be?" Tyson, one of Ettore's best men, asks me.

"Go in to use the bathroom and then wait for me there."

"How are you going to get in?"

"Don't worry about me. I always find a way." I smile. I send him on his way and then enter through a locked alleyway door with my lock breaker. Making my way skillfully through the long corridors, I find Tyson and lead him to the back room where their safe room is. *A keypad lock?* They are just making this too easy for me. In no time I am in, and while Tyson goes through their security and sets up the bugs I created, I go through their computer systems and download everything they have and transfer it to Ettore. Stealing from the criminals never bothers me.

"Okay... we have two minutes to get out of here. Are you about done?" I ask Tyson.

"I am ...now."

"Alright, let's get out of here." We step out of the room, and I lead him back "Leave me and step back into the restroom where you came from; wait less than a minute and leave, quickly. You understand?" He nods, and I think we are free and clear, so I leave him to escape out the alleyway door again. I get back out onto the street, look behind me, and see him being chased. *Motherfucker.* I quickly take out my phone and call Antony. "He's coming your way. Be prepared to go and fast; he's being followed."

I hang up and begin walking the opposite direction, expecting to meet them a few blocks down, only I find Austin driving around, apparently searching for me. Damn, she tracked me. I really should have left my phone at home. "Ah damn." I walk by, keeping my head down, but I don't get far before she is chasing after me.

"Dace! Dace please talk to me!" Austin yells after me.

"Go away, Austin. We have nothing to say to each other and stop tracking my phone." I stand at the meeting spot, waiting impatiently as Austin approaches me. "Austin, what are you trying to do? Get us both killed? Go away."

"I will do whatever I have to in order to talk to you. Please, Dace, I only want to talk. I can't believe you can just let what we had go?"

"I can, and I am. Now please, I am begging you, go."

She gets a look of determination over her, and I become instantly worried. "What are you up to?" I roll my eyes, sighing. "If you won't talk to me then I will arrest you and force you to talk to me."

"You're going to what? You're insane. Go find your friends. Better yet, go find my brother. He would love for you to arrest him, I'm sure."

"You're being an asshole," she says. I throw up my hands as I spot Antony across the street, wondering whether to approach me or not. "That's it." She grabs me and throws me against the wall and ties my hands together. "You're under arrest."

"Oh you have got to be kidding me. You are insane. Damn it, Austin, let me go!"

"No, not until you agree to talk to me."

"Okay we will talk later. Let me go now, and I will give you a call."

"No, now." I twist in front of her, cursing under my breath. "You can throw a tantrum all you want, but I am going to get you to talk to me one way or another." She pushes me to her car and shoves me in. Shaking my head, I sit silent as she drives us to a secluded spot and parks. "I'm sorry I didn't tell you I was a cop, but after you said you hated them, I thought …"

"You thought better to lie to me. I get it, typical cop."

"No, that's not what I meant at all. Besides, you lied to me about who you are."

"I was protecting you from getting involved with people you shouldn't be."

"Liar," she says, not relenting when I glare at her. "You were afraid I wouldn't have anything to do with you if you told me. Everyone in this city knows who your family is. I know you love me. I see it, and I love you, Dace. No matter who we are, we can't change how we feel."

I huff, shaking my head. "What is the point in telling me that? Am I supposed to say, 'oh I love you too let's see if we can work this out'? Oh, I know. Let's get our families together. Dad this is my girlfriend, Austin the cop, and her father, the chief of police, and Austin, this is my Dad, the known mob boss. And the best part is, we can get my older brother to marry us. Yeah, Michael, marry me and your girlfriend. You don't mind, do you? Oh what a happy family we will be. We will spend our afternoons with you trying to arrest me and then our nights making love and trying to coax information out of each other. Now, will you stay with the kids or get a babysitter before you go out to track me down and stop me from committing a crime?"

"So you admit you're a criminal?" she says sarcastically.

"Oh, that's funny. Austin, my family would kill us both."

"But then why is Michael chasing after me?"

"Because I'm not Michael! Michael is the first born. He dictates what happens. He makes the rules. Not to mention, he's a politician now. He wants nothing to do with the old ways of the family; he wants to change it to better his political career which isn't sitting to well with Ettore. My family is on the brink of an internal war. The last thing I need is for them to change their focus from each other to me. Michael would disown me if he found out I was with you. It would break his heart, and I couldn't do that to him. And Ettore, Ettore would use my connection to you as a sure sign of betrayal to the family, and without Michael to protect me, I would be as good as dead and so would you." She looks down with sad eyes, and as much as I want to console her, I can't. *Mostly because my hands are tied behind my back!*

"I don't know what to do, Dace. I miss you."

"Get over it. Get over me. Go find someone else. That's what I am going to do."

"You can just walk away that easily?"

"Yes. It's not that difficult, Austin. We had some great times, and now those times will be some great memories that we can never tell anyone about. We both have to put it behind us and move on."

She gets out of the car, pulls me out, and cuts my ties. "Go then, go have ... fun ... with someone else since it's so easy to do." She turns away and slides back into her seat. I go to her as she hides her face with her hands.

I am not sure what to say or the right thing to do to make this all better for her. "You'll be better off without me." She doesn't move, and then I see tears falling down her face. "Hey …" I reach out for her and then stop myself. I am not sure what love is, but something inside me aches and pulls at me to help her, to make her happy. She does deserve to be happy, there is no doubt in my mind about that. "Michael is a great guy. You couldn't do much better than him. I promise you." I walk away with every part of me wanting to run back to her and tell her to forget what I said and love me only. I stop and look back … *Who am I kidding?* We are from two different worlds with two completely different views. I am the villain, and she is the hero, the improbable story of the fallen angel in love with the angel. It would be laughable if the truth of it didn't hurt so much. I stop and look back over my shoulder while my heart beats in an unstable rhythm. I, Dace Colletto, curse the day I was born and the family I was born into. I curse the circumstances that are forcing me to walk away because, no matter how much I want to run back to her, I know that even hell itself is against us. So if I can't have her, at least I can make sure she is with someone I know will treat her like I want to, love her … like I do. She will be happy with him, and I will be happy once she is.

I text Antony where I am. He comes to get me and, thankfully, doesn't say a word to me when I get in the car. Tyson, however, is rightfully curious as to what happened.

"Why did that cop arrest you and then let you go. Is she the one we are paying for info?" I look at him, wondering who he is talking about. "No, that's not her. She's a blond, and our person is definitely not a blond or that tall."

"She was harassing me is all. She's Michael's girlfriend. I am sure he put her up to it," I say with Antony looking at me with a sudden understanding of what I have done. We have never had to say much to understand each other completely.

CHAPTER 16

Austin

It's been a couple of weeks since I have seen Dace. I am not sure if he moved out of the building or if he is doing a really good job avoiding me. I have never been one to need someone, especially a man to be happy, but then I lost *him*. I hate my bed these days; it seems bigger for some reason, so big that I almost took a man home from the bar the other night, and I would have had he not disgusted me before I got a chance to make the offer to him. It's so hard to not care—to simply stop and walk away as if the feelings never existed.

So, here I am, taking a chance, on someone new. I probably shouldn't be doing this, but my father begged me to give him a chance, and maybe, deep inside, I want to prove that a Reed can be with a Colletto, or maybe I just want to prove it to Dace. No matter my reason, I owe this to myself, to try and be happy. I owe my family and even Michael this. He has been nothing but respectful and nice to me. No matter his reasoning, I do like that spark he gets in his eyes when he sees me. As soon as I walk into the room, he lights up as if the sun moved out from the darkest of clouds. Although, it still doesn't compare to how Dace made me feel when he smiled at me. His smile was earned. Michael's is given and with hopeful expectations, expectations I am not sure I can meet.

"Wow, you look amazing. I don't know what finally changed your mind, but I am certainly glad it did," Michael says, taking my hand and kissing the top of it with respect. "So, Miss Reed, let me escort you to dinner." He helps me with my coat and shows me out the door, holding my hand sweetly the entire way. "You know, my brother lives in this same building. I can't believe you two have never run into each other."

"Oh, I have seen him, but he isn't exactly approachable. Not to mention the women he is usually accompanied by are not exactly

..."

"Oh, no need to go any further. I love my brother, but his time away from home was spent with some pretty rough people. I am glad he is back so that maybe we can coax him back into a more socially acceptable attitude at least. Hey, how about your partner? You think she might be interested in going out with him?" I cringe at the very idea of Jamee with Dace. I think I would rather cut off my own arm and beat her with it before I would want to see her with Dace. "From that expression, I guess that would be a no. Okay. I won't mention that again."

"Let's talk about us and not about other's dating issues," I say, smiling up at him. He nods in agreement as he helps me into his incredibly immaculate car. It's so expensive that I am almost afraid to let my cheaply clothed ass fully touch the leather seat.

When we arrive at the restaurant, men come running at the car to help me out and greet Michael as if he is royalty of some kind.

"Mr. Colletto, welcome. We have your table ready for you," the maître de says as he takes my coat and escorts us to our table, or I guess Michael's table. We sit down, and two waiters come up to take care of us, one for each of us, and then a water man comes out just before the wine waiter greets us.

It's all a little dizzying, and I must have an expression of the same because when I look up at Michael, he holds back a smile until I laugh. "I'm sorry. I have no idea what is happening," I laugh, giving him permission to laugh with me.

"No, it's my fault. I was trying to impress you, and I guess I overdid it. Next time I promise to scale back a bit, if you allow me?"

"Sure, maybe we can try a restaurant with one waiter per table. I won't make you go buffet style yet," I laugh.

"Thank you, not sure I even know what that means, but the prospect sounds scary enough. My father was never one for the common places. Mostly, he likes places with good music; he always had to have music with dinner, and the band here is amazing. I would love to prove it to you with a dance later?"

"I didn't know you could dance."

"Of course. My mother made us all learn, and in fact, when the rug rats started getting older, Ettore and I were made to dance with them and teach them. It was torture, but when our mother wasn't around, we would have some fun. Ettore and I would tell them they had to be the girls and had to wear dresses and heels." Michael laughs so hard he can hardly explain the story. "They were so cute and completely confused on why we dressed them up that way. Dace, oh poor Dace, he would keep saying, *'But I don't want to wear booby holders. Michael, I don't want to have boobies'*. He looked so cute and pathetic. I finally turned to him and said, *'Okay Dace, what would you like to wear?'* That kid didn't even hesitate. He said, 'A hat'. He wanted this guy's hat who was a professional tap dance instructor. He said if he had that hat then he could dance like that man does. Antony though, he didn't care what we had him do as long as we paid attention to him and loved him. That kid was so loveable. I didn't have the heart to be mean to him… much. I am still the older brother." He laughs. "My little girl, she reminds me of him. I can't get enough of her little smile."

His love for his brother, his family, is apparent. It's a wonderful thing to see about a man. "You love your family very much, don't you?"

"Without a doubt, I would die for each and every one of them, but especially my little girl. Since her mother died, I try to be around as much as possible for her. I think it's important for a child to have their parent around, not just a nanny. Even as young as she is right now, she knows her mother is gone, and I have to do everything I can to make up for that. Do you want to see a picture?" I start to nod, but he has his phone out and ready with pictures before I can say a word.

"She's adorable. Do you want more kids?"

"Definitely. I love kids; I would have a whole house full if I could. What about you?" Michael says with obvious enthusiasm.

"Oh, yeah. I love kids too. I would like to have my own one day, when the time is right."

"And when is the right time?" he asks.

"I guess when the job stops being fun and when I meet the right man."

"So when Prince Charming comes along and sweeps you off your feet, you would consider quitting your job?"

"Quit? I don't know … I …I."

"I'm sorry. You don't need to answer that right now. I am being way too nosey. It's hard to answer a question so important and serious without all the information. Let's change the subject and talk about you."

"What about me?" I ask nervously.

"What is your dream prince charming, and how can I become that man for you?" he asks sincerely with a sparkle in his eyes that sends butterflies through my body. "How about telling me while we dance?" I smile with an excited nod, and he instantly stands, holding out his hand to me. As hard as I try, I can't help but compare him to Dace. Sure, they are brothers, but they are so different and not just in their hair color. Dace is ruggedly built, sexy as hell, unattainable, and oh so seductive in every move he makes. Michael, despite being much older than me, is still handsome. He greets me with a respectful hand, always has an encouraging word or two, a true politician along with being the perfect husband and father material. I am sure he is closer to what I should want. *Right?*

My father walks into the station with his head held so high I am surprised he notices me, but he gives me a quick glance before meeting with my boss and then talking to Aaron, his pride and joy. We may be twins, but I am the daughter he could care less about, the one who can't carry on the family name, traditions, or long history of police chiefs in the family. As far as my father is concerned, a female cop is only good for keeping the feminists off his back. I spent years trying to change his mind, prove to him that I was more than worthy of the position he now holds, but one day, I realized, he doesn't care. No matter how hard I try, he will never see me for anything other than a daughter that he has been burdened with. He has never known how to talk to me or treat me. When I first got my period, he had a female neighbor come over and talk to me. It was incredibly uncomfortable to talk to someone I barely knew about something so personal; however, it was better than having to talk to him. I am not sure how my mother stayed married to him for so long, maybe it was the many men she was sleeping with behind his back, at least that's what my father told us. I don't remember her ever being with anyone, but I guess she wouldn't share that kind of thing with her children. My father wouldn't even allow us to go to her funeral. I hated him for that, and at times, I still do. Now, I am the typical little girl trying to get her daddy's approval. It's disgusting and for some reason, knowing that, I still keep trying.

"Austin," my father says sternly from behind me.

I stand and immediately begin adjusting my clothes. "Sir, how are you today?"

"Good and you?"

"Doing well, thank you."

"How is Michael?"

"He's good, I guess."

"You guess? Are you even trying to make him happy? How can you keep a man interested if you're not in tune with his wants and needs or if he is at least doing well?"

"That's not really up to me Father. That's up to Michael. I can't control his happiness." His glaring eyes tell me he disagrees. "I really wish you would see me as a valuable officer and not a value as a whore to make your connections happy."

"Come with me!" he snaps. I follow him to a meeting room and he shuts the door behind us. "Sit down, Austin."

"I don't have time for this. I have a lot of work to do,

Father."

"You will make time to listen to this. Our family has built a perfect reputation in this city. We have gained importance with each generation, and next, Aaron will be taking over for me to help continue that tradition. The best contribution you can make is to marry Michael Colletto."

I stand up with force. "Marry him?! How can marrying into a crime family help our family's reputation?"

"Sit down!" I slowly ease back into the chair while my father leans down into my face. "The Collettos have had past issues, I will give you that, but they are a strong, prideful family, and now they are making huge strides to better their own. Michael is a good man, and his ability as a politician and leader is something to admire. He is going to be president of this country one day, I promise you. If you play your cards right, you could be his first lady, and that is something I want for you and our family. You have a chance to be part of the history books, Austin."

"Oh yeah, as the wife of a crime boss, who is able to trick people into voting for him, or buy votes, is probably more like it!"

My father smacks me in the face, leaving a burning hand print behind. He stands tall in front of me with a scowl as Aaron runs into the room and quickly puts himself between me and my father. "Dad! What are you doing?"

"Your sister needed to be reminded of who I am."

"Why are you forcing her to date Colletto? He's a dirt-bag. I don't understand why you would go against everything you have taught us, and I am sure she doesn't either."

"Because sometimes you need to align yourself with the powerful to stay ahead and to stay powerful yourself. This is the way it is, the opulent control the world."

"I think we could do much better if we would put them behind bars for life."

"Don't be a fool, Aaron," my father says through his teeth. "They are beyond punishable. They are the leaders, the kings of this world, and if we want to succeed against our enemies then we need to align ourselves with them to do it."

"We have the law on our side. We don't need to align ourselves with anyone! You are the chief, a king in your own right. We control them! They should fear us!" my brother stresses with his whole body beginning to shake with anger. "I'll make it my personal mission to put their whole family away."

My father grabs Aaron's face with both hands. "You listen to me. You will do nothing of the sort. You're being foolish, Aaron. There are the laws of the common man, and then there are the *Laws of Kings*, and Lord help those that go against the King." My father grabs my arm and pulls me out of my chair. Looking Aaron and I both over, he breathes heavily, "Our family has always done whatever it has to do to stay in power, and now it is your turn to take the reins and lead this family to even greater heights. You both have the opportunities to go so much farther than I had ever anticipated for you. Trust me to direct your lives to greatness."

To make my father happy, Aaron and I both join him for dinner, and it is no surprise that Michael shows up as well as Jamee, my father's sudden choice for Aaron, something we only just learned of the day before. I didn't even know my father knew who Jamee was; it's not as if he takes much of an interest in my career. My father's new cook made a delicious meal, thankfully so good that I can pretend it is too good to bother talking. Michael and my father do most of the talking, all about the city and their concerns for its future, while Jamee does her best to get Aaron's attention. She must know of my father's plans to make him the next chief; otherwise, why would she be so interested in him? He doesn't make enough money for her standards.

"Michael, how do you feel about a woman concentrating more on a career than having a family?" my father asks with a cocked brow in my direction.

Michael smiles at me from across the table. "Well sir, I think it's important that everyone follow their dreams, whether that be a career or a family. It's all worth concentrating on if it's important to that individual. A happy family can only begin with happy parents, don't you think?" Michael says with a wink in my direction. I don't bother to look my father's way. I know he doesn't agree. I simply mouth a "thank you" in Michael's direction.

"Well, I would quit my job in a heartbeat for the good of my family," Jamee says suddenly.

"That would be more for the good of the people working with you, wouldn't it?" Aaron laughs.

"Aaron!" My father tenses. "That is very admirable, Jamee. Please excuse my son's smart mouth; he hasn't quite reached maturity."

After dinner, and after some more boring conversation in the living room, Aaron is forced to take Jamee home while Michael volunteers to spare me from the bickering between the two and takes me home.

"Thank you for the ride," I say as he parks in front of my building.

"Well let me walk you to your door. I am a gentleman, after all." He jumps out of the car and rushes to open the car door for me before I can do it myself. I suddenly realize that he means all the way to my front door and not just the building door, and I begin to get nervous. I have yet to do much more than kiss Michael on the cheek. I know he wants more. What man wouldn't at this point? We have been out more than a handful of times already, and I have always managed an excuse or a maneuver to keep from going beyond a friendship with him. I don't know why he hasn't given up on me. He should have, and I wish he would, it would make things so much easier. I have tried to find a flaw within him, so I don't have to feel so guilty about not sharing his feelings, but as hard as I try, I can't find one. Taking my hand, he walks me up the steps and into the building before grabbing the elevator for me. I walk in first, and he follows in after Dace.

"Hey, little brother, how was your evening?" Michael asks,

taking my hand again.

Dace looks down at our intertwined hands and forces a smile. "It was good, had a few drinks with Antony."

"You went to a bar and you're coming home alone? Are you sick?" Michael jokes.

"Ha ha, no. I'm just not in the mood to … I'm too tired to… entertain," Dace says, glancing my way.

The elevator door opens up to my floor, and Michael leads me out while I look back at Dace and meet his eyes, aching inside. The moment we reach my door I already have my keys in hand and feel that overwhelming dread take over as I turn to face Michael. *He's so handsome, Austin. Why can't you love him?* Michael smiles at me, cradling my face in one hand and wiping away a tear from my cheek with the other.

"What's wrong, Sweetheart? Are you still upset by what your father said?" he asks and I instantly take advantage of the idea and nod. Falling into his arms, I rest my head on his chest and somehow feel comforted. "Do you want me to stay with you for a little while?" I don't seem to have control over my own emotions anymore, and I nod yes. *Why? Why would I do this to him?* I am so selfish wanting to be comforted by one man because of another, because of his own brother. Yet I still don't push Michael away. No, instead, I bring him in even closer and allow him to kiss me. It's a sweet kiss and seems to satisfy him enough to allow me to sleep against his bare chest for the entire night without pushing me to go any further. How did I get here? I don't even remember how all this torment started.

CHAPTER 17

Dace

It's an early morning when Michael wakes me up and asks to talk to me. He shows up at my door with his shirt untucked and hair obviously fingered back into place. My brother, who is the epitome of perfection, is anything but this early morning.

"Good morning, Michael. You look …a mess. Don't you iron your clothes anymore or change them?"

He smiles happily. "Okay, okay, yeah I spent the night with Austin last night." He moves into my place, floating on air. "Things have been moving annoyingly slow with her, I have to admit, but there is something about her that keeps me coming back. I guess you could say she is worth waiting for. I have never met a woman like that. Have you?" he asks.

"Me? Um… no, I don't know what you're talking about. You must still be on a sex high," I say, dashing towards my kitchen and opening my refrigerator door to relieve my steaming body within the cool air.

"Well, I wish I could say that was true, but we didn't have sex, we only slept. She was upset and crying about her father, so I stayed to help her feel better."

I slam the refrigerator door shut and turn back to him. "She was crying?"

"Yeah, her father is a real bastard. He treats her like shit," he says as if he knows her.

Austin could care less about what her father thinks of her. I've heard her talking to him before; she ignores most of what he says and is unfazed by his criticisms soon after she hangs up. She's too strong and independent for anyone's comments to bother her. I look my brother over and realize he will never see this about her. He will only see the perfect representation of a politician's wife at his side, representing all that he believes is right. Austin is more than what he sees; she's a lot more. It pisses me off that he doesn't realize that.

Michael begins talking about business and asking me to help with one thing or another, but all I can think about is him lying in bed with her and feeling her warm body against his chest while he slept. The more I think about it, the more I want to punch him in the face, and then he turns towards me.

"You okay, Rocky?" Michael asks, reminding me of the nickname he gave me as a kid. He was always the one that would play with me and let me pretend to beat him up. It used to make me laugh so hard when he would pretend that I knocked him out. He looks me over as he always does when he is worried, and I surrender my anger within seconds. "Maybe you should stay home and rest, you have been working non-stop since you have been back. I'm sorry, I didn't even consider that. I'll have Antony handle this. He's been learning a lot from you lately and begging for an opportunity to prove it."

"No, I'm fine. I promise. I would rather be working than sitting around here bored out of my mind. What do you need, Michael?"

Michael steps back with an odd look. "I just told you a few minutes ago." He sighs. "Stay home and watch some old movies, maybe call a girl to come over and take your mind off of things. Hey, whatever happened to that girl you were telling me about, the one you were so excited for me to meet? You seemed to really like her."

"Oh, it turned out she wasn't really meant for me."

"Sorry to hear that. I was really happy for you, but if you came close once, there is no reason to believe you won't find someone even better. Right?" He grabs the back of my head and rubs it.

"Right," I say, forcing a smile.

"Alright, I will call you later to check on you…" He reaches into his coat pocket and pulls out a tiny box. "Oh damn! I meant to give this to Austin. Do you mind giving this to her for me?"

"Me?! Why can't you do it?"

"Because I am afraid she won't like it, and I hate to see disappointment in her face."

"You really like her, don't you?" I ask him as he lowers his eyes away from me.

"You know I have always been attracted to her, and I thought she would be a good fit for my political career, but she is so much more than I could have ever imagined." He smiles and shakes his head before walking out with a wave. I walk over and pick up the little box he left on the table. Opening it, I see a tiny elephant charm. It's not quite the same as the one I gave her. Instead of being completely carved with dramatic detail, it is adorned with a cute diamond trunk. *Sigh. I need a ride.*

I grab my helmet and head out, being sure to stop by her door on my way out. *Don't bother knocking, just put it in front of her door.* I squat down as her door opens. *Of course.* I stand up and quickly hand Austin the box.

"What's this?" she asks with a smile.

"Michael forgot to give it to you. He was afraid you wouldn't like it, so he asked me to give it to you instead, but I thought considering…well I was going to leave it at your door."

"Oh. Thanks."

"Aren't you going to open it? I'm sure he is going to ask me later." She lifts the top and looks in with a sigh.

"It's very pretty." I nod. "He saw the one you gave me, and he asked if I liked elephants. I told him I that I love them."

"And how did he see it exactly?" I say sharply.

"I wore it! Do you have a problem with that? Or maybe you want it back? Maybe you want to take it all back, every word said, every kiss given. Is that it, Dace? Am I one big regret now?"

"I told you, my brother would have us both killed. He is very paranoid, and he has never really liked me or Antony. He doesn't need much of an excuse to have me killed."

"Then why have anything to do with him? Talk to Michael. I am sure he…"

"Austin, it doesn't work that way. If my family looks the least bit weak then we take a chance of being attacked from all sides, and then we are all dead. As much as I love Michael, Ettore keeps our enemies in check; we need him. They are terrified of him. As much as Michael likes to think everyone likes him and will follow him, our enemies are only staying away from him because of Ettore. My father knows that, and I know that. That's why I help him, because I love Michael that much to help make his dreams come true. Otherwise, Antony and I would have never come back here. We would have disappeared forever."

"That's really sad. You know that? Are you never going to allow yourself to be happy? What about Antony? Is it all about Michael?"

"You don't understand. If it wasn't for Michael, Antony and I would be dead. He was the one that talked our father into sending us away and keeping quiet about us being alive. Our father was too distraught to make decisions at the time; he didn't speak to anyone for weeks. Michael took over the family the day after my mother died and saved Antony and I from being sought out for revenge. It's an eye for an eye in our world, and I killed theirs, Austin, to protect my brother and myself. I killed part of their family. I grabbed my father's gun and shot the man. No matter how young I was, they would have surely hunted me down and killed me if not for Michael's quick thinking and overprotective love. My family isn't like others, Austin. We have to live by a different set of rules. I don't like it, but that's the life I was born into, so that's the life I have to live." I look down and start to leave her but turn back around to reassure her. "And I am happy." I smile wide. "See?"

"Sure you are. That's why you can't look me in the eyes," she says, waiting for me to do so. With a huff and lot of swearing, I look into her eyes and … "Dace please, at least tell me I mean, something, to you?"

"Something? Food means something to me. Water means something to me. You … well you mean more than simply *something*." I walk away, run down the stairs, and jump onto my bike, riding away, letting the open air ease my misery.

Chapter 18

Austin

Wearing Michael's elephant on my wrist, and Dace's around my neck, I sit with my brother at lunch, trying to avoid the question I know he wants to ask.

"Do you really like that guy?"

"Who?"

"You know who. Colletto—Michael— or whatever his name is?" I look over at him with a shrug of my shoulders. "Oh, well that's good. I was afraid you were falling in love with him, that maybe Dad was getting to you."

"Honestly, Michael is a great guy. He really is. He's comforting, respectful, and everything a girl could ever want…"

"But?"

"You know me too well," I say, sipping my coffee.

"Well enough to know that there is someone else. Who is he?" My eyes widen as Aaron smiles, shaking his head. "I am a better detective than you think. Don't worry, I will let you keep your secret since it seems to be over for some reason. I don't need to dig up any more trouble than you already have. That guy is trouble, the Collettos are trouble. I don't know what they are up to or how they got our father on their side, but I assure you, I am going to find out."

"Do you think they are paying our father to help protect them?" I ask him.

"I don't know. I don't want to think that, but something is not right. I can feel it." Aaron looks up at the door and leans back, groaning. "Oh no, I thought you told her you were going home for lunch?"

I turn to see Jamee walking in with all smiles. "Hello you two sneaky devils," she says, swaying her hips into Aaron's side.

Aaron looks up at me, repulsed. I have to take a drink to keep from laughing. "I need to go. Billy is supposed to be meeting me somewhere, I am sure of it." Aaron gets up and kisses me on the head, leaving before Jamee can say another word.

"Huh. I think he is finally coming around, don't you think?" Jamee says with optimism.

"I don't even want to know how you found us. Let's just go. I got a lead about Paltrow, Ettore Colletto's money launderer, and where he is getting his funding from."

"You got a lead? When? From who?" she asks, and I am sure expecting for me to give her a reasonable answer, but for some reason, I don't feel I should. I still have Nelson's notebook, or rather Mr. Martin's extensive notes he somehow managed to get on what I assume are Ettore Colletto's complex business dealings. It is still too early to tell, but I am getting closer, and I don't want anyone to stop me, especially my father, who Jamee is making a special effort to suck up to lately.

"Merlin introduced me. He wouldn't give up his name, and he would only talk to me over the phone."

"Merlin? You got this info from Merlin? Yeah, I am not going to get too excited then."

"Don't. We'll just have to see," I say, urging her to go anyway.

If there is anything that can take my mind off of my trouble with men, it's work. Right now, I am sure Myers Paltrow is supporting his criminal actions through a company called Elision. I found a company account under the Elision name, and though it is small most of the time, there are minutes where it contains large funds, and then it all quickly disappears again. Since I haven't been able to sleep much lately, I have been watching it constantly, and I have tracked down an access point from a particular address.

"I don't know what we are doing her. It looks like a mom and pop hardware store." We walk in, and we are immediately greeted by an older man with a cane while a similar-in-age woman behind the counter waves at us. "Oh yeah... hardened criminals, I am sure."

"Shut up," I tell the sarcastic bitch. I smile at the old man, flashing my badge. "Hi, Sir, do you have an internet connection for your store?"

"Oh yes, it's in the back, we use it for orders and talking to the grandkids, not much else. Is there a problem?"

"I'm sure it's nothing, but do you mind if I take a look at it?" He nods and shows me the way. Jamee follows with a huff, but I don't let it bother me. I move into the little office and sit down in front of the surprisingly high tech computer. "Wow this is something," I say to the man.

"The wife and I could barely figure out how to turn it on when it came, but it was free, so who are we to turn down a brand new computer?"

"Free?" I ask.

"Yes, we apparently won it in some contest. Our old one is over there on the file cabinet."

I look behind me and see the large monstrosity that is clearly decades past its time. I give Jamee a look as her eyebrows raise. "Are you interested now?"

"Maybe. It is a little suspicious, I will admit," Jamee says, leaning down over my shoulder to look over the brightly lit computer. "What are you looking for though? I don't know how you can tell that there is anything odd about it other than the old people nose prints on the screen. Gees, they are blind." Disregarding her smartass comments, I type away, looking deep into their system. "Wait how did you get there?"

"It's something I learned along the way. And here, right here, is where the bug is hidden."

"How can you tell? It looks like everything else."

"Because it is trying too hard to blend in," I say, recognizing the trick I learned in the military.

"What are you doing now?"

"I'm going to upset it and make it sick so someone has to come and heal it."

"I doubt anyone will come. They will probably just set it to a new location."

"Oh I think they will." I nod assuredly.

"Well, I am not waiting here all day and night for someone that may or may not show."

"Fine, go."

"Austin, this is ridiculous, and I have to be at the dinner tonight to see your father's speech. Aaron's going to be there; don't you want to be?" I roll my eyes. "I am not working overtime again only to get yelled at for working without approval."

"I said 'fine'. Go."

"You're going to get into trouble. You're going to get in over your head and get killed, and then I am going to get into trouble because you're dead. Then, I will have to bring you back to life so I can kill you for ruining my career," she hisses in frustration.

"I will wait safely across the street. Will that make you feel better?"

"Not much."

"Fine, then stay and miss your chance to be around Aaron when he's drunk." She instantly stands back, thinking about the possibilities.

"Bye," she exclaims, running out the door.

"Have a good night." Once she's gone, I make myself a nice viewing spot across the street and wait. It isn't long before someone comes rolling by on their motorcycle. He doesn't stop; he continues past, but the coincidence is simply too perfect. Jumping up, I rush out the door and across the street, running to the back of the store. Making my way quietly through an alleyway, I find someone opening a back door. "Stop and put your hands up," I say, holding my gun steady on him. Dace slowly turns around with his hands up all the while shaking his head. "What are you doing here, Dace?"

"I'm helping out some old family friends with their computer, Austin. I'm a giver."

"Sure you are."

"Ask them, if you don't believe me," he says as the door opens wider and the little old lady walks out.

"Oh my! What is happening here?"

"Mrs. Brooks, this woman thinks I am breaking into your store."

"Oh no." She wraps her arms around his waist. "Dace is a lifesaver. When you said there was a problem, we called him to help. He is so smart about these things and nice to help us out whenever we need him. Oh, please don't think badly of him. He might not look it, but he is a very sweet boy." Dace smiles, and I roll my eyes.

I put my gun down. "Do you mind if I talk to the sweet boy alone for a few minutes?" She nods and walks back inside after some persuasion from Dace. "There's an interesting program on their computer that hides business dealings for a company called Elision." I watch his expression carefully, but his poker face doesn't give me anything. "I know you know what is going on with that company, and whatever you programmed onto their computer is causing disruption in the system to block anyone from seeing what is happening with that company's accounts. Good idea by the way. No one would ever suspect these people."

"Then why do you?"

"Because I know how you people think."

"*You people*? Wow, that's harsh, Trouble," he says, nearing me with a smile. Clearing my hair from my ear, he leans down and whispers, "I'm just a sweet boy helping out some old family friends." With a soft hand down my arm, he continues, "You remember how sweet I am, don't you?"

I jerk my arm away from him. "Dace, you are up to something, and I am going to find out what."

"Let it go, Austin. There is nothing to be found here. I'm not sure what led you here, but whatever it is or whoever it is, is going to end up getting you killed," he says, walking away.

"I'm not. I'm not ever going to let it go. I am going to arrest you and your brothers," I yell out to him, causing him to stop and turn to look at me with frustration.

"You can't win this one, Austin. I swear … you're only going to get yourself killed."

"If that's the way it has to be, then so be it," I say, lifting my chin up to him in defiance.

"Don't look for me to help you." I shrug, and he hisses, "You're a damn fool. Stick with Michael and stay away from Ettore as much as you can. He is beyond your reach, Trouble. Trust me." He smiles briefly with a slow upward movement of his eyes along my body.

With a sudden reach, I grab hold of his coat and jerk him to me. Looking into his dangerous, steel blue eyes, I smile. "And you? Will you stand back and watch me die? Or will you stop the bullet from reaching my skin?" His eyes dance around my lips and to my soul before denying me my answer. I watch him walk away knowing if the words are that hard to say, then they must not be the ones he wants to admit to himself.

"You're not eating. Is there something wrong with your food?" Michael asks.

"No, it's fine. I just have a lot on my mind."

"Work?" I nod. "Dare I ask what you are investigating now?"

I look him over and consider what he may know. Maybe I should see if my so-called "boyfriend" is up to no good right along with his dangerous brother. "Oh, just a small unknown company named Elision," I say with ease, carefully watching his expressions. He stares down at his food with barely a glance in my direction. *Nothing?* "Are you not even curious as to who they might be?"

"Of course. Who are they?" he asks with no sign of any knowledge at all. The perfect poker face must run in the family.

Shaking my head at him, I sigh, "I thought maybe you could tell me."

He wants to deny me, but surprisingly, he looks up at me and grabs my hand from across the table. "Austin, clearly you know enough, and I will be honest with you. I don't get in the middle of my brother's businesses if, indeed, it is his. If you want help taking down my brother, I can't help you. I wish I could, but I won't." Michael squeezes my hand, looking away from me. "Austin, I am not about to tell you, of all people, what to do, but I will ask that you be careful. Please. I would very much like to spend a very long time looking into your beautiful eyes." His words instantly make me smile. I am not even sure what happened within me, but I felt something, and that something seemed obvious to everyone around us as even the lady at the next table smiles with a nod in my direction. Michael squeezes my hand, and I squeeze his right back with a shy laugh. "Wow, there are no words for how beautiful you are right now. I love to watch you blush. I'm not sure what caused it, but it looks good on you."

"You make me so uncomfortable when you say things like that."

"I'm sorry. I don't mean to. I am simply overwhelmed sometimes and can't help myself. It's insane really. You know, I have to be honest. Originally, I pursued you for my political career, but you know what? After spending time with you and getting to know you, I would give it all up just to spend another night simply talking and holding you."

"That's so sweet. Okay JFK, you have my attention. What do you want to do with me now?"

He looks at me with an odd expression. "That's funny. My brother is the only one that has ever called me that. What made you think to call me that?" I shrug my shoulders, suddenly recalling talking to Dace late into the night about his brothers and him referring to his oldest brother as JFK. I didn't think much of it at the time, but now it makes sense. Wow, he was trying to tell me who he was without telling me.

"Don't change the subject. I asked you a question …" I wink at him.

His smile brightens up the whole room. "I told you …" he says, sitting back holding my hand. "I want to spend the entire night in this moment."

Michael's kiss is warm and soft. I can't help but feel lost within it. The only thing that keeps me from staying lost is the kiss that made me soar. How to forget one for another? Maybe it can be done; I am just not sure how much time it will take.

"I would like for you to have dinner with me and my daughter?" Michael asks. I look up at him in shock. "Don't be scared. She is only three, and she is amazing—just like you. You two are surely going to get along. I really want you to meet her. I have told her all about you."

I don't know what to say to him, but his hopeful expression and tender touch makes me want to please him. "Okay, if you think it's a good idea."

He smiles happily and hugs me tight. "I know she will love you as much as … well, you will love each other I'm sure."

I smile as best I can, but I am terrified on the inside. Not of his child but of the idea of being in his home, his turf, and the expectations that are surely to come.

I know how to dress for work, or even a date, but how do you dress for a date with the future governor and his three year old daughter? I have been through everything in my closet, from a pantsuit to my college sweatshirt and jeans. I don't know why it's so difficult to make up my mind; my closet only holds so much and I have nothing more outside of it. No, there is simply no perfect outfit for this occasion. The best thing to do is to go with something in between incredibly comfortable and terribly uncomfortable. With that part of my decision making out of the way, I now have the horrible responsibility of trying to decide what to bring to dinner, wine? Probably not the best for a three-year old. However, wine for me and a charming little bunny purse for the child might work just fine.

Michael saw to it to have his driver pick me up and his butler help me out of the car and escort me inside. His maid announced my arrival to him while another took my coat before I followed the house manager to where Michael was waiting for me. It's not exactly what I am used to, this life, and this mansion of a house with all its servants. I don't know how anyone lives with people constantly around you. Michael waits for me in the sitting room with his daughter in his arms. The little girl has a tight grip on her father and eyes me with a shy awkwardness. "Sage, honey, this is Austin. Say hi."

"Hi," she says sweetly.

"Hello Sage. I brought something for you." I lift up the brightly colored package to her, and she promptly lifts her head up off her father's shoulder and leans forward. "Here you go."

Michael sits with her and helps her open it with a smile. "Wow, that is so cute. What do you say Sage?"

"Tank-you," she says sweetly, playing with the purse with an open mouth smile.

"That was very nice of you, to think of her. You certainly didn't need such bribery to win her over. All you have to do to make my daughter happy is offer to play with her for a little while. She's not hard to please. Although, she is a little spoiled, but you can't blame her for that."

"She is beautiful," I say, admiring the picture perfect family that they are together.

Michael lifts her up with pride, kissing her face while she

giggles happily. "I tell you, there is nothing better than the laughter of your own child. Are you hungry?" I nod, and he, along with his daughter, takes my hand and escorts me to dinner in the opulent dining room. Staring at the layout in front of me, I begin to become overwhelmed by it all. Wow, this is certainly not a college sweatshirt and jeans room.

After dinner, I play with Sage, but mostly I enjoy watching Michael play the goofy father for his daughter. Seeing him act like a child and be whatever she would like him to be, whether it be a barking dog or a roaring lion, he obliges, giving her every right to imagine all the possibilities. Suddenly, Michael's phone rings, and he responds with a worried expression.

"Do you mind watching her for a few minutes while I take this call?"

"Of course." Michael leaves his daughter with me. *With me?!* I am not exactly a woman that has ever dreamed of having children. Sage looks at me and begins speaking to me in a language I am not familiar with. It sounds like English, but the words are not clear. Maybe best to change the subject. "So … great weather we are having, huh?" She laughs. "Yeah, you're right. It's terrible. I am not sure why I even mentioned it. I am sure you would rather talk about something else, like um … politics maybe? Your Dad is in politics. That's impressive." She giggles. "Right, you probably don't care much about that." I sit down on her princess bed and think. Surely I can come up with something to entertain this little girl. I, after all, was a little girl at one time. What did I want to do at her age? Suddenly, she comes at me with a big hug and a book. I take hold of it for her, "You want me to read this?" She nods, settling into my lap comfortably while I begin reading it to her. Apparently she is sleepy because she curls up under my arm and begins to fight her eyes from closing. Her little blanket is not too far away, so I reach out for it and cover her up, wrapping her up as my mother once did for me.

"Tank you," she says with her eyes closed and a soft sigh.

I could stare at her all night. "Oh wow, I didn't know how much I wanted one of you," I whisper with a soft kiss to her head.

"She is a heartbreaker," Michael says, coming over to pick her up from my lap and getting her ready for bed. "Alright Honey, it's bedtime for you." Once we put Sage safely in her bed, Michael takes my hand and leads me to a quiet place by the fire. Curled up next to him with a glass of wine, he cuddles me, nudges me, kisses me, and encourages me in every way he can to get me to return his affection. I feel obligated to try, and so I do. I am afraid that he will want more, and I am even more afraid that I won't be able to give it. If not for Dace being in the back of my mind, I am sure I would fall for Michael, in a heartbeat; any woman would. Maybe I need to stop thinking so much? Let him have control of me? I give up my glass and enjoy him removing half his clothes to show his long lean body off. It feels so good that I even allow him to loosen most of my clothes, squeeze my breasts, and grab my ass to pull me in against his erection. I breathe out heavily as he kisses my neck and breaks through my shirt, enjoying my freed breasts. Michael pushes me onto my back and is desperately trying to get me fully naked as he is himself, his erection protruding fully in my sight. Giving up control at this point seems more to his doing than mine. My arms are pinned, my body is forced back, and my clothes are disappearing rapidly, and suddenly, I am having trouble breathing.

"Stop. Stop! Michael stop!" I yell at him, doing my best to break free.

He sits back looking at me confused while I struggle to breathe. "What's wrong?" He leans over me as I continue gasping. "Are you okay, Honey?"

I quickly grab my clothes and get dressed. "I need to go."

"Austin?" Michael questions me trying to get a hold of me while I push away from him.

"I want to go home, please, I need to go home."

"Okay, but first I want to know what I did wrong. Please, whatever it is, I assure you I didn't want to pressure you."

I have no idea how to answer him. "I can't breathe. I suddenly don't feel well is all. I'm sorry, I really need to go."

"Alright, I'll have my driver take you home immediately," he says, throwing his hands up and walking away from me.

He barely says goodbye to me, not that I expect him to. I am not sure what I should have expected after what happened. I am not even sure what happened. I stumble out of the car and send the driver away, telling him I can make it the rest of the way on my own. I fall into the elevator, shaking and still desperately trying to breathe. When the elevator is stopped from closing completely, I open my eyes, and Dace walks in, looking me over. I jump towards him and grab his arm, but he shakes his head at me with wide eyes. I don't understand until I notice someone behind him.

The large man walks out from behind him, looking me over with a cold stare, sending chills up my spine. "Good evening." Ettore nods towards me. I nod towards him and step back, avoiding eye contact at all costs. This is the closest I have ever been to the man, and now I understand why people are so scared of him. There is a deadness about his glare, maybe it's the scar near his right eye or maybe it's the lack of any feeling or emotion at all, as if he is the walking dead. I can't get out of the elevator fast enough. I rush into my home and find Preston casually lounging in front of the TV.

"Hey, you're home early. I assumed you wouldn't be here until tomorrow afternoon" He laughs while I stumble to my room and crawl into bed. "Austin." Preston follows, placing a hand on my head. "What happened?"

"I am a disaster, and ruined for good. Why can't I love the right man and not the wrong one? I panicked, Pres. I was in the moment; I wasn't even thinking of Dace. Everything was great, but then I couldn't breathe. It felt so wrong. I don't know why I can't love him, even though he's perfect."

Preston sits on my bed, sighing. "Have you ever thought that you do love the right one, that maybe your body is reacting to some type of intuition that you're not realizing yet? You are so good at sizing people up, but this time, you keep talking about him as if he is flawless. You know no one is flawless. Your instinct is telling you something is off, but you're trying not to listen to it for some reason." I sit up and look at him, hopeful. "Yeah, maybe you picked the right brother the whole time, but the circumstances have you running from what you know is the right decision." I hug him tight with a smile. "Never give up on what feels right, even if he is too stubborn to realize that you two belong together."

"Do you think I am crazy? I mean, most women would kill to be in my shoes right now."

"Oh, yeah, you are definitely crazy." I look up from his shoulder. "Sorry, but you are. I mean who wears those ugly ass shoes on a date? I'm sorry Sweetie, but ain't no woman going to kill to be in those shoes."

"Oh shut up!" I laugh, smacking him with a pillow.

Preston helped me forget about my issues for a while and laugh about the ridiculous things we get into sometimes. He even talked about Antony. I don't know why I assumed they had stopped seeing each other, I guess because Dace had put a stop to our relationship. Not that he was wrong. I understand his reasoning, but there has to be a way. I don't know much about men and dating, but I do know I have never felt the way I do about him.

Preston has been asleep for a couple of hours when I am still up watching old Cary Grant movies, trying to understand what makes a man a man. The light knock on the door gets me up, but with my gun in hand, I peak through the peep hole and lay my gun to the side as I open the door. "What are you doing here?"

"You didn't look so good earlier," Dace says, leaning against my door frame.

"I'm fine now."

"Good, I'm sorry I couldn't talk to you on the elevator, but …"

"Yeah… I get it, you work for a ruthless killer and can't have anything to do with a cop. I got that now."

"You don't understand anything, and unfortunately, I can't explain it to you now or maybe ever. I don't want you to be hurt or upset, Austin."

"I'm not. I'm fine. I'm completely fine." He looks me over

not seeming convinced. "I am, Dace. No reason to worry about me, if that is what you are doing." He starts to say something, but I stop him. "I'm fine, I promise," I say with a smile.

"Okay, good." He reaches out his hand towards me but pulls back. "If … um, if you need anything, let me know. I do live right upstairs. You know if you need uh … sugar or something." I laugh, and he smiles before leaning in and taking hold of my head and pulling me towards him. I don't want to want him, but the feeling of his chest, his hands, and his lips against the side of my face is too much. "Good night, Trouble," he breathes with a soft inhale of my hair and disappears.

CHAPTER 19

Dace

Austin was upset, and I know she was with Michael tonight. He was making a big deal about the meal that was supposed to be served and how to dress Sage for their first meeting. It was all I could do to listen to him go on and on about his expectations for the night. He actually spent money to have his bedroom decked out in roses and candles, strategically placed for multiple possibilities for the night. I don't know what happened, but if he forced himself on her, or pressured her, I swear I will … Damn! I can't imagine him doing that, but something happened, and as much as I should probably let it go … I can't. I can't rest until I know what happened. I storm out of my own building and to his house. When the door opens, I suddenly realize I have nothing to say to him, no way to ask what happened without giving away my past relationship with Austin.

Michael's doorman escorts me to the study to wait for him while I figure out what to say. "Dace? What are you doing here so late?"

"Ettore, he came home with me tonight, and …um … well your girlfriend was in the elevator and she nearly gave me away. If you want me to play the distant, unfeeling role, I can't have your girlfriend talking to me as if I'm a … close friend or something. "

Michael sighs, walking around me in his robe. "I'll talk to her, but …" I look up, hoping that he is going to confess what exactly happened. "Yeah, I'll talk to her," he says with a forced smile.

"What's wrong?" He shakes his head. "Don't do that. I know something is wrong. I assumed she would still be here. Did you not pull the infamous Michael Colletto move?" I laugh, fighting my own urge to slug him if he says the wrong thing.

"Yeah… I guess my moves aren't for everyone. I don't know what happened. I had her right here, enjoying the moment. I had her naked even, in my arms ..." I tense, thinking of her on the sofa that's in front of me. "She was fine, it was exciting, and I was ready ... you know? And then..."

"Then what? What else is there, but to fuck?"

"Don't say that, Dace. That's a disgusting way to put it."

"Then what Michael?!"

"Why are you getting mad at me? You probably had sex several times today. You should be completely relaxed."

"Just answer the question, Michael."

"Fine, we got right up to that moment and then she started to hyperventilate." *What?* "I don't know what happened, but she panicked and ran out of here as fast as she could. I am not even sure if she will ever see me again. There has to be something, someone holding her back."

"Wow, that sucks," I say, hiding my smile.

"Do you think it's because I am a Colletto? I mean... do you think she is still having a hard time letting that go?"

"Oh probably, I mean she is a cop. She has learned to hate us."

"I need to figure out a way to get around that. I need to figure out how to get her to forget her beliefs and marry me."

"What?" He is unbelievably determined. "I mean, what can you do? She doesn't like you like that, maybe you should find someone else?" I can't believe it took this to make me realize I don't want to see her with even him. It's too hard.

"No, I want her. I need her, and I will do whatever I have to in order to get her." He turns to me with a look I have only seen from Ettore, and I begin to wonder if my brothers are all that different when it comes to getting what they want. "I bet it's that other cop, the one that partners with her brother. I have seen the way he looks at her and she smiles at him. I need to have her followed and make sure. If there is someone else, then I want to know who they are, and then I will have them removed from the equation."

"What are you saying, Michael? She can't be involved with anyone other than you?"

"I only mean to make sure that no one is able to capture her heart before I can.

"And if they already have?"

"Then I will dig up enough dirt on them to make her change her mind." He looks up from his folding hands and smiles. "Like I said, I know she is the one, and I only need to find a way to convince her that I am her one. You know I will treat her better than anyone else."

"I think you need to take a step back and let her come to you and stop chasing her. Your desperation is clear, and it is probably clear to her."

"You're right. So I guess I shouldn't have her followed?" He laughs, but for some reason, I don't think he is giving up on the idea. His head lowers as he picks up a picture of Wendy, pregnant with Sage. "I miss her so much. I miss having her here to talk to, to hold, and to love ... I miss being in love and feeling it back. I want that feeling back, and then I am going to do everything I can to keep anyone from taking it from me." He closes his eyes tight, and for the first time, I see what Antony has been telling me—Michael is completely heartbroken, a feeling I can understand.

I spot the public chessboard tables in the park and walk towards them, and after passing a couple of tables, I spot the coin on the third table at the right side of the south end on the empty chessboard. Picking it up, I put it in my pocket. Before moving in any direction, I check my surroundings and move south to the third walkway on the right. There is nothing but the homeless and drug addicts out this late, not exactly a relaxing walk through the park. Our meeting spot is clear, and I find him waiting nervously for me.

"Maybe we should start meeting in a safer place for you to be, Father."

"Don't worry about me. This is fine. Besides, any other place would make it too easy to be followed. So, tell me, what do you know so far?"

"Not much more than I did the other day. I told you he doesn't fully trust me yet. Brotherly love doesn't mean much in this family."

"All I want you to do is find out who he is aligning himself with, if anyone. What he's planning? I know he's up to something, and it's going to be a problem for us all. He is quiet and keeps his opinions to himself too much these days. My own son and I can't trust him not to stab me in the back in order to take my seat at the head of the family." My father slams his cane into the ground, cursing his own son. "I use to think his determination was something to be encouraged; little did I know that determination would eventually overpower everything I have worked for."

My father is so paranoid. I have been around Ettore constantly for weeks, and he is already more powerful than my father and certainly too powerful to bother killing him. "How could Ettore possibly take over for you? Michael is next in line and you made sure that was how it was going to be with the way you set up the funding for everything. Michael has the ability to stop everything and ruin Ettore, if he so much as thinks about making a wrong move. If Ettore has found a way around that system, then I don't know what you want me to do." My father was careful to set up his will so that Michael has control above all, then Ettore. Ettore began working through my father, and my father took advantage and weaved each new business through an old so the confusing web would take him forever to unravel if he didn't wait his turn in line or get Michael to sign it all over to him. Michael may not want the role, but his campaign is funded through the same sources. He was smart, too smart for his own good, because he knows damn well that someone is going to be able to figure out his money puzzle and steal everything out from under him.

"You just keep me informed. I don't want you any more involved than you have to be. I will take care of whatever it is and cut him off before he can make any major moves."

"If Ettore truly wants to kills us all and take over, then why would he ever tell me anything?"

"Because he needs you," my father growls. "I saw it in his eyes when he realized what you could do. He will confide in you eventually; he is waiting for the right moment, the right time, to force you to trust him. Be careful what you share with him, Dace. He's smart and always waiting for you to make a mistake so he can capitalize. Is Michael giving you anything to report back to Ettore?"

"Nothing of value, or of any value to Ettore. Michael is purely political right now. Ettore could give a rat's ass about any of that."

"What about that girl Michael has been seeing?" he asks.

"What about her?"

"I'm assuming it's only a matter of time before Ettore suspects her of spying, which I am sure she is doing, not that she will get anywhere. She should be enough to get Ettore upset and make a mistake, hopefully the mistake will cause Michael to wake up and take Ettore more seriously. "

I jerk my head in his direction. "What? You're using her to start a war between them? You are going to get her killed!"

My father stops our casual walk and looks me over. "She is a cop, right? I am sure she can take care of herself. Besides, Ettore will only use her for leverage. Killing her would be a last resort. If she is going to be worried about anyone, it should be Michael. Michael's last wife, I suspect, would still be alive if she hadn't of been cheating on him."

"What? I thought they were so in love that they were devoted to each other?" I ask him, considering what could happen to Austin.

"Oh, don't listen to me. I am sure they were; it is primarily speculation on my part. She was a beautiful woman, Wendy. I only assumed she didn't spend all those lonely nights by herself while Michael was working late."

"I think you need to tell Michael to find someone new, someone other than a cop. Austin deserves better than to be pushed into a middle of a war."

"She does, does she? What was the name of that woman I saw with you the other night?"

"I don't remember. I wasn't that much into her."

"Uh-huh. Anyway, I could be wrong. I imagine there could be some faithful women out there somewhere. Maybe this 'Austin' is one of them?" he says oddly. I shrug. "It was a sad funeral …" My father's concentration drifts off, and I wonder whose funeral he is speaking of—Wendy's or my mother's? Considering he is twisting his old wedding band that has never left his finger since their wedding day, I assume it is my mother's. He looks up at the sky and smiles before sighing back in my direction. "You were always a good kid. I find it ironic that you're the one I trust the most."

"Oh yeah? Why? Because I am the one always running away."

"No, but now that you bring it up, you're ability to know when to stay and when to leave is what will keep you alive. If you're the only one left standing against Ettore, I left you something, an apology you could say. It will help you regain whatever stronghold you may need."

"An apology for what?"

"It will all be in the letter. I have someone assigned to give it to you after I die. Look for a man named Hayden Stryker, he will know what to do."

I sigh, shaking my head. "I told you I don't want to take over. I am only here to help you and Michael, and then I'm gone. Let Antony be your prince in waiting."

My father grabs my coat and forces me back to him. "You listen to me. You are the best of both your mother and I; I know it, I see me in you." I nod with a sarcastic roll of my eyes. "You are my son!" My father looks into my eyes, vibrating with intensity.

"You are my son."

"Yes, I am," I say with my hands out as he clamps down on my coat and stares into my eyes as if he is searching for something.

"You will honor your heritage, your birthright, and claim your position at the head of this family if it is necessary. My name cannot die."

"Are you planning on dying soon or something?"

"Not planning, expecting. Like you, I know when something is coming. I don't know from which direction it is coming, but it's coming for me. All I can do is wait for it. A word of advice: if it is Ettore left standing with you, then you fight like all hell to claim that sovereignty from him because he won't let you run free without getting blood on your hands. You just make sure it's his blood," he says with an odd sadness about him. All I can do is nod in agreement to something I don't even understand. This family was always considered the tightest, most solid family there ever was. That's what kept us strong, but now, all of a sudden, all hell is breaking loose.

My meeting with my father has bothered me ever since I left him. I am feeling a weight on my shoulders like I have never wanted. I really don't care if Ettore takes over; I just want out of here—out of this city and away from this insane family.

"Hey, sexy, you want a date?" I look over and laugh as Antony smiles his goofiness in my direction.

"Get in the damn car, dumbass. We got shit to do."

"So what's on your mind that you look so serious?"

"What's on your mind that's made you look so happy?"

"Do you really want to know what I was doing last night?" He glances my way, letting me know all I need to know. I shake my head, looking away. "Oh come on. He was really good. It might be enough to sway you?"

"No thanks. I'm good, but nice to know someone in this family is having sex."

"Wait, who's not having sex? Obviously not Dad and his old boring balls. Ettore ... uhhh ew. Michael ... oh yeah how did the date go?"

"Not well. She was coming home as I was coming in with Ettore. She grabbed my arm and looked at me with those pitiful eyes of hers. Nearly killed me to act like she was a nutcase and turn away from her. And fucking Michael is obsessed with her."

"Sounds like Michael."

"What do you mean? How am I the only one that didn't know how obsessed he can get?"

"Because you weren't here right after Wendy died. He's been crazy obsessed about perfection ever since. Nothing can be out of place or done even a second late. Now that he has it in his head that Austin is perfect for him, he isn't going to settle for anything else, better or not."

"Oh great, both of my brothers are insane. Why would you let me tell Austin she should be with him then?!"

"Excuse me, asshole. I wasn't there when you fucked that up. You should stop pushing people away and start letting life work itself out rather than forcing it on everyone." I look at him with annoyance. What the hell am I supposed to do? Continue seeing her and risk her life? If I didn't live here, if I was back with KTR, then it might be different. "It's your life, Dace. If you can't control your happiness then the world will, and that is not going to ever work out in your favor. You might end up with Shirley over there." I look out my window at the large woman in yellow heels and tight mini skirt that is barely covering her backside.

"She isn't even bothering to shave anymore." I take notice of the facial stubble on her face.

"Why bother? That snake is hard to miss. Good news, she

said she has nearly got enough to pay for a boob job."

"A boob job? Shouldn't he, I mean she, get the snake taken care of first?"

"I asked that, but she said there is a lot of money to be made in dick fucking a guy with big boobs."

"What?" I shake my head, trying to rid myself of the visual. "Okay, let's talk about something else."

"Went too far with the gay info this time, huh?"

"Little bit."

"Awesome. I love grossing you out."

"Just drive asshole. At the next light, take a right." He does as asked, and I see the building up ahead. "Pull off here and let's walk." Antony and I both get out and carefully approach the broken down building. It doesn't seem to be much of anything but the amount of internet activity coming out of this building is staggering. There seems to be something going on here; the Aksakovs must have something more going on than they appear to. There are only a few guards posted around the building, which makes it easy for Antony and I to sneak in. The computer system is surprisingly out of date. The only thing odder are the security cameras showing Austin and her brother walking in and asking questions, both of their partners behind them.

"Is that Austin? Ooh yeah, and that's her brother. Can't miss him." I look back at him and roll my eyes. "Sorry."

"What the fuck is she doing here?"

"She seems to show up wherever you are. It's like you two can't be broken apart, no matter how hard you try to push her away." He laughs while I stare impatiently at him. "Not funny? Okay, maybe later then."

"Shit!" I yell as an alarm goes off and the cavalry rushes in around us. Men are coming in from everywhere.

"Did we set that off?" Antony asks. I shake my head, looking around for anything that we might have triggered, but there's nothing. "Maybe Austin and her brother caused them to set it off?"

I watch them, and the guards seem as surprised as they do. "Doesn't look like it. Someone set this off from somewhere else. This was a decoy. We were set up. Fuck!"

"What do you mean?"

"There is nothing here, nothing that they couldn't afford to lose. They must have found the bugs we set in Rory's house. They are trying to get us. We need get out of here and quick."

"How?" Antony asks as I look up at the monitor and watch Austin and her brother sneak past the guards and in towards us. I look over at Antony, and he realizes the same thing. "Okay, but hopefully she isn't still mad at you and we don't end up in jail."

"Like it or not, she's our only way out."

"So how do we get to where she is?"

"That's the hard part, but I suggest we take out whoever we have to in order to get there." I breathe in deep and ready my gun as he does and we take off out the door, taking on fire immediately. They were waiting for us. Unable to go much more than a few feet down the long corridor, we dive into another room. "Okay, that didn't work out quite like I had hoped."

"No, that fucking sucked!" Antony snaps at me.

I look around, trying to think of something, and then I notice the sprinkler system. Okay, let's try that. I cut some wires and cause enough friction to get some sparks, lighting up the mounds of paper and files they seemed to have stocked up on for decades. I open the door next door and push Antony in, with me following. It's not overly secure, but it's a few steps closer to where we need to be. Once the full blaze gets going and the sprinkler system goes off, I peek out the door and tell Antony to go while I cover him. He takes off through the raining sprinklers, and outside of a few slips and slides, he makes it safely around the corner. Taking a deep breath, "Here goes nothing," I say, rushing out the door, firing at anything that could possibly kill me. I get lucky at first, but one spots me and gets me in the leg as I slide into a wall and sends me crashing to the floor. Antony makes it to where he needs to be, but

I get trapped. Then, my girl, who seems to have a lock on my location at all times, rounds the corner. I crawl into a janitor's closet and wait, hoping for the best.

"This is the police. Put down your weapons now!" she yells.

"You are being surrounded mother fuckers. You can either come out of here in a body bag or in handcuffs, but either way, you are leaving here on our terms," Aaron yells.

The men begin running the opposite direction while I wait and hope to either be missed or discovered by someone I can convince to get me out of here. I hear them running around outside the door and slow moving footsteps follow after them — all but one set. I steady my gun as the shadow walks slowly past the door and then stops and turns back. The doorknob begins turning, and the door slowly opens.

"This is detective Reed …" she says and then slams open the door with her gun aimed right at me.

"I knew Trouble was coming for me," I smile.

"Son of a bitch, Dace. What are you doing here?"

"Getting set up apparently," I say with a groan.

"You're shot?!" she shouts, rushing to my side.

"And soaking wet, not my sexiest wet look, but it got you to come running for me," I laugh.

"Making jokes? Really, Dace? Your sense of humor is a little twisted. Now, tell me what you need me to do."

"Can you help me get out of here?"

"Sure, I'll call an ambulance." I look up at her with wide eyes. "Oh yeah. I should arrest you. You deserve to be arrested." I don't bother saying anything; I simply wait until the lecture is done. "I swear you are …"

"Oh, good, I am finally getting to repay the favor," I say as she helps me up. She guides me out through the side door and has me wait for her. I start to wonder if she is ever coming back when I see her pull up with the car and my brother.

"Hey! Look who I ran into, Dace," the smart ass says as he helps me into the car.

"You two dumbasses please keep your heads down. If I am going to commit a crime, I would prefer to do it without getting caught."

"Oh… her first crime, and we get to be a part of it. It's a Hallmark moment," Antony says as I laugh.

"Oh this is funny, real funny. Now, can you tell me where to take you to get that bullet out of your leg?" Austin asks.

"Just take us to my place, and I will get my own help."

"No good. I can't have anyone I know seeing you getting out of my car. We do live in the same building. Plus, I would prefer to make sure you get proper help." She doesn't listen to me and ends up taking me to Michael's. As soon as we pull through the security gate, I roll my eyes. *Great.*

Austin runs into the house and comes back out with Michael while Antony stares in the opposite direction, shaking his head as I do.

"What the fuck were you two doing?" Michael yells. "I swear you knuckleheads are a constant pain in my ass. No, take them somewhere else because they are not staying here."

"But Michael, Dace is hurt. He needs a doctor. He needs attending to," Austin pleads in her drenched clothes that are sticking to her well-formed body. Unless Michael is blind, I doubt he says no to her right now. I would give her whatever she wanted, even if I had to run on this bad leg to get it for her. Then again, I am clearly an idiot. I was much happier in the middle of nowhere with nothing, but no I came back to the big city with my family, buy a big penthouse with everything, fall in love, and become miserable. I look back over Austin as she continues to sweet talk my brother with his dreamy eyes looking down through her white blouse. Damn her breasts look amazing. Have I seen that bra before? Oh yeah, the one with the little pink flower on the front. That one didn't stay on long—cute but it was unnecessary for what we had planned. Shit, now I'm horny and in fucking pain. This sucks. I glance Antony's way as he nods with a smile.

"Shut up," I say as he laughs.

"And why are all of you so wet?" Michael curses some more and paces away before finally calling some of his people over to come and help me out of the car. "Put him in a room and call Doctor Gallagher and have the other idiot checked out too before sending him home."

Michael looks down at Austin with a smile. "The things you get me to do for you."

"They're your brothers. You should want to help them."

"I do, but sometimes they need to accept responsibility for their stupid mistakes. You should have arrested them, not risk your career to save them, Austin."

"Well …" Austin looks over at me as I stare at her. "I felt I owed you something for my horrible behavior the other night."

Michael takes hold of her face and makes her look at him. "Hey, I was more worried about you than anything. Don't ever feel that you can't talk to me," he says to her as I lean down into the seat with a deep exhale.

The doctor nearly kills me taking out the bullet and stitching me up; he is not exactly gentle. Michael must have told him to be harsh. When it's all over, I lie back, ready to sleep, when Austin walks in. "Ah damn! Don't you have cop shit to do?"

"You're welcome, Dace. Don't worry about me. Luckily, no one found out what I did. They did ask where I went suddenly, but I told them I was chasing down a suspect that got away."

"Thanks, I do appreciate that. By the way, why were you there in the first place?"

"I found some information on this place in some notes I found."

"Some notes you found? And where did you get these notes?" She shrugs. I laugh sarcastically. "Where the fuck did you get these notes that are going to get you killed, Austin?"

"Don't be so overdramatic. It's only a notebook from one of Michael's campaign people that died. They seem to be of Ettore's comings and goings and other things."

"Why would one of Michael's men have information on Ettore? It wasn't Ettore's anyway, it was the Ask…" I shut up quickly and look in another direction …*fuck*.

"It was whose exactly? Fine don't tell me, but I know the information I have is slowly revealing itself, and it all has to do with Ettore."

"That's how you keep ending up wherever I am lately." She smiles simply. I sit up and grab her arm. "You listen to me. You burn those notes and forget them if you know what's good for you."

She jerks her arm from me with a scowl. "No! I will not. This is the best lead I have gotten in a long time, and don't you dare say a word to him or anyone. No one knows I have them."

My jaw drops, and I look up at her in shock. "You're hiding them and working the case by yourself? Oh that's a lot better. You're an even bigger idiot than I thought you were!"

"I'm not working it by myself, I have my partner, Jamee, and my brother and Billy."

"They know about the notes, too?"

"My brother does… sort of." I turn my head away from her, cursing under my breath. "Don't judge me. I shouldn't have even told you, but I was hoping …"

I snap my head back in her direction. "No, don't even think about it."

"Come on, Dace. I know you don't want to be in this life any more than I want you to be. If you help me, we can get you to a better and safer life."

"Oh yeah, six feet underground. I will surely be safe there. Forget it, Austin. You're fighting a losing battle. Go fight normal cop crime, like domestic violence, gangs, serial killers, or something. I don't know, but stay away from my family."

"Except your brother, right? I don't think Michael is the best one for me," she says, looking me over while touching my bandaged leg and my bare chest. I take hold of her hand and start to move it away from me but hold on to her a little too long.

"You shouldn't be here, Austin. No matter what we may feel, there is no future for us."

"Okay, I understand, but I still wanted to make sure you were alright. I am allowed that, right?"

"Sure, thanks." She leans down and kisses my forehead, and holds her lips to me as I wrap my arm around her and feel down her ass. She smells so good. I grasp her ass before needing to feel along her thigh and making my way in between her legs. *Stop, Dace! Stop before you can't. Fuck! It's too late.* I push my face down in between her breasts. I dive in and kiss my way around her wet bra until I can taste the tip of her nipple. *Damn, I miss her.* Her hand feels down my chest and takes hold of my cock, stroking it with intent. My hand slides down her pants and feels inside her pussy, fingering her in sync with her every stroke of my dick. *Fffuckk.*

She grips the back of my head, whispering my name as she asks for more. "Dace, it feels so good."

I lift my hand up a little more into her and kiss her cheek. "I could do better with my tongue."

She fists my hair. "Damn I know …" she moans, "but … oh." Austin breathes heavy and suddenly my fingers are covered in her cum. I lie back with a smile as she tries harder to make sure I come too, I groan and grip the sheets under me when she goes down and wraps her lips around my cock, drinking up every drop. She stands back up, gripping my hand as she licks her lips clean. We stare at each other silently when Michael suddenly walks in. I quickly maneuver the blankets over myself.

"Did he thank you, Austin? If he didn't, tell me, and I will make sure he remembers how to show his appreciation properly," Michael says.

"Oh he showed his appreciation perfectly." I take a deep breath, avoiding eye contact with everyone, out of fear of what feelings I may give away.

CHAPTER 20

Dace

A strange noise wakes me up, and I do my best to try and get up. The pain medicine the doctor gave me isn't helping much though. Making my way downstairs, I find Michael on top of Austin, removing his clothes and hers. At first I think to leave until Austin whimpers something. I can't make it out at first, but then she says it again.

"I want to go home. Please, I just want to go home. I don't feel well."

"Everything is going to be alright, I promise," Michael says, continuing to enjoy himself with no sign of concern or stopping.

"Michael what are you doing?!" I yell at him, realizing she's drugged. He jumps up at me, ready to slam the door in my face but I knock him back. Even drugged myself, I can still out maneuver him. He tries to punch me, and I knock it out of the way, jerking him back into a headlock. "Michael, what the hell is wrong with you?"

"Let me go, Dace. I'm doing what I have to do."

"You're raping her!" I scream at him, realizing the truth of it myself in the same moment.

"I love her, it's not rape, if … I'm going to marry her. She just needs to relax and realize …" he says, suddenly relinquishing his fight and dropping to his knees in tears. "I'm sorry. I am. I was going to leave her alone, but she gave me a kiss on the cheek! She kissed me on the cheek, Dace! I have done everything right, everything, and still she doesn't show anymore love for me than that of a close friend. I don't know why. I have had her followed and checked out, and she isn't seeing anyone else, not even that other cop. He's sleeping with some other woman. I don't understand what she wants."

"So you drug her and try to rape her? What good can come from that?"

"That wasn't my plan at first. At first I thought maybe a few drinks and she would be put at ease, but when she wouldn't take more than a few sips, I became desperate and thought I could coax her easier this way and once she found herself in bed with me she would get used to the idea. Maybe I could even get her pregnant." He tries to look me in the eyes, but no doubt, he is too ashamed to do so. I begin to realize his desperation is insane, and I am afraid for him, for her especially. "Please don't look at me that way. I really didn't want to hurt her. I only want to love her. That first moment I saw her, I tell you, I felt the sun come out again. When Wendy died, I didn't think I could ever feel love again, but then Austin was assigned to her case. I complained that nothing had been done to find Wendy's killer, and I demanded their best, and they sent me Austin. I thought it was fate. She was so determined and so abrasive with me; she clearly disliked me from the first moment we met. I am sure it was because of my name, but I didn't care. The more she wanted to dislike me, the more I liked her and the more determined I was to get her to like me. When she slowly started to come around—that first smile, that first laugh she made at one of my jokes—I knew I was in love because it was the greatest feeling in the world to make her smile. I knew it was just a matter of time. I thought I was finally going to be able to be happy and have that family I always wanted." He eases back into a corner with his head in his hands. "I know she is a lot younger than me, but I know I could make her happy. She is tough as nails but, at the same time, so innocent, and when she looks at me, I want nothing more than to take care of her. I wouldn't let anyone hurt her."

"So instead you hurt her?" I ask, and he looks up at me, seeming to finally realize his mistake. Closing his eyes, he curses himself. "What happened to you, Michael? Since when do you become so desperate for perfection that you can't appreciate what you already have?"

"Before you judge me, maybe you should know what it feels like to watch your wife die in front of you, carrying a child you will never know!"

I turn my focus back to Austin and dress her back perfectly, covering her up with a nearby blanket before sitting in a chair near her. "Go to bed, Michael. I am going to sit with her and make sure she is alright, and then I am going to make sure she gets home. I will tell her that you both had a little too much to drink and you left her to sleep while you passed out upstairs."

He stands and turns to go to his bedroom but stops and returns to stand right in front of me. "Something happened. She was falling for me, I know it, and then, something happened. I don't know what, but I'm going to damn well find out and put a stop to it," he says to me with his head held high. He stops near her and adjusts the blanket on her, kisses her gently, and whispers, "Goodnight, my darling," before leaving for his room.

Taking her hand, I understand how he fell in love with her because it was the same way I did. She has an effect on us Collettos unlike most women. She wants so bad to dislike us, and we want so bad to change her mind and convince her to love us. Maybe we are all crazy and should learn to let go?

There is something to be said for having people wait on you constantly. I think they would call it being one lazy ass motherfucker. I can't take much more of this. I practically have to run away and hide from Michael's people just so I can brush my own teeth. The moment I see Franklin, my assigned caretaker, coming, I dart into another room and down the back stairs to find myself in the kitchen where I make my own meal. I'm not sure where Michael is, so I wander his house, looking around at things, seeming to get to know my brother for the first time. I didn't even know he had an interest in artwork. The extensive paintings and sculptures are amazing and extremely expensive. Why would he keep such things in his house? He has a lot of faith in the idiots guarding this place. The idea makes me curious, exactly how secure is this place? It doesn't take me long to find a control room to tap into. At first, it seems reasonable for most people, then I find something odd. This place is heavily wired with a secret passage and cameras everywhere, even inside. *Inside? Fuck?* Scrolling through the camera views, I search for my room and stumble upon Michael talking to someone in the stables. When she turns around, I know her immediately, Austin's partner—Jamee. *Son of a Bitch.* What the fuck is she doing here? I can't make out what she is saying, but Michael is clearly pissed. He throws something into a wall and waves his finger at her until she laughs. He grabs her throat and pushes her into a wall, hard. One of his men calms him down, and he backs off and sends her away. The only thing that makes this even more interesting is when Rory Aksakov walks out of the shadows, shaking his head. Michael seems to be listening to him, and what's worse is he allows him to leave unharmed. I step out of the control room and get back to the kitchen, crashing into a seat to eat my sandwich where Michael finds me. I look slowly up at him and nearly see the steam of his anger coming from his skull. "Hey, something wrong?"

He doesn't say anything at first, only his eyes bore holes into me, and I suddenly become uneasy. A slow, unnerving smile forms across his face. "I'm fine. How are you today, Dace? Glad to see you are getting up and around okay."

"Yeah, I'm sure I can go home now."

"No, no reason to do that when I have so much here for you to take and use as you wish. You stay here, I insist. As your big brother and protector, I truly insist." Michael leans down and kisses the top of my head with a tight grasp of the back of my head.

I stand up and away from him. "Is there something wrong Michael?"

"No, everything is great, perfect even." He walks off whistling a tune that sounds neither cheerful nor unhappy but some sadistic level in between. *It's time for me to go.* I try packing my things, but Michael sees to it that a large group of his men stay at my side. I am pretty sure I am fucked when my father comes in and orders the men to leave me with him.

"What did you do?" I look away from him and refuse to say a word. "Never mind. I have known about you two. I knew when I saw her clothes on the floor at your place. It was the shoes, not too many women where those kinds of shoes, especially not ones that my sons would be interested in."

"So he knows."

"He thinks he does, but I told him that his informant was a liar, that you started to go after her, but she turned you down like she did him. It drove you crazy for a time, but you have since gotten over it. I went on to say that she is actually involved secretly with her brother's partner. I had some pictures made up to prove it. I have had them ready just in case this happened."

I stand up and get in his face. "That won't work! He said he had him followed and that he is seeing someone else."

"Sit down, Dace! It will work. That other woman was nothing more than a distraction to make Austin jealous. Do you understand me? Everything is going to be fine. Michael knows you would never betray him, and that you will stay away from this woman." He looks me in the eyes, waiting for me to agree.

"I love her," I admit to him.

"I don't care. Your life depends on you getting over it and making sure she does the same. Now, get your things and come with me."

"Where are we going?"

"I'm taking you to stay with Ettore until you can find a new place to live."

"I'm not a child, Father. I will do what I want, and I'm going home." He turns to me in shock. "Do you hear me? I'm not doing this. I'm not going to live by some rules that I never agreed to. If you want to take me anywhere, then take me home. If Michael wants to kill me, then let him. I'm not afraid of death. I'm afraid of not living."

"And you're willing to put her life in jeopardy too?"

"No, I'll stay away from her for her, not for you or anyone

else." I walk out around him and call for Antony to come get me and take me home.

With all that is going on, I find no problem at all telling Ettore about Michael meeting with Rory Aksakov. After he curses and throws his fists around, he turns to me with a look of validation. I begin exclusively working for Ettore and going after the Aksakovs, despite our father and Michael's wishes.

I go meet up with a contact for Ettore at his boathouse. Olsen supposedly has information for us on the Aksakovs. The man has some interesting things to say, but I still feel as if he is holding back. He says the Aksakovs are searching for ways to make more money and have looked into converting one of Ettore's drug suppliers to their side, but drugs aren't really what Ettore deals in anymore. He has become more interested in internet trade deals. It's a lot easier and a lot less liability since he has no direct handling of anything. He simply contacts this person to move this product to this person who then transfers from that country to the next and hands it off to the next person who handles the trade for either product for someone else or money. If it's money, then it gets laundered back to Ettore. He enjoys it; however, he still has an interest in all the old family businesses as well. I guess that's why we are here, trying to head off the Aksakovs before they win even one part of Ettore's stronghold. Ettore constantly reminds me that even the slightest weakness can encourage dissent within the organization.

"So you will tell your brother that I am doing everything I can to get him more information, right? I am sure they will trust me more soon."

"Sure, don't worry about it. I'll make sure you are in good standing with him. Now, did you get that thing I asked for?"

"Oh yeah." He rushes out of the room and comes back with a

thumb-drive. "It has everything you asked for, but I don't understand why you want it."

"Sometimes there is important information hidden within the unimportant; it's the best place to hide," I tell him with an exchange of some money and the untraceable gun he asked for.

"Wait. What was that? Did you bring someone with you?" He rushes to look through some windows. "Damn, who is that?"

Going to the window, I look out and see Austin walking up to the boat. "Son of a bitch! What is with her?"

"You know her?"

"Sort of, but I don't want her to know I'm here. Do you have some place I can hide until she goes?" He points to the ridiculously tiny bathroom. It's a tight squeeze for me, but I manage while he talks to Austin and gets rid of her for me. He doesn't do a great job; she moves right past him and inside the boat.

"Can I help you find something?" Olsen asks her.

"Maybe. I was told you are getting money from all directions, and I was wondering exactly which side are you really working for?"

"Excuse me? Who the fuck are you?"

"Don't worry about it. I just wanted to know why you are getting paid from the Collettos twice. It's one thing to be playing both sides, but both sides within the same family? Is there going to be a war between them?"

"Get the fuck out of here lady before I call someone to take care of you." Olsen's voice lowers to a defensive tone.

"I wouldn't threaten me if I were you," Austin says, unafraid.

"Oh, no? Why is that?"

"Because I could arrest you and make sure the Collettos know all about your willingness to tell me everything. I would imagine you wouldn't survive to the next day."

"You're a fucking cop?!" he yells at her.

"I promise I won't tell anyone I was here if you tell me one thing. Which Colletto brother are you working for—Michael or Ettore?"

"Get the fuck off my boat, bitch, before I call someone to have a talk with you, and trust me, your people are not nearly as scary as the ones I know." Olsen goes silent as does she, and there seems to be a light scuffle, but I can't tell what it is. I open the door, allowing a glimmer of light in and hearing some whispering between them before she walks off the boat. "Okay she's gone."

"What did she whisper to you?"

"Nothing important. She just threatened me is all. She thinks she can intimidate me, but no cunt is going to scare me," he snickers, obviously trying to lighten the mood.

"What was she talking about? Who all in my family is paying you? Are you double dipping or something worse?"

"No, she's crazy. She's trying to start trouble where there isn't any."

I grab my gun, hold it on him, and call Ettore. "Hey it's me. Your man Olsen seems to be getting paid by more than just you and by more than one Colletto."

"Kill him," Ettore replies with a low roar.

"Done." Olsen's death is not for Ettore. It is not for me or anyone in my family. It is for her. I would have never considered it if not for her; her presence here was going to be known the moment I left. Getting permission from Ettore not only secured my loyalty to him, but gave me cause to kill Olsen without questions needing to be asked.

After a long day, I return home and walk into the elevator with Austin following in after me. *I swear!* "What is with you?" I ask her. She looks at me as if I have lost my mind. "You know what? Forget what I said …" I stare hard at her. "Stay away from Michael. He's not right for you. In fact, stay away from my whole family."

"Oh really? Why is that?" she asks.

"What is with you and the questions all the time?" I say in frustration.

"Dace, if you want me to listen to you, then you should answer a few questions, don't you think? Why in the world should I stay away from the man you said I should give a chance to and also stay away from the man you said is dangerous and I should stay away from you because it's dangerous for us both? But, for some reason, you have not bothered to move out of my building and continuously show up where I am at."

"I show up where you're at? You're following me!"

"I am not. I have no interest in whatever dumbass thing you're doing." She has the nerve to say.

She turns away from me and walks out onto her floor, and I follow. "Oh no you don't. You don't just get to walk away from me." She huffs and continues on, entering her condo and trying to shut the door in my face.

"Sorry, no criminals allowed here," she says with an annoying smile.

"What are you going to do, shoot me?"

"Maybe. Maybe in the other leg."

I move in closer to her. "Oh really? Maybe beat me up, hurt me somehow?"

"I could. I could hurt you good, and you know it," she says, easing back against the wall and wetting her lips.

"Oh I know." Her hands shift to my face, and I move in, taking in her lips and pushing my hands down her body and up again. *She's not meant for him …*

She suddenly pulls away and looks at me with an odd

expression. "You were on the boat today!"

"What?!"

"You were there. I should have known. You are trying to find out what I know, and that's the only reason you're here."

"Are you kidding me? I was kissing you, not talking. I am not *Ms. Question A Lot.* That's you. Kissing! I was kissing you, nothing more."

"So you were there. Why? What was there? Does he have something to do with Ettore? I knew it."

"You're impossible."

"You're a criminal."

"I'm leaving. I know I have a great ass, but try not to follow me."

"Dace, tell me. Please tell me. Maybe I can help you. I know this is not what you want to do. You're not your brother. I see something better in you, and I'm never wrong about people. It's you that's paying Olsen, too. You're paying him to help you keep tabs on Ettore, aren't you? You are working with him for a reason; otherwise, you would have left. Now, tell me what it is. Tell me so I can help you. It doesn't have to be on the record. Talk to me like a friend, not a cop."

"But you are a cop, Austin! You're a cop, an annoying one at that. I am here to work in the family business, nothing more. I am perfectly happy with my life. Now leave me alone."

"But …"

"No buts, leave me alone, and stop following me everywhere."

"But you followed me into my home," she says with a cock of her head.

"Right. Then I should go."

"Okay, see you tomorrow, Dace." I roll my eyes and go home.

CHAPTER 21

Austin

A new tip leads us to an abandoned building at the edge of the city line. I have no idea where the tip came from; all anyone knows is that it came from a woman and to my brother. Most believe that Aaron knows who it is and is protecting a key informant, but he isn't talking, except to me—his informant. I had to get some help, and in order to get the proper help, I had to tell someone I could trust about the notebook and the information I am slowly deciphering from it. Aaron wasn't the least bit happy about me keeping it from him this long; however, he was real happy about the information, and I am real happy to have a little bit of this weight off my shoulders. We dress in full protective uniform as we get ready to head in.

"I want this guy, Austin. Rowen Rodecker. I can't believe we figured out who he was."

"Once Brandi told me about the steel toed boot with the skull and cross bones engraved on the metal, I knew who he was. I had seen him hanging out at Wendy Colletto's car accident. He looked strange then, and that's why I questioned him. Cocky son of a bitch smiled the whole time I asked him questions and didn't say a word.

"He was involved in her murder and our mother's. I can feel it, and not far behind him is Ettore Colletto." My brother won't give up his pursuit of this man. Not that I blame him. I have, after all, been searching for him myself. "We still don't know for sure what is being run in and out of this facility, but for a supposed abandoned building, it sure is wired for some major access. It is heavily guarded and secured by monitors everywhere." Aaron hands me binoculars so I can see for myself.

"Aaron, what have you stumbled upon?" I see the trip wires to alarm the building of anyone coming within a hundred feet, something I haven't seen since our military days. "It's sophisticated."

"Extremely. They paid someone well to design this," Aaron says, licking his lips.

"Keep calm. One wrong move and this could all go wrong very quickly."

"I know that, and I know you, my sister, can find a way inside any building there is. Let's get in there."

"Without a warrant? Are you being a bad boy again?" I laugh.

"It's an abandoned building, right? I am only here making sure to clear out the vandals I saw running through." Aaron smiles his big cheesy smile.

"That fucking smile gets us into trouble every single time," Billy says, shaking his head. "That's the idea he has had in mind ever since we got word on this place. I have been trying to talk him out of making a move and simply keeping an eye on it. Eventually, someone or something has to come and go from it."

"I'm with Billy. This is a bad idea. Watch it? Yes. But breaking in and getting ourselves into the middle of something that could cost us not only our jobs, but possibly our lives, too?" Jamee expresses, already retreating from our group.

"So maybe we keep it simple then. Aaron and I will go in, and you guys stay out here and watch our backs. That keeps you guys from getting into trouble and puts all the responsibility back on us," I say, returning Aaron's already nodding head. We begin to map out our entry, laying out our path and procedure for communication. We don't waste any time deciding on our plan of action, and as soon as we do, we move in.

I love this. I love the adrenaline rushing through my veins, anticipating what will be waiting for us, what we may find, or who we will take down in this surprise attack.

"You know, it would be nice if you guys would fill us in on what's going on before you make decisions?" Jamee gripes from behind us. "And maybe you should tell us who the informant is, in case you two get killed?"

Aaron and I both look back at her and smile. "We got twin

powers. You can't kill us," Aaron brags. "Stay behind and wait for us to tell you to call for backup." Aaron looks at me with his adrenaline clearly rushing as much as mine. "Ready?" I nod, and we move in. The tunnels and overly wired corridors are tricky but fun to figure out. I follow one guard after the other without being seen until I can get to a place where I can control the cameras and alarms. Then, I signal Aaron to move in as I do. I communicate with Aaron from my end to his with simple pings back and forth, all the while taking pictures and mental notes along the way. Then, I happen upon it—a vaulted room. Analyzing it carefully, I try to decipher its entry key.

"Hello, baby. What's your secret?" I mouth with anticipation. I take the face off and rework the wires to connect to a device I invented to get it to tell me its entry code. The iron door tells me exactly what I need and opens up wide. I walk into the freezing room and take in all of the elaborate computer systems before suddenly being grabbed from behind and held against a wall.

"You need to leave here now. They know you're here, and they are coming to do you in."

"I'll arrest them all," I admit happily before twisting and turning to try and get at him face to face, but he counters my every move. "This isn't a game, Trouble. Get out of here and seek your fun somewhere else."

"I don't consider this fun. I don't consider going after my mother's killer fun at all. Revenge maybe, but not fun."

His long sigh is heavy. "Damn it, I should have known. Your determination has been too great to be purely professional." He jerks my back to his chest, and I feel down his body. "Stop that," he breathes. "Get out of here, please."

"Why should I, Dace?" I ask.

He pushes my chest against the wall and leans his hard body into the back of mine. "Because I would miss you if something happened to you," he breathes against the edge of my ear. "Give me time, that's all I ask. Give me a little time, and I will come back for you when I am done and tell you anything you want to know." His lips caress my cheek. "Just give me some time, Trouble, and I promise you, I will make it worth your wait." His hand moves up my thigh, to my waist, and with a gentle tug of my ear with his lips, I begin to hunger for him.

"You better tell me everything or I will come after you," I say, earning a kiss to my lips.

"Promise. Now get your ass out of here and take your brother with you. You got two minutes." He pushes me towards a path. "Go that way. You'll meet up with your brother at the corner. There is a passage through the second door on the left; go right through and don't stop." I nod and move towards the path he gave me until he jerks me back to him. "Go home, take a hot bath, and get into bed, and then … I'll take care of the rest." A quick kiss and I rush to meet up with my brother.

Aaron looked at me as if I had lost my mind rushing him out of the building, but the shock on his face when we just made it out and away before an army of Ettore's men came rushing into the building was hard to ignore, and I tried. The last thing I need is questions I am not sure how to answer, so I come with whatever excuse I can to get away, and using Jamee seemed to be the best option. I meet him head on before he can get the question out of his mouth. "Aaron, Jamee is asking if we can all go have dinner at her place and discuss the details of what we know so far. She is planning to show everyone her new bedroom suit. She is very excited to show you especially."

His attention is clearly distracted as he looks over my shoulder at Jamee who gets excited by his sudden attention. "Not sure I can do that. I suddenly feel very ill. Besides, Billy is feeling neglected lately and wants some bro time."

"I do?" Billy asks as he is dragged into the conversation.

"Yes, you do. Remember how sensitive you are? You need some good bro time to strengthen our friendship," Aaron says with his arm around Billy, shaking him close like he is a teddy bear.

"You better stop touching me like that or our friendship is going to turn into a beat down," Billy says with a scowl.

"Okay, we will talk tomorrow." Aaron kisses my cheek with a quick hug as Jamee looks on confused. "Love you."

I turn towards Jamee with a shrug. "His adrenaline is flowing too much; he gets goofy that way."

"If I didn't know better, I would think you two are hiding something. Did you find something in there? Why did you run out so fast? Did you know those men were coming?" she asks, watching me reaction closely.

"I found a camera room and saw them coming down the road. I planned our exit from there," I say, turning away with a proud smile. Now to get home and get into that bath.

I am on such a high by the time I get home that I can barely contain myself. Thankfully, the hot bath eases all of that. In a tranquil state, I exit my bath with a towel around me and drop my hair from its clip. Staring at my bed, I wonder whether to prepare for him or assume he lied and go to bed as I would normally? I don't want to look like I am willing to put up with his games or his criminal behavior. No, I should not show any sign of acceptance of his behavior at all. So, I am going to bed naked. *That'll teach him.* Time passes quickly, and I begin to believe he did lie to me, that he isn't going to be here at all. Then, I feel a strange sensation and open my eyes to see his beautiful thick waves moving their way up my body. His tender lips kiss my legs and my thighs before I feel his heated breath against my clit and his plush tongue sending a titillating vibration up my body. I sink my hands deep into his waves and guide him back up to my lips.

"You need to understand something. I do not approve of

your criminal activity or your behavior, and I will not condone or participate in any activity that goes against my values. I need you to understand that." His blue eyes smile with a cocky attitude behind them. "Do you under … oh …stand," I say as his hand fondles me roughly into position, spreading my legs wide around his hips. "So do you?"

"Do I what?" he asks, continuing on as if I didn't say a word.

"Do you understand that I don't agree with your criminal behavior?" I breathe with a deep moan.

"I understand a lot of things, Trouble, but the one thing I think is clear after your illegal entry into a privately owned building today is this…," he takes my lips in deep with a simultaneous push of his cock deep inside of me. He tugs on my bottom lip and continues. "You love to be bad and are a lot naughty. Admit it, you wanted to fuck me right there in that moment." He raises up and back down again, sending me back into my bed with an exhilarating exhale. "I know I wanted to fuck you, strip your ass naked and bend you over in front of me and slide my dick between your legs and right into your pussy." His dirty mouth tastes so good that all I want is more. "Is that what you wanted, Trouble, to be captured by the criminal and taken from behind?" His pulsating cock swells more inside of me, and I suddenly have no breath to speak. With a kiss to my cheek, he whispers, "I know I briefly considered doing just that, teach you a lesson for breaking into my vault like you did." His hips thrust into me, and he leans back with a groan. I call out to him, pleading for leniency for my bad behavior, but he continues on and on until I meet his eyes and watch him rise up with a roar, coming inside of me. I caress his face, and he kisses my hand. "I would have done all of that to you today, no matter who was coming for you, that is, if I was really a heartless criminal. Instead, I am a criminal in love. I don't want you with Michael, Austin, I want you with me. Damn them all."

He stares deep into my eyes, completely vulnerable. My heart beats more rapidly now than it has all night. "I love you too, Dace."

Lying in his arms, I can hardly believe the feelings I am having. I can't stop smiling or touching him. I don't want to let go of him—ever. Then, I realize our situation. "Dace what about your brother?"

"Which one, the one that wants to kill you or the one that wants to marry you?"

"Oh this is worse than I even considered." I shut my eyes in panic.

Kissing me on the head, he pulls me in. "Trust me, I know. I have thought about it a million different ways. Every time I knew you were with Michael, I wanted to kidnap you and run away. And I will, I only need to take care of something first so Antony will be okay."

"Runaway where? What good does that do?"

"That gives us the opportunity to be together without scrutiny and allows Michael to move on without us rubbing it in his face. Besides, I have these friends who go to all these amazing places and help people. You would love it. You'd get to help people and kick bad people's asses all at the same time." I look his way as he raises his eyebrows with a nod of expectation. "See… I knew that would get your attention."

"That does sound like fun, and I guess since my career here is obviously never going to go anywhere, thanks to my father, then I wouldn't be opposed to getting away for a while. But what about my brother? Your *brothers*? Are they going to let you go? Are they going to leave my brother alone?"

Dace sits up and grasps my chin to look at me. "I have thought about it all. It doesn't have to be forever. Like I said, once Michael gets used to the idea and finds someone else—which he will—we will build our life together. My brother is prince charming in a suit, and he'll find the perfect woman for him. While he does, we will settle in a place we both love and make sure to have plenty of room for family when they come to visit."

"I take this to mean that you're planning for Ettore not to be an issue at all anymore? That scares me, Dace. You keep telling me how dangerous he is, and you seem to be deeper than anyone into his dirty deals."

"Let me worry about him. I have help, trust me. It's all working out fine. We just have to keep *us* a secret for a little while longer." Dace leans in with a tender kiss. "What do you say, Trouble? Want to run away with me and kick some international bad guy asses?"

I climb on top of him with a smile. "I say, yes. I love adventure, you know that, but I love you more than anything."

He wraps his arms around me, kissing me with a crazed happiness. "You know there is this quaint little white chapel on a cliff that is amazingly beautiful in the spring. Maybe we could ... if everything works out with us ... we could?"

"Wow... is Dace Colletto really speechless, stumbling over his words?" I laugh as he shakes his head and pushes me away. I pull him back and kiss his smiling face. "All you have to do is ask, and I will be there—anywhere—at your side, forever. Of course, I will be the one in the better shoes."

"Probably, because you most likely stole my shoes, knowing your affinity for men's footwear."

"Argh!" I yell, smacking him with a pillow until he pulls it away from me and pins me down underneath him.

"I love you, Austin," he says with an honesty that highlights all the wonderful edges of his masculine face, seeming to release a great weight off his shoulders.

Chapter 22

Dace

"Why are you smiling so much?" Ettore asks, interrupting his meeting with his valued associates. I shrug, not understanding why he is bothering to pay attention to me at all. He never has before unless he wants something. "Don't shrug at me like I'm crazy, you're smiling and happy. What, did you finally screw that blond bitch in your building? She seemed like a good fuck," he says, pissing me off.

"Oh I'm sorry, Ettore, I forgot that happiness was not allowed in your house, only grief and misery," I say happily until I notice his squinty stare. I instantly change my expression to match his. Ettore rolls his eyes off of me and back onto his business at hand. My mind checks out of the monotonous conversation until Ettore gets a call, and we are excused. I try to rush out but don't get too far …

"Dace, come back here and shut the door," Ettore creaks out of his enlarged neck. He continues on talking on the phone while I wait. With a deep sigh, I step back in and shut the door. "Have Mays take care of the evidence. Call our attorney, and get my plane ready. I want him taken to my house on the island. Send someone with him and make sure no one else knows where he is. Call me when it's ready." He hangs up and folds his hands in front of him as he looks at me.

"What do you want?" I ask him impatiently.

"Why must you always have an attitude?" he asks with his own type of attitude.

"Why must you, Ettore? Don't talk to me like I should be afraid of you like everyone else, because I'm not."

He rolls his eyes. "Sometimes, I wonder why I bother with you. Then I remember you're the only family member that actually is similar to me. Our family is full of bullshit, and you know that as

209

much as I do." I nod, sitting back in my seat. "I understand you don't want to be here. I get it, and for your great work lately, I am rewarding you with a little trip."

I perk up curious, but then I notice an odd change in his mannerisms. "What's that? What are you getting ready to lie to me about?"

Ettore laughs, shaking his head. "Damn you're good, and that's why I'm doing this. I need you to go away for a while until I take care of something. I wish you would just go and not ask me questions, but I know you better than that, so I'm going to be honest with you. Somehow, the police think you're involved in Olsen's murder."

I sit up with wide eyes. "I thought you said everything was taken care of, that everything was wiped clean?"

"It was. There is no evidence that you were ever even there, but someone knew you were there and is setting you up. I don't know how you made enemies so quickly, but you did, and apparently, a very serious one because the police are listening to whoever it is and they are trying to build a case against you or rather make up evidence against you."

"That's crazy. Who would hate me that much?"

"I don't know, Dace, but please take my plane and leave with one of my guards and stay put until I tell you to come back. I need some time to investigate this closer and remove the threat."

"You know who it is, so tell me. Who is it Ettore?"

"You don't need to know that right now. All you need to know is that you are in danger, and I need you to leave right now for your own good. It shouldn't be long before my people can have this taken care of. While you're there, you can relax at my home on the beach. Enjoy yourself, but make sure while you're there you don't contact anyone. I can't have you alerting people to where you are until I take care of this."

"Wow Ettore, are you being nice to me? I didn't know that was possible for you. Why should I believe you? Maybe this is a set up?"

He sits back, sighing. "You need to trust me, Dace. Whatever you have been told about me is a lie, and I will prove it to you, but for now, I need you to use that incredible instinct of yours and realize that I am helping you."

"If this is true and you trust me, then I need you to do something for me—approve something for me when I get back. Then, let me go back to my friends and live my life the way I want to. I don't want to be a part of this business, Ettore. I want to dictate my own life without worrying who is trying to stab me in the back," I say, leaning forward and hoping that maybe Ettore really is out to protect me. If I can get him to be on my side, then I can convince him to trust my relationship with Austin is not a threat to him.

"I really would prefer you here with me, but if you can promise me that you will stay here long enough for me to get our father to fully step down and hand me the reigns then I promise to approve whatever life you want to live. Now, what are you doing?" Ettore snarls at me.

"Nothing, why?"

"Stop the damn smiling. I swear you look like a human Snoopy." Now, I roll my eyes. "Just go, and by the way, my plane will be ready to take you out of here in an hour, so don't take time deciding on your favorite outfits to pack."

"An hour?! Ettore how am I supposed to be ready to go by then?"

"Fuck Dace! What exactly do you need to do?" he yells, but I can't say why I need more time, not yet, so I give in and accept the time frame. "Oh, and Barrett is going with you. He's packed and waiting for you outside. I have made sure he understands that you're not to leave his sight. You may think you're fine with taking care of yourself, but I'm not."

"Ettore! I swear I can take care …"

"Of yourself! I know! I have heard you say it a million fucking times, but you can forget trying to persuade me to leave you alone like you did with Father. You're too valuable to me right now." I glance his way, and he looks up. "Oh and also because you're my brother and shit." I sigh. "Go, and don't worry. Barrett is only going to stand guard; he's not going to sleep in your bed. Please feel free to fill that spot with whomever you like."

"Thanks," I say, walking out and meeting Barrett immediately. I try to find a way to text or call Austin, but fucking Barrett won't give me any kind of breathing room as he constantly reminds me of the time and our destination time. I decide to go with him and explain everything to her when I get back.

CHAPTER 23

Austin

I couldn't be more on top of the world when my father calls me in a panic and asks me to see him. It's never a good thing when my father calls me, but when he asks me to see him, it can only be something horrible. Dreading the possibilities, my curiosity forces me to go to our old family home, despite the unknown. I walk into the house and find my father sitting in the dark, crying.

I rush to his side and grab his hand. "Dad?! Oh my God what's wrong? What happened?"

"I'm so sorry, Austin. I am. I just can't help myself."

"What are you talking about, what did you do?" I ask, suddenly noticing the wrecked house and the papers thrown across the room. I find myself picking up betting forms, past due bills, and even a foreclosure note on the house. "What did you do? What did you do?!" He buries his head under his arms, but he can't hide from me. I grab his arms and jerk him up to look at me. "What did you do, you stupid old man?!"

"I tried to win it back, but the only one who would give me any money to try was a man named Beringer, and as it turns out, he works for Colletto. Michael Colletto helped me the first time for a trade of favors." I stare at him in disbelief. "Yes, I gave him my support for office and …"

"And me!"

He holds his shaky hand up to me as if he is asking for forgiveness. "I have only been setting up meetings and encouraging the relationship. I did not promise anything, but now, things have changed."

"What things have changed, and where is Aaron? Why call me and not your favored son?"

"Because they have him." My body goes weak, and my father

213

stumbles to my side to support me. "I called him to meet me some place safe, but when he got there with Billy, they ambushed them."

I push away from him. "Where's Aaron?" I am barely able to breathe.

"They took him. They shot Billy and took Aaron to force me to find the money any way I could. Billy is in a coma, and I don't know where Aaron is. They have friends everywhere. I am not even sure they are going to allow Billy to live. We can't say anything. We have to just let the police think they walked in on a drug deal that went bad."

"How much do you owe?"

"Too much for you to handle on your own. But if you go to Michael and ask him to give you another chance, then maybe …"

I shove him away from me. "Are you insane?"

"It's your brother's best chance, Austin. We need the money and who else can talk a Colletto into surrendering a man but another Colletto." Shaking my head, I step away from him, holding my weighted head and heavy heart. "Austin, you have the power to get your brother back safely and save this house that your mother loved."

"Why did they take Aaron? He's a cop. That's a huge mistake. Ettore will have every cop in the city after him. Not to mention the chief's son?"

"We can't tell them why, or who, all we can do is let them spin in circles looking for him. They think he's dead. They have fake leads pointing to some small time drug dealers. We have to let them continue on believing that; otherwise, I will lose everything."

"You're worried about your own skin right now? You got him into this, and you are worried about yourself?!"

"I am worried about both of your futures. What do you think it will do to you both if anyone finds out?" One look in his direction, and he knows my answer to that question. "Fine, but do you really think anyone can touch Ettore, right now? It will only lead to someone who covers for him. It will only lead to Aaron being killed with no chance of ever bringing the person to justice for it." The silence doesn't help me think any clearer. My brother's face keeps flashing in front of me while Dace's image begs me to consider other options.

"Maybe I can get a loan from the bank, maybe we both …"

"No, it won't be enough," my father says, hanging his head in shame.

"Why? How could you let it go that far?" I ask, suddenly realizing it wasn't just him that allowed it. He was tempted to continue on and on. "What else do they have on you? What proof do they have of the horrible things I know you had to have done?"

"They showed me pictures, video, some of me placing bets, some of me taking bribes to help pay my debt, and some of me … with professional women," my father says, picking up a package to hand to me. I take it and begin to look through it and find the last pictures of Aaron, blindfolded and badly beaten.

What are my options? Who do I have to go to for help? Can Dace help me without blowing his cover? He has money, I know he does, but can he get Ettore to release Aaron without getting himself killed? I'm not sure. Still, I need to talk to him. He will know what to do. He knows his brother much better than me.

"You stay here and wait to hear from them, and let me know if you do. I'm going to go see what I can do," I say to my father.

"Are you going to go talk to Michael? He would help you, I know it. He loves you. He would do anything for you, and if anyone has the power to clean this up and make it go away, it's him," my father presses annoyingly.

"Right now, all I know is that I don't want to hear your opinion or advice on anything. I really don't want to hear your mouth open to me until I ask you a question." I leave him in his dark room, whimpering over his failures, his problems, and his sorrow. It has always been about him, and now all of his egotistical ways have devoured not only his wife but his own children. I'm not sure what to do, so like I always do when Aaron isn't available, I go and see Billy.

I can barely contain my horror when I walk into the ICU and see him. As expected, there are cops everywhere. My presence is expected, as well as my emotions; however, it is still hard to face all my fellow officers knowing I could help them get the fuck that did this. Out of the corner of my eye, I notice a man walk by, and I look over and see the boots I have been looking for. Rowen is on the elevator and gone before I can say anything to him, but I know now he had something to do with this. I collapse in a chair next to Billy's bed and take his hand. "What am I going to do Billy? I need you to be here. I need you and Aaron both. I am so sorry this happened, but I'm going to fix it, and I promise you, I'm going to get that fuck," I whisper.

"Austin, honey, are you okay." Michael peeks his head into the room with a sympathetic expression. "I heard what happened, and I was afraid you might have been caught it in the mess, too. Have they found your brother yet?" I shake my head, and he leans over me with a warm hug. It feels good for someone to care, but for some reason, I am suspicious of why he is here, not that I should be. It is perfectly reasonable for him to show up for the press at least, but still, he's here and at the same time as Rowen?

Billy's family is with him now, so I go home and wait for Dace to come home, but the later it gets, the more desperate I become. I even try calling him from Preston's phone. He doesn't answer, and he doesn't return my call. He doesn't seem to be anywhere. What's happening? Where is he? Desperation sets in, and I go to his penthouse, only I find some men guarding his place.

"Can I help you?" one says with a harden glare.

"I was looking for Dace Colletto."

"Mr. Colletto left town," he says, looking back over my shoulder as if his response should have satisfied me.

"What? When? For how long?"

"Miss, please, Mr. Colletto is handling business out of town. There is no set time for him to return. Now, if you don't mind?" he says, waving his hand back at the elevator for me to leave.

Nodding, I turn around and walk into the elevator, dazed. Why would he do this? He went back to his friends. He must have had enough. I thought we were going to leave together. Did he have something to do with this? *NO.* No, why would he leave without a word said to me? I walk into my condo and immediately collapse to the ground. Preston runs to me and tries to help me up, all the while nervously asking if I'm okay, but I have no voice, no energy to speak, so he calls someone to help or at least tries. Aaron, of course, isn't available, neither is Billy. Dace is nowhere to be found, and my father is in such a desperate state that he is too scared to answer his own phone. I guess I can't blame Preston for what he does next, who he decides to depend on for help. I mean, he thinks he is helping me, and maybe, just maybe, he is.

Michael shows up on his white horse, picks me up, and carries me to the safety of his home where one of his physicians can look me over, all the while holding me and trying to coax me into telling him what's wrong.

"I tried calling everyone I could think of for her, but no one is answering. I wasn't sure what else to do. If I call 911, they will report it and possibly cause problems for her at work," Preston says as Michael runs his fingers through my hair and his hand down my back. His comforting touch soothes the pain enough for me to see him and return his smile. I have no options anymore. I only have him, and maybe I can solve everything with …*him.*

"Michael … I need your help."

CHAPTER 24

Austin

Michael has been wonderful, supportive, understanding, and dogmatic in his efforts to get my brother back. During the process, he's done everything he can to make me smile and give me what he thinks I want. You couldn't want for a better man ... *they* keep telling me. *Love will come over time,* my father says. Maybe. Maybe it doesn't matter. Maybe I'm a fool for questioning what seemingly is a perfect situation for me. I stand and look over myself in the mirror. The modest white dress fits nicely on me, it's not overly feminine but something I am sure Michael will love for the press pictures he is having shot after the wedding.

"You look beautiful," my father says, stepping into the room.

I turn towards him with a pointed glare. "You don't get the right to speak to me with any happiness in your voice. You don't get to feel good about anything. I despise you and everything you have done," I say to him before walking out and taking Preston's arm. I walk out into Michael's large party room and walk up on Michael greeting someone happily.

"I am so glad you could make it back in time," Michael exclaims.

"In time for what?"

"I'm getting married."

"Married? To who?" Dace asks as I step out and stare at him in horror.

"Oh there's my beautiful bride," Michael says, taking my hand. "We better hurry. The pastor only has an hour before he has to get back to the church," Michael says as he escorts me into the overly flower-adorned room. I look back over my shoulder and look into Dace's eyes, seeing nothing but betrayal staring back at me.

I don't even remember the ceremony, the words said, or the papers signed. I don't remember anything until we are dancing and I am suddenly handed off to one brother and to the next until there is no one left but Dace. The touch of his hand sparks the longing for him that I had hoped was taken over by the fury and the rejection I have felt for him. Unlucky me, his masculine scent, strong hands, soft lips, and the waves of his hair touching my cheek as he leans in for a respectful kiss, they are all so tempting that it's impossible to hate him. Then, I see it, the hatred I felt for him is now in his eyes, and I'm not sure what to say anymore. The things I have wanted to say since he left now all seem wrong. "I …"

"Shut up," he says with a forceful smile. "I have nothing to say to you, and I don't want to hear your voice or your explanation for anything. Three weeks. I was gone for three weeks, and despite my brother's advice, I tried calling you a million times, and now I guess I know why you never answered."

I suddenly realize my phone hasn't rang in weeks. I haven't even gotten so much as a text from anyone. I have been so concerned about my brother and why Dace left that I hadn't noticed. I have made countless calls out, but none came in. Shaking my head. "No, Dace, I …"

"Shut the fuck up," he huffs, looking down at me with a controlled anger. "Enjoy fucking my brother, Austin." He lets go of me and nearly shoves me back at Michael.

"Hey, Sweetheart. I have a surprise for you," Michael says as I follow the wave of his hand and see my brother.

"Aaron!" I run to him and wrap my arms around him so tight that he has to adjust my grip so he can breathe.

"Hi, Knothead. Good to see you again, or what I can see of you." Aaron's wounds are clear, despite them cleaning him up for the occasion. "I wish you hadn't of done this for me. You should have just given them the notebook."

"They said this was about father's gambling debts. I thought that sounded wrong."

"Yeah, it was a good excuse to take me and beat me until I could tell them where the notebook was, but they must have figured out that I don't know where it is. I never told him, Austin, but I have a bad feeling they know you have it and that's why you were set up to do this. They have you living within their walls. I don't like this at all."

"I know what I am doing, Aaron. This will be good for both of us. I'm a Colletto now, so everything has to work out for me, right?"

"So you love him, Michael, I mean? If everything works out for a Colletto, then you must be in love with him."

I grasp his face, gently stroking the marks near his right eye. "Everything is fine. I'm fine, especially now that I know you're okay. That's all that matters. I lay my head against him and do my best to hold back my tears. No one sees me cry, a promise I made to myself when this all started. No one will get that satisfaction. "I will make sure they pay for what they did to you, Billy, and our mother."

"*We*. We will make sure. You understand me? It's you and me kid, as always, it's you and me." I nod silently, still pressed hard against my brother's chest. I look up at Dace who eyes us with a puzzled expression. I think briefly that he might give me a nod, anything, something to tell me that he doesn't hate me, but he shakes his head, grabs his coat, and leaves, racing off the estate with a roar of his bike.

CHAPTER 25

Dace

I was gone three weeks. I nearly went mad, and I was at one of the most serene and beautiful places in the world, but none of it mattered because I couldn't be with her. Three weeks, and I come back here to find her marrying my brother after spending so much time trying to figure out ways to call her without anyone knowing how to find me. Three weeks, and suddenly Ettore says I'm good to come back. *Good to come back?* The cops still showed up at my door to greet me. They still questioned me as if they are never going to give up on arresting me. If not for Ettore's attorney, I would be sitting in jail right now. I thought maybe I could go to Michael and get him to use his connections to get them to back off, but instead, I walk in and find *her*, marrying my ..." I pick up a vase from my table and slam it against the wall. "My fucking brother! Are you kidding me?!"

"Still upset, huh?" Antony says, following me into my place.

"Fuck you!"

"Don't take it out on me. I had nothing to do with it. I didn't even know about it until yesterday when they asked me to come. The whole thing is very strange."

I point to him. "This is your fault. I would have never met her if not for you."

"Me?! It's not my fault." I shake my head at him until he begins to nod. "Alright, I guess it is." I crash into my chair, resting my pounding head into my hands. "What are you going to do?"

"What can I do? There's nothing I can do. I just need to finish this bullshit with Ettore and then get the fuck out of here. Go back to my life," I say, thinking hard until I realize he hasn't responded. I look up at him as he snarls at me. "Now what's your problem?"

"You know there is more than just you suffering in this crazy family. No matter the rest of the family, I would like to think you would want to be around for me at least. I love you, Dace, and I'm sick and tired of you running and making me feel like I don't matter to you at all. I get enough of that from our father," he says, fisting his hands and slamming one fist against the wall as he walks out.

"Antony!" I yell after him, but he leaves before I can get a chance to apologize. I love my brother more than anything, but this city has become too painful to be a part of.

I avoid Michael like the plague, but I find no comfort in being around Ettore either. He is so boring that I can't keep my mind from thinking about her. The only relief I get is when I am out working on his arrangements and deals.

It took me many calls and a lot of apologizing before Antony would finally forgive me for what I said. He never lets me get away with being self-centered. Thankfully, he did and now we can both get back to business as usual. Antony is worried about me and is trying everything to make sure I fall in love with this city again and stay with him—here at home, or what he considers our home. Right now, he is continuously making jokes while we wait for our next meeting at a local dive, a place criminals come to talk business because the owner is known to take bribes to help anyone out with an alibi. Ettore needs the owner to do him some favors, and we're here to give him the details as soon as he finishes up some other business. "Stop Antony, I'm not in the mood for your jokes today."

He sighs, sinking down into his seat. "You know, I was over at Michael's this morning."

"So."

"Well, I saw her come out of the spare room, not his room. That's strange… don't you think?" I shrug, continuing to stare out the window. "You know, I hate her for what she did to you too, and for what she is doing to Michael, but something is really off with this whole thing. There is something missing, something we don't know."

"There's nothing that could explain why she did what she did, Antony."

"I guess not, but aren't you curious as to why they would get married so quickly?"

"No."

"Damn, Dace, you have to be torn up like hell. I think it would help if you talk to her."

"No! Now shut up about it."

"Okay, then I guess you don't want to hear that Father wants us all over for dinner tonight."

"Oh fuck! No, tell him I'm busy. Tell him anything you want, but I'm not going."

"Dace, come on. Eventually you are going to have to face her. Michael is going to call you and force you to come somehow, you know he can guilt you into anything."

"Then don't tell him I'm not coming until you get there, and I won't answer my phone when he gets pissed and tries to talk me back into it."

"I could, but you might as well tell him yourself because he is walking up behind you," Antony mutters with an innocent smile.

Cursing under my breath, I stand up and turn to greet him. "Michael, how's it going?"

"Save it and sit back down, Dace." Michael harshly motions me back towards my seat before sitting down with us. "What are you two doing here? So help me if you are helping Ettore with his quotas by giving money to that slime ball, Paltrow, I am going to kick both of your asses." I look away from him, shaking my head.

"That's kind of funny how you just show up out of nowhere and come in here accusing us of doing illegal shit and all, but we are only here having lunch, nothing more. And how did you find us anyway?" Antony laughs sarcastically.

"I don't find it funny. I find it ridiculous that you two waste your life away doing this bullshit and that you let your own brother use you like this. I want you both to stop this and come work for me and leave Ettore alone. He's getting in too deep and is going to get you both killed."

"Michael, mind your own damn business! We're old enough to make our own decisions. Stop trying to dictate to us," I push back on my bossy brother's demands.

"What the hell would we do for you anyway?" Antony asks, not expecting much of an answer I'm sure.

Michael sits back with a smile. "Glad you asked because I have some great ideas for you both." I make eye contact with Antony and then roll my eyes. "Don't roll your eyes at me. You, both, are coming over tonight for dinner, and we are discussing better lives for you. Safer and more legal lives."

"No, thank you," I say clearly.

Michael leans forward and slams his fist on the table in front of us. "Did I ask you? No, I'm telling you. As the head of this family, you are going to follow me and you're going to do as I say. I'm digging this family out of the dark shadows and putting it out in front of the world, and I can't have anyone fucking it up."

"Oh, yeah? What are you going to do about Ettore? I seriously doubt he's going to go on the straight and narrow. You going to get Ettore to handle your press conferences, let him flash that big ugly frown on TV for you?" I laugh.

"Dace, don't worry about Ettore. I'm handling him in my own way. He's had his warning to straighten up, and now he's on his own. I have had my people hunt you two down, and now I am making sure you two get out before he buries you both along with himself." Michael's phone vibrates, and he picks it up to read a text with a nod before standing up and adjusting his suit back into place. "Now, I'm not asking, I'm telling you to get out of here and get out of here now," he says, walking out a little too quickly to make me feel comfortable about ignoring him. Antony and I look each other over briefly before we both jump the table and take off out the back. We barely make it back to the car and down the road before the restaurant explodes.

"Damnnn ... so I am thinking Michael isn't planning to handle Ettore the legal way. Why do you think he chose that place and today of all times to start going after Ettore?" Antony asks, nodding in my direction.

"I don't know, but I think I better not skip dinner tonight."

The table is set for eight, and I quickly try to do the math in my head when Austin walks into the room. "Hi, Dace."

"Hi."

"I'm glad you came," she says standing there in her well-fitted dinner dress, reminding me that Michael likes everyone to dress for dinner even if it is at home. I'm sure my outfit is not going to pass his inspection.

"Dace, glad to see you made it okay. Although, I would have preferred to see you in a dinner jacket. I guess I will just be glad you're not wearing a t-shirt and a leather jacket."

"Dace!" Sage yells, running up to me with her arms held out for me to pick her up.

Smiling, I do as asked. "How are you beautiful? Have you been keeping your nanny busy playing all day?"

"Yes," she giggles as I kiss her face playfully.

"Yes, well that's good. You must have made me pictures today then? I haven't gotten a good picture to hang in a long time," I say as she nods excitedly and points to her room. I hide out and away from the other dinner guests in her room until we are called to eat. The moment I walk into the dining room, I want to run back to Sage's room and away from this sure to be awkward meal.

"Dace, you are in between Aaron and Austin. And do you know Jamee, Austin's partner?"

"No, nice to meet you," I say.

"Nice to meet you as well," she says with a wink as if we hold a sweet secret between us.

"And this is Jack Reed, Austin and Aaron's father and our humble city's chief of police," Michael says as I shake the man's hand and exchange nods. Antony makes eye contact with me, looking as uncomfortable as I am, especially with Michael's tie, tied tight around his neck. Cops and a mafia family sitting down for dinner together? This is about as right as Hell's Angels being invited to the White House for tea. The worst part of all this is sitting by my brother's wife, all the while picturing her naked and all the amazing things I have done to her and, better yet, the incredible things she has done to me. It's difficult to keep my dick down, but I feel a little satisfaction when I reach for the salt causing her to lose her train of thought as I push into her to reach. I am not sure if anyone noticed the odd exchange of looks between us, but why would they? We barely know each other, as far as anyone else knows. Throughout dinner, Michael makes polite small talk, and everything seems to be moving along without trouble, at least for a brief period before announcing his plans to take down Ettore and using it to win the governorship. He explains his plans to get the chief to lend police support and concentrate their efforts primarily on putting Ettore in jail. The whole idea that this man would agree to such bullshit is laughable, but for some reason, this supposed proud man agrees without hesitation. Austin and Aaron both breathe with a rumble against their lips, obviously wanting to protest, but they keep quiet. Antony and I are slated to go behind the scenes and get information for them to use to take him apart. We are to use what we know now and step up our efforts to turn people against Ettore, getting them to give up vital information. I, especially, am supposed to continue to be loyal to Ettore, gaining his trust until he gives up enough that will put him away for the rest of his life. It goes against everything our father has taught us: You stand up for family, not take them down for your own gain.

The lines in this family are getting blurred, lost even, and I'm not sure which side to choose anymore. I wish I didn't have to choose, but I see no way to stop the war that is surely coming.

"So we are going to be working with cops to take down our own brother?" I ask, nodding with a laugh.

"This is serious, Dace. Michael has thought all this through, and I, for one, am standing one hundred percent behind him," my father announces with his wine glass held up to his pride and first born son.

"You are all delusional if you think this is going to work. That this isn't going to somehow blow up in your face. Ettore is smart, and do you not think he has his own spies in every corner of this city?" I say forcefully.

"I agree with him. For once, someone has some sense. This whole dinner and sudden family relationship is making me sick to my stomach. Thanks for the lovely meal, but I can't handle much more," Aaron says as Austin sits quietly, but their father stands and chases Aaron down, apparently trying to reason with him.

I don't know how my father got this man to bow down to Michael, but I am clearly missing a huge piece to this puzzle. "What's happening here? Why all of a sudden are these two families together? Someone needs to explain to me why I should suddenly trust the cops after they killed …?" I hold off talking about Mother. This is not the time or place to bring up an argument that should be had among family only.

"Because, Dace, we have a similar enemy and goals," Michael says coolly.

"Oh, well that explains absolutely fucking nothing. I'm following Aaron and getting the hell out of here."

"Dace, come with me." Michael stands up and motions for me to follow him into his den, and Antony doesn't miss the opportunity to tag along.

Michael looks at him oddly when he barges into the room with us. "I'm just as confused as he is," Antony says, defending his presence.

"Fine, but I don't want what I am about to say to you to be talked about outside this room," Michael says as my father walks in and shuts the door behind him. "Jack Reed has a gambling addiction, something me and Father have known about for some time." I step back as the puzzle pieces suddenly start lining up. "Jack was in heavy debt to one of Ettore's men. The man was about to lose their family home and I am sure his job too by the time Austin came to me to help them. Their whole family would have come under suspicion if their father's gambling issues had gotten out." My eyes widen as I watch my brother explain the man's hardship that he put his children under. "She needed a lot of money to get him out of debt, and I am glad that I was able to help eliminate that burden from her."

"And you were able to pay off his debt in exchange for a wife? Is that what you are telling me, Michael?" I ask as my heart begins to race and my blood begins to boil.

"It's not quite like that. Austin and I were already dating, and I'm sure would have married eventually. This simply propelled it a little bit. I didn't simply pay off his debt; I secured his son's future and his daughter's, and in the process, I bought their allegiance to me. I don't have to tell you that his endorsement is a huge help to my campaign. This is the first step, gentlemen, and the next is to get rid of Ettore and clean our slate before I win the votes."

"Okay, so what does that mean for Dace and me? If we work for you and Ettore finds out, we become a target."

"With my bid for office, Ettore can't touch us. Any attempt would bring more attention to him than he could ever want," Michael boasts.

"Also, Antony, we would like to make you a celebrity of sorts with your permission," my father says, putting his arm around my brother's shoulders as Michael crosses his arms and smiles. "We want you to know we fully understand who you are and we support you in every way. In fact, we would like to make a public announcement in support of you." Antony looks around himself nervously as if he is suddenly being surrounded by hungry predators. "I'm sure Dace agrees that you are an excellent spokesman for gays in this city."

"Antony, I would like to make you my gay rights advisor," Michael states proudly. "You have grown into an amazing man, Antony, and I know you can really do a lot of good things." Before I can say a word, I notice Antony's expression as he is praised by our father and brother and shown more attention than he has ever gotten from them, attention he has longed for since our mother's death. Something about this bothers me, but I have never seen Antony so happy. The praising continues as they discuss details with him about what they would like for him to do. This night has been exhausting, and the first chance I get to excuse myself and walk out, I do, but on the way, I spot Austin walking into one of the spare bedrooms. Antony was right; she's not sleeping with him. *What happened, Austin? You obviously don't love him, so why go this far?*

CHAPTER 26

Austin

Sitting down to breakfast, Michael playfully teases Sage to make her laugh. I enjoy watching them play together; it's so innocent and pure. "It's good to see you smile again. You have been so down lately. I was beginning to worry."

"I'm fine. It's just a lot to get used to in such a short time."

He reaches over and grabs my hand. "You know you mean a lot to me, and I want nothing more than to make you happy. Please tell me how I can do that?"

"I'm happy, Michael. I only need a little time to get used to things."

"How about a trip together, get away from it all, just the two of us?" he says, savoring the idea already.

"I couldn't possibly get off of work right now. You need to ask for vacation months in advance."

"Hmm, okay. You know you don't have to work. I can take care of you."

"I love working. I…"

"I understand. I didn't say you shouldn't work; I am only giving you an option. And maybe you quit this job and do something else you have always wanted to do but couldn't afford to? Something a little safer."

"I can take care of myself. I'm very good at my job, and I love it." He nods and seems to give up his pursuit to have me quit, for now. His tender touches and sweet smiles assure me that he is never going to give up on getting me into his bed though. He promised to give me some time, but I'm not sure how much time he is really willing to give. I am his wife, and I should be "performing" as my father said, right before I smacked him. I feel awful whenever he kisses me goodnight and holds my hand tight, gazing over me with desire. All I can do is force a smile and kiss his cheek before walking away from him to go to my room by myself. I want to give myself to him, I do, and I had planned to. It's not as if he isn't handsome or desirable, it's that … he's not Dace. If Dace had not come back, I might have been able to move on and do everything I had set in my mind to do when I agreed to this. There is no way to change anything now, so I need to move on. I need to give myself to him and forget.

"Okay, I have to go. I have a ton of meetings today. Goodbye, little one." Michael kisses his daughter before leaning towards me. I turn my head towards him and allow him to kiss my lips which excites him more than I expected. He kisses me again and breathes a slow groan against my cheek. "See you tonight?" I nod. "I can't wait." His excitement is written all over his smiling face.

I still can't believe I'm here in this place, in this life. Things happened so fast, and I was so scared for my brother that I would have done anything to get him back safely. Michael had tried everything to convince Ettore to let him go and even paid my father's debts, but still, they held him, beat him, all because of me. Because I held onto that notebook with the notes, and they thought he had them. After a long conversation with Michael, I was convinced that I needed to confess:

"I have something I am sure they want Michael."

"Like what, Honey?"

"I found a notebook full of information on him, and that's how I have been able to follow his trail of activity. I am sure they think Aaron has it since he claimed he had the informant giving us the information. It's all in code, but with each place, I find the code becomes clearer and easier for me to figure out. I know I'm close to getting him, I know I am, but I can't risk my brother."

Michael takes my hands. "Thank you for trusting me enough to tell me that, and now that you have, we can use it for leverage against them. Do you have the notebook with you?"

"No, I put it in a storage unit under my mother's name. I keep her things in there that I hid from my father until I was old enough to store them. I

need to give it back to them to get my brother back, don't I?"

"I think it's best, but don't worry. I will make copies, and I will help you take my brother down."

"What? Why?"

"Because I don't want any part of that business he is involved in, and I have tried and tried to get him to get out and let it die with our father, but he won't. I told him it will get him killed one day, like it did my wife and child. That world is harsh, and it's hard to build a happy, healthy family from it. It's not as if my father doesn't have enough money to support us all for as long as we live. Ettore doesn't have to do the things he does; he chooses to because he enjoys it. He enjoys the killing and the twisted games he plays with people. You can't change a person like that. You can only lock them up and keep them and everyone else safe."

"I want to trust you, I do, but that notebook is a huge help in prosecuting Ettore. Aaron would be irate if I gave it up."

"I tell you what. We will go get the notebook together and make copies of it, and then I will take the original to give back to them, but I need you to do something for me first. I need you to agree to marry me."

"What? Why?"

"Because that's the only way I can protect you and your family. I need to make you all a part of my family and, in the process, put a barrier around you that would scare Ettore from coming after you or killing Aaron. Even if we give the notebook back, there is no guarantee they won't kill him after they have it. The only way to guarantee that is to make him family, make you the wife of the future governor, someone he won't want to harm. So marry me, Austin, and guarantee your brother's life will be spared and he will be returned safely. I promise not to force you to do anything you don't want to, but I know I can make you happy and keep you safe while we both hunt down my brother. Once I'm governor, then getting rid of Ettore can't hurt us anymore. I will be too powerful for our enemies to touch. All I ask is that you give me a chance and stand at my side to help me win. After that, if you are not happy with me, then I will agree to an annulment."

We are interrupted when Dominic Colletto walks into the room. "Michael, do you mind giving us a minute?" Michael kisses my hand and leaves me alone with his father. "I know the idea of marrying my son right now *must be hard to consider, especially since you have been sleeping with his brother."* I snap my head in his direction. *"Yes, I have known about you two for some time."*

"Are you going to tell Michael?"

"No, there is no sense breaking his heart, not because of you, but because of his brother's betrayal."

"Dace didn't know who I was, and he certainly didn't know about Michael and me. If he had, I am sure he wouldn't have even considered being with me."

Dominic holds up his hand to me. "The facts of the past don't matter. What matters are the facts we have now, which are, that you need Michael's help because I promise you, Austin, Dace isn't coming back. He is still in love with a woman he was running around with before he met you. You were only a distraction that he thought he could replace her with, and as soon as she called him, he went running to her and left you here without a second thought. Dace is in love with someone else, Austin, and he is never, ever coming back to you. That's how he is, he's a wanderer, not someone that settles down and makes a life with someone. He gets bored and he moves on. I imagine he finally got what he wanted from you, accomplished what he wanted to and ran back to his adventures. However, Michael loves you dearly, and he will do anything to make you happy. He's handsome and intelligent and thinks the same way you do about the law. It's your decision, of course, but if you say no to Michael then what are you going to do? Are you going to wait around forever for a man that doesn't love you while risking your brother's life?

I consider his idea as I play with the elephant around my neck. I hate him for leaving me. I hate him for not even saying goodbye. We had plans, and he changed his mind that easily? Why? Didn't I deserve at least a note of explanation?

"Can you give me a second?" Dominic nods, and I walk away with my phone in hand and try calling Dace one more time. He never picks up, and his voicemail is turned off. Ring after ring pushes me to my breaking point. I rush back to Michael and jump into his comforting arms, instantly feeling as though my pain is a little easier to take. "Okay, I'll marry you. I'll marry you, Michael."

Even Antony didn't know where Dace was and had assumed the same thing I had, that he wasn't coming back. What else could

I have thought or done? I wanted revenge, and I wanted my mother's killer, and if I had to sleep with the enemy to do it then I would. What do I care about my own happiness when I can have revenge?

I still have a few hours before work, and instead of going right in as I would normally do, I stop by to see Preston. Only Preston isn't home. I guess I should have known that he would be at work by now. I start to leave; I even make it to the elevator, but I don't push the lobby button. Instead, I push the button that sends me up. As soon as the elevator doors open, I spot him in his doorway, waiting for me.

"You shouldn't be here, Austin."

"Why? Tell me why you left me? I need to know, Dace. Why? You said I am supposed to be with you, right?"

He steps back looking at me. "I didn't leave you. I had a job Ettore gave me at the last minute. I was coming back. I tried to call you a million times, but you never answered." I shake my head. "I did, but you never returned any of my messages either, and I shouldn't have even left any. I thought something was wrong. I was worried sick about you, and then I came back and find you marrying my brother. Tell me why? Why would you go that far? To help your father?"

"I don't care about my father."

"Then why, Austin. What could possibly push you to make that kind of decision?"

"They told me you weren't coming back, that you went back to your old life with another woman."

"Who told you that?"

"Your father did. I don't know why. I had to do something, Dace. They said Ettore took my brother, and I know Michael knows Rowen Rodecker."

"What? Who?"

"They took him because of the notebook I had on Ettore; they thought he had it. I needed to get my brother back and keep him safe. Michael said he could make that happen." Dace seems in disbelief. "I thought you had lied to me, that you left me for another woman. I needed help, and you weren't here to do that. So I decided to handle things on my own, and to get my mother's killer, the man with the steel toed boots," I say, falling against his chest. "You weren't here, and I needed you."

He looks down with an odd expression. "Steel toed boots? I thought you said you didn't know the person that got away? You never said anything about boots or anything."

"He wasn't the one that was there. He was the one that organized the murder. One of the guys who was caught said he was paid to do it, but before he could say by who, he was killed. I found his brother's girlfriend, and she told me about Rowen, or really about the boots, and then I figured out Rowen. I saw him at Wendy Colletto's accident scene." Dace stares at me in disbelief as the wheels seem to be spinning in his head.

He pulls me inside and shuts the door, locking it tight. I stare at his back, watching him breathe in and out until he turns to face me. "The man in charge of my mother's murder wore steel toed boots with an engraved skull and crossbones on the metal." My eyes widen as I understand his reaction. "I was told the police had her killed to get back at my father, but now, I'm not so sure that it wasn't someone within my own family."

"Do you know Rowan?"

He shakes his head. "Does he work for my brother?"

"I don't know who he works for, but I have seen him at the oddest of times, like he haunts me."

Dace lays a hand on my back and lends a kiss to my forehead, but then, he pushes me away. "You shouldn't be here. You're my brother's wife now, and I ... we both need to accept that and move on with our lives. No matter why or how it happened, that's how it is."

"Do you hate me?" He shakes his head, still pushing me away. "Well... I hate you, and your family."

"Michael will be very good to you, if you let him, much better than I ever could."

I step back, shaking my head with anger. "Did you set me up too?" I ask, but I don't bother to wait for an answer.

"Austin! What do you mean? Austin, why did you ask me that?!" he yells through the closing elevator doors.

Jamee sits next to me with a giant smirk on her face. "What are you smiling about?"

"I am just amazed at how fast you moved from the sexy, bad-boy brother to the debonair politician brother. Then to get him to marry you?! Wow, I guess you could have them both whenever you want. And why exactly are you working still? I mean, you're rich now, go be rich and enjoy life."

There is nothing I can say to her that she would ever understand, so I ignore her comments and go back to work. "So Merlin said he heard from Nelson, and apparently, he has more information for me. He wants to meet. I don't want to scare him, so I want to go alone."

"Wow, I can't believe he would actually trust someone he barely knows," Jamee says with an attitude.

"What are you saying?"

"I'm saying you're being a fool. I need to go with you and back you up. What if this is a setup?"

"I don't think it is. This kid is really scared and really wants to stop running. If I can help him, Jamee, then we have a great witness."

"At least tell me where you are meeting him so, if you don't come back, I know where to go to find your dead body."

I laugh. "I don't think there is much of a way anyone will hurt us in front of all of those people, but if it makes you feel better, then fine, I am meeting him in the park near the south side entrance."

"Thank you."

"See you in a couple of hours, partner," I say as she waves at me.

The park is busy today, which will hopefully ease Nelson's mind a little bit and encourage him to come out to meet me. When he does, I need to talk him into coming with me. I already have my speed dial set up to get him protection. I walk near a large tree and see him vibrating with a cigarette in his hand.

"Nelson?" I ease closer to him until he jumps back from me. "It's okay. I'll stay right where I am. Merlin said you had something to tell me?"

"Yeah, there are more notes that I didn't tell you about, a lot of them, and I know where they are."

"Oh yeah? And how do you know this?"

"I followed him one night. Mrs. Martin, she was scared he was cheating on her, and since she was always so nice to me, I wanted to check it out for her. He wasn't cheating, he was hiding his notes and a bunch of other stuff. I don't know what exactly."

"Can you take me to it?" I ask him, hopeful.

"Yeah, but are you going to get me some protection first? These people are killing my friends to try and find me, and I don't want anyone else to die because of me."

"Sure, come with me, and we will take you somewhere safe, and on the way, you can tell me what you know."

"Okay," he says looking around himself and slowly walking

with me to my car. He gets in and shuts the door, and I take a deep breath of relief.

"Are you hungry? We can get you something to eat on the way."

"Yeah, but where are you hiding me?" he asks, nervously looking around the area.

"A motel just outside of the city."

"It's safe there?

"It'll do until we can get clearance to take you somewhere better," I reassure him.

"Alright, then here's the key to that storage unit."

"The notes are in a storage unit?"

"Yeah and a lot of other things too. He kept the key hidden nearby, so I was able to take it after he left and get in. I slept there a few times."

"Is that where you have been?" He nods.

"There is some scary stuff in there though, so I only sleep there when I really have to."

"What kind of scary stuff?"

"Just pictures of dead bodies and guns and stuff."

I take the key and slide it into my car's sun visor with a smile. When we arrive at the motel, I go to get Nelson checked in while he waits for me in the car. By the time I get back, two men are there, trying to drag him off. "Stop!" I try to get a clean shot at them, but I can't. I race after the car when another car pulls up followed by another. They surround me, and I give up my weapon and let them go with my key witness, but when they come after me, I fight. They clearly want me alive, so I have nothing to lose. I throw an elbow at one man and give another a high kick to the head. They back off, staring at me in shock. "What's wrong boys? Never met a woman that could fight with men? Although, to be honest, none of you are much of a challenge." They bravely come at me again only, this time, they stick a needle in my leg and inject me with something. I go weak all over and collapse.

When I awake, I am tied to a chair and blindfolded. "How are you doing there, Blondie?" A man roughly runs his fingers through my hair and laughs when I jerk my head back from him. "Don't worry. This won't take long. All you have to do is tell us what you know."

"He didn't tell me anything. I wanted to get him somewhere safe first," I quickly say, letting them know where I stand.

Another man leans down and whispers in my ear. "This isn't a game. We will kill you, and no one will ever find your body. Not your cop friends or your family. They will live in agony not knowing where you could be or what happened to you." I laugh, and the man picks me up off the chair, throws me to the ground, and begins kicking me. "Do you want to die, bitch? Tell us everything you know, and we will forget ever seeing you with the kid. Understand?" I nod. "Okay, good. I have to get back to work on my own interests. You take care of her and let me know when you're done." The man leans down to my side and grabs my face. "You really should have stayed away and stuck with arresting your drug dealers. Continue," the man says to the other.

"Okay, I'm going to ask you one more time, what did the kid tell you?" I'm not telling them anything, and I make sure they know that. I hear the wisp and feel the hit to my arm. The blow goes down deep into the bone forcing me to scream out in pain. "Tell us what he said to you!"

"Nothing!" I yell. "I told you my primary goal was to get him somewhere safe first.

"Yeah, well you did a great job at that, didn't you?" the asshole reminds me. I hope they don't harm him. Hopefully someone can get to him before it's too late. "This is getting ridiculous cop, just tell us what the kid said, and we will let you go."

I hold my head up in defiance. "Go fuck yourself!"

"Screw this. Let's go. She doesn't know anything more than the kid anyway." They grab me and hold my head still as they place a gun to my temple. The cold metal of the barrel buries into my skin, and the painful pressure of it begins to give away to the realization that I'm going to die. I have nothing to say to them. I'm not going to give when my brother never did. I can do this. "Fine, unless you have something to add, cop, then goodbye …"

"Wait!" I scream with a trembling voice, damning myself for being weak.

"You have two seconds, and then we don't care what you have to say anymore," the man says. All I have to give them is the key to the storage unit, but I know Aaron will find it and figure it out eventually. I shake my head, being instantly halted as the man holds my head still and presses the gun deeper into my head. "You have something to say?" I can do this. I take a deep breath as he fingers the trigger…

KWACK

KWACK

I heard the gun go off, but I don't feel the pain of it.

The silence in the room is strange. *Are they dead? How?* Then I hear someone breathe deeply. "Who's there? Please, tell me what's happening?" I plead, scared of what could be coming for me now.

A warm hand touches my face, scaring me until I realize it's him. "It's okay, Trouble. Your brother is on his way," he says, holding my head with a soft hand and placing his lips on my temple before disappearing.

"Wait! Come back!" I yell for him, not understanding why he would leave me here alone. Within a few minutes, I hear Aaron calling for me. "Aaron! I'm here! Aaron I'm here!"

CHAPTER 27

Dace

I knew about Austin's father having gambling issues, then she told me about her brother being kidnapped, and now after watching the news, I find out her brother's partner is in a coma and they are still searching for suspects. The wheels in my head begin spinning as I consider what Austin said about the man with the boots being seen around Wendy's accident. She must think he is involved with Michael not Ettore. Can't be. Michael would never associate with a man like that. I need to relax. I step into the shower and try to calm, but then my alarm goes off. I jump out to check it out, and I spot Jamee coming up to my place. I open my door as she gets off the elevator. "What are you doing here?"

"I wanted to talk to you about something," she says, walking past me and into my place. She looks around my home as if she is already sizing it up to own it.

"Oh yeah? And what exactly do you want to talk about?" I ask, crossing my arms as I move in front of her and stop her from moving any further into my home.

"Wow you look even hotter all wet. Do you need someone to help you get your back or anywhere else?" she says, twisting her fingers into my towel. I take a step away from her and impatiently wait for her to tell me what she wants. "I think you and I should have some fun together."

"No thanks, I think you should go."

"I can go but if I do then I am going to have to tell my good friend Michael about his wife and his brother still seeing each other. She confessed to me you know, that she still loves you and only you. She is never ever going to have sex with Michael while you're still around. I think Michael should be aware of that don't you?"

"Are you threatening me?"

"Yes, you see I tried Aaron. I have kind of lost interest in him lately though, but you, you are way more interesting and fun and obviously have more money. I promise I could make you very happy, all you have to do is make me happy and give me what I want and if you do I will keep yours and Austin's secrets. Like the sex secrets she told me about, the things you used to do to each other. Hell I even copied the pictures Austin took of you two together at some cabin. Great pictures, and so sweet, I am sure Michael would love to see them. I am not sure that you are aware, but Michael has a slight temper." She says almost assuring me that he had something to do with Billy being in the hospital.

"You are something else."

"Thanks, so want to get started now or …"

"I think you need to go, and I'll get back to you on that." I insist.

"Alright but just so you know, I will be home tonight waiting in a special outfit I bought just for you." Jamee smiles up at me touching my chest with a purr as she places her address in between my towel and my abdomen.

I march to my door and show her the way out. She walks out like she's the queen of the world. I can't believe her, she has got to be out of her damn mind if she thinks I am going to fuck her to keep her quiet. The alternative is to let her tell and prove to Michael that it was me all along and not Billy who is now in the hospital, because of me and my family. I need to get some dirt on her and turn the tables. After I get dressed I head out to break into her place and dig up whatever I can on the bitch.

Aaron comes rushing at me as soon as I step outside of my building. "Where's my sister you son of a bitch!"

I push the maniac off of me, "I don't know what you are talking about!"

"I'm talking about my sister who's missing. She was meeting a witness a few hours ago and hasn't been heard from since. We found her car sitting in a motel parking lot wide open and empty, no witness and no Austin. Now tell me where she is, I know you are still working for Ettore, and I know he's the one that took her."

My heart beats rapidly as I begin to understand why he is so upset. "Go home Aaron, I don't know where she is, but I am going to damn well find out." I rush back up to my place and quickly open up my system. Searching for her phone I find the last ping signal near the motel she was taken from, and then I search the phone signals pinging thereafter, narrowing down the numbers to a specific timeframe. I begin looking through each one and follow their paths until one stands out. There, that's where you are. I head out the door to find Trouble and hoping I can make it in time to save her.

They are holding Austin in an abandoned apartment building in a drug infested part of town, where no one is going to call the police no matter how much screaming is heard. I pull through the building and park my bike inside. Moving into the stairway I move up one floor at a time listening carefully until I hear someone move. I don't hear anything, but then I get a whiff of her perfume and feel her presence on the third floor. Opening the door slowly I move in.

"I'm going to ask you one more time, what did the kid tell you?"

"Nothing!" Austin yells. "I told you my primary goal was to get him somewhere safe first.

"Yeah well you did a great job at that didn't you?"

I peak around the corner to see her tied up with a blindfold. I text her brother where she is and plan to stay long enough for them to get here, but nothing ever works out like you plan for it to.

Her captor takes a gun and holds it to her head, "This is getting ridiculous cop, just tell us what the kid said and we will let you go."

"Go fuck yourself." I shake my head with a roll of my eyes. She is hit across the face and still she stays silent, they hit her again and again. She stays silent. I'm not sure I can stay in the shadows much longer, but I know these men, and they know me. I'm either going to have to kill them or risk them killing her.

When I hear her cry out, I cringe. *Where the fuck are the cops when you need them?*

"Screw this. Let's go. She doesn't know anything more than the kid anyway."

"You have two seconds, and then we don't care what you have to say anymore," the man says. "Fine, unless you have something to add, cop, then goodbye …"

"Wait!" she screams, sounding completely breakable.

I look at Austin shaking and scared and more vulnerable than I have ever seen her, but even with a gun to her head, she stays silent. "You have something to say …" I take aim and...

KWACK, KWACK. I kill them both with one shot each as she remains trembling and gasping for breath. I go to her and look her over for any major wounds but find nothing, but a skull and crossbones imprint all over her swollen skin. *Son of a bitch, I swear I'm going to kill him one day and leave an imprint on him for eternity.*

"Who's there, please, tell me what's happening?"

Reaching out I touch her face and she flinches, "It's okay." I kiss her lips and leave before the cops find me here.

Austin was taken to the hospital and to satisfy my own fears I meet Michael there as a concerned brother. "Dace, thank you for coming."

"You're welcome, when I heard what happened I wanted to make sure she was okay." I say as Antony walks up next to me. Michael smiles at me with a quick hug then he takes off into Austin's room.

"And how did you know she was here Dace?" Antony asks.

"You called me remember?" I say waiting for him to nod in

my direction. I make my way into her room and watch as Michael wraps his arms around her and nearly in tears as he does so. "Oh my dear God I am so glad you are alright. Thank you Aaron for finding her and bringing her back to me."

"No problem." Aaron says glancing my way. I am sure he has questions for me so I need to get out of here before he asks them.

"I want whoever is responsible for this to be dealt with immediately. Find them! Do you all understand me?" Michael announces to his entourage of people. They all scramble around him talking about how to make this happen. "I can't believe they would attack my innocent wife like that, a cop even." Michael turns back to Austin holding her hand, "I am so sorry Baby, this is my fault I'm sure. Whoever is responsible for this was obviously doing it to get back at me. I am sorry to tell you this, but I can't have my wife put in this kind of danger anymore. You are going to have to quit."

"No! No why? I can handle myself, this is a part of the job, it has nothing to do with you. It was about the runaway I told you about. I found him and they followed me somehow and took him and me to see what I knew"

"Austin they didn't need to take you and you know it. They took you to get back at me, so it has everything to do with me and I am sorry, but even your captain agrees, you could put your own partner in jeopardy. No other cop wants to work with you."

"Aaron would."

"And you want to put your own brother at risk? That's selfish. Honey, take some time away for a little while and then we will revisit the idea of you going back or maybe you can do something else that's fun and safer for you. Maybe you can help me with my campaign I would really like to have you at my side at these campaign stops. My speeches could be so much better if I have someone beautiful to stare at while I make them." She smiles a weak smile and nods. "Wonderful, okay let's get you checked out of here and home."

Austin looks up at me touching her lips and I give her a smile with a wink. She leans back into bed with a sigh. It's time to go, I walk out of her room only to be chased down by her brother.

"Dace wait up please!" I stop and wait for him trying to think of the answers to his questions before he can ask them but when he reaches me he seems to not want to know the answers any more than I want to tell him. "I had in my head what I wanted to say to you, but now I am not so sure. I do want to say thank you, I don't know how you found her, but thank you." I nod and wait in silence as he breathes in deep. "You're the guy she's in love with aren't you?" I stop breathing. "Don't worry I won't say anything. I should have known. I guess I'm not as great of a detective as I thought. Anyway, thanks and if you ever need anything let me know, I owe you one." I nod and shake his hand.

"Actually Aaron, I'm curious, who knew where Austin was meeting that kid today?"

"As far as we know only Jamee, they must have been already following Austin because I don't know how else they would have known. Jamee would never betray Austin like that, she's a pain in the ass, but she is loyal to Austin, like a sister."

"Right, like a sister, so I'm sure she wouldn't." I say, considering a new tactic to handle Jamee.

I show up at Jamee's door ready and willing to do whatever I have to, to protect Austin. She opens the door in next to nothing. "I knew you would show."

I walk in looking around the room, "So where do you want to start?" I ask her and she smiles wide. "Oh but I have one question first. Who are you working for? Ettore? Michael? Who?"

"I don't know what you are talking about." She says standing back from me.

"You set your partner up to be killed today."

"You're crazy, I would never do that." She snaps at me.

"No, you would just inform to whoever you're working for her every move." She stands in front of me with a smug look.

"You should realize by now, that once Austin gets something in her head she won't let it go until she resolves it. I tried to deter her, but she wouldn't let it go and you know as well as I do what can happen when you go too far and run into the wrong people."

"Yeah I do, I also know what can happen when you threaten the wrong people and hurt the people they love."

"Oh yeah, well no matter what happened to Austin, your brother will still be very upset to hear what you two had been doing behind his back. Considering what is going on in your family right now, I wouldn't think he would hesitate to kill you or someone else you love, for your betrayal." She wiggles back and leans over a table showing off her body openly to me. "Our original deal stands if you care about your own life and Antony's."

I laugh with a smile, "Threatening my brother now? That was the worst thing you could have done. By the way, Austin is alive and safe." Jamee's confident expression changes dramatically. "Yeah she knows it was you, but no need to worry, I'll take care of you." I pull my gun from my coat and shoot her dead in the face. "Nice knowing you Bitch."

CHAPTER 28

Dace

I wake up this morning to a call from Antony, "Hey Dace wake up, I need you today."

"Why is that?"

"I have decided to make an announcement to the media about being gay and Dad and Michael are going to stand at my side while I do it." He says proudly.

"Antony, that doesn't sound like a good idea? Why didn't you talk to me about this before you decided?"

"I don't have to tell you everything Dace, I can make decisions on my own too."

"I know that, but this seems like a big one, one that I'm not sure you should do."

"Why? Because it means I don't need you anymore, that I have support from someone else in the family? Like our own father, which you have always wanted to please yourself."

"That's not it at all, I just wish you would have …"

"Why can't you just be happy for me Dace?"

"I am Antony."

"Good, then that means you will be at the press conference too right? Standing at my side with the rest of our family?"

"Sure if that's what you want?"

"I do." Antony exhales happily, "Thank you, this is going to be a great moment just you wait and see. Dace, make sure you dress for the conference, otherwise, you might have to stand in the back with the spectators." Antony laughs.

"Cute, I'll do my best to be presentable for you."

"Thanks Dace."

"I'll see you soon." I am happy for him but nervous all at the same time. Before I can get ready to go, Ettore comes by and pushes the buzzer to come into the building. Security must be on break. I click on the speaker which annoys him immensely, "Who's there?" I ask laughing at his annoyed expression.

"Your fucking brother dumbass. I want to talk to you about our father." Ettore creaks out through coughs.

"Yeah, what about him?"

"Just let me in!" He yells at me. I let him in and open my front door for him to come into my place and have to laugh again when he passes me with a huff.

"Okay Sunshine, what is it you need to tell me?"

"I have been doing some digging and found out some things I think you should know. But first off our father needs to be taken down. He's not making wise decisions these days. He's being horribly misguided by Michael."

Shaking my head, I respond. "Ettore, I'll talk to the old man for you if you want, not that I think it matters. He is going to end up letting you have it because who else is there to give it to? Do what you want with it already and don't worry about ..."

"I am not concerned with you or Antony. What I am worried about is Father getting me into a war that I can't win with Michael."

"What are you talking about?"

"The Aksakovs. Michael is making a deal with them to have us all killed. He's using you to distract me while he arranges to have me, you, and Antony killed and hands over the keys to what's left over to them. Don't tell me Michael doesn't want it. He may not care about the business, but he does care about the name and the power. He gets off on it, and if you would open your damn eyes, you would realize that."

I stare at him, looking for any sign of deception. "How in the hell would you ever expect me to believe that bullshit?"

"Think about it, Dace. He wants nothing more than to have a clean slate and develop this family into the next Kennedys. How am I the only one that sees that?"

"You're paranoid."

"Am I? Open your fucking eyes, Dace! Ever since you have been back, you have had one foot out the door, ready to take off again. You're so concerned about getting out of here that you don't even realize what's happening right in front of you. You think I don't know that Father is meeting with you? Hell, he's meeting with Antony too. He's the one that got him to call you back here, to make it easier on Michael. You know Antony. He would do anything to get Father to pay attention to him, make him feel loved. Not that you're much different. You both have been gone so long that you only remember what you want to remember. Michael is not who you think he is. He was the one to send the cops after you for Olsen's death. I found out about it and sent you away for your own protection. I'm not sure why, but he is suddenly desperate to get rid of you, and quickly."

I turn away from him, considering what he is saying, and if it's true, then Michael still suspects me and Austin are together. "Why are you telling me this Ettore?"

"Oh, trust me, I don't have to. I could have went ahead and let him kill you. One less brother to worry about stabbing you in the back, but ever since you have been back, you have impressed me. You are worth saving, Dace."

"And Antony?"

"I respect you enough to give you the information. Do what you want with it. I like the kid. I won't harm him. I have no reason to, but if you want to keep him alive, you better stop him from doing that favor for Michael today." I stare at him hard. "Ah... you're starting to understand, aren't you?" Ettore looks at his watch and back up at me. "You don't have much time there baby brother."

I rush out of the house and jump on my bike, trying to call Antony, but he won't answer. My heart is pounding, and my mind is racing. I pull up on the crowd of press in front of the LBGT

Rights city headquarters and instantly begin searching for a way to get to him. I spot the group making their way towards the makeshift stage. "Antony!" I yell at him. He turns and looks at me confused, but only for a second. He's my brother, and we know each other better than anyone. Just as I had hoped, I don't have to say a word. He takes a step back while I jump off my bike and run towards him. "Antony get down!" I yell as I spot the car driving towards us and realize my whole family is here, even Austin. Everything I care about is right here and in danger. I take out my gun and fire at the car that is now spraying bullets towards the stage. The attackers come in strong, aiming right for where Antony is, and then another car comes from another direction, heading directly for me. I find cover and look up to see Austin reaching for me. Michael comes after her and looks back at me briefly. He doesn't hesitate to get her safely out of harm's way, giving me the opportunity to concentrate on getting Antony out of here. "Antony!"

"Dace," I hear him softly call for me.

"Antony, where are you?"

"Here!" he yells painfully. I work my way towards him, firing as necessary. I manage to find him, bleeding and wounded. I check him over. Can you walk?" He nods. "Where's your Glock?"

"Michael said to leave it in my car because it wouldn't look right to the media," Antony says, holding onto me as I help him up.

"You're getting out of here now." Taking hold of Antony's jacket, I drag him along with me while trying to maneuver through the onslaught being directed at us. I make it to a door and kick at the base to try and get someone's attention to open it. "Open the damn door!" I yell, kicking and screaming until someone finally unlocks and pushes it open for us. Austin reaches out and helps bring Antony in while I cover us until we get the door closed and locked. I check Antony's wound and realize my father and Michael have been safely hiding inside. "Where were you?"

"Dace, calm down. Everyone is fine, and the cops are handling it now," Michael says.

"You left him out there by himself with no way to defend himself!" I yell at the bastard.

"I was trying to protect my wife and my father. I thought he was right behind me. I didn't realize he wasn't until we were already in here. I was working on a way to get to him, but then I saw you with him, and I knew you could help him. It's not my fault he got caught in the middle of the people targeting me."

"Not you! Antony was the one being targeted today, and me."

"What the hell are you talking about? Why would they target Antony, or you? Neither of you are running for office."

"Oh shut up, Michael. Not everyone cares about your race to the fucking White House!" I scream at him.

"What is going on with you, Dace?"

"Ettore told me what was going to happen. He told me you were setting up Antony. Why, so he can be your cause? Guilt people into voting for you because of your dead, gay brother who died coming out to the world with you at his side," I say, dramatizing every word clearly to him.

Michael looks me over, shaking his head as if he is insulted at my accusation.

"Dace, I wanted to do this. I am the one that suggested it. My counselor said I needed to finally let go of being scared to admit it fully to my family. When I told Michael about it, he said he would be at my side only if I wanted him to be. He didn't ask me to do this," Antony says, putting a hand on my shoulder and trying to calm me down.

"Yeah? Then who did? Who put this idea into your head?" I ask, looking over at my father who eyes me carefully.

"Ettore is messing with your head. I guarantee you," my father says to me.

"What he says makes sense though Father."

"And what did he say?" Antony asks, struggling with his wound.

252

"He said that Michael is working with the Aksakovs to kill us, to help Michael have a clean slate for his path to political greatness, and that Michael has Father fooled. He is making him think that Ettore is up to everything and that we are only getting caught in the crossfire."

Michael laughs, looking back at our father, shaking his head. "Are you kidding me? Why in the world would you ever believe that bullshit?" Michael steps to me and grabs my face. "Listen, baby brother, you have got to stop believing everyone is out to get you. You have to trust someone at some point. How you could possibly believe that I or Father would set something up to kill our own family is beyond me. I'm going to go talk to the police and see if we can help catch these fucks."

There are deep sighs all around as I stare down at the floor, trying to catch my breath. Michael helps Antony up and to a waiting ambulance with Austin following after, but my father stays. "Have you been lying to me? Did you set me up?" I ask him.

"I always do what is best for my family, and if knowing that you still believe I would kill my own, then so be it. I doubt I could ever convince you otherwise with nothing more to defend myself than words."

"You could at least try!"

"I told you he wanted you and he would do everything he could to find your weakness, find that person that you love so much that you would give your own life for. He's playing you like a violin, and you're letting him. I told you. He likes to make sure he can control everyone, and he just figured out how to control you." My father swears under his breath and walks out. I chase after him.

"You don't give a damn about anyone but yourself! You don't try to defend yourself because you know you can't, and you don't care enough about me to try. You're the one that set this display up. You're the one that talked Antony into doing this, and you're the one that benefits if Michael wins the governor's office. Ettore doesn't stand to benefit from any of it; he has no reason to risk his men to pull off what happened today. He has no reason to bother, and if he did, why would he tell me?"

"To convince you to turn your back on me." My father smiles arrogantly.

"You mean like you did to me and Antony?" He stares at me in silence. "You act like family is everything when it only means something to you when you can gain something from it."

"Like I said, believe what you want, Dace. Just make sure before you choose a side that you know all the facts; otherwise, you might choose the wrong one," he says, walking away from me without another word said.

Antony is well-drugged now as he lies in his hospital bed. Michael is out talking to the press about his goals and desires to bring people to justice. I'm afraid to leave my brother's side. Michael was right; I don't trust anyone, but why should I?

"Are you okay?" Austin asks, peeking in shyly from the doorway.

"I'm fine. I wasn't shot this time."

"This time." She seems to be trying to make a point, but I am not taking the bait. "Someone killed my partner." I give her nothing more than a glance. "I guess I should be more broken up about it, but I am pretty sure she is the one that set me up to be killed in the first place. No one would have believed me if I had ever accused her before, but they do believe that she did now. For some reason, she stupidly left out her bank account information which shows a lot of money going in and one sizeable payment made the same day Nelson and I were taken."

"Doesn't sound good."

"No, it doesn't. I guess I am lucky someone killed her before she killed me." Austin moves near me and runs her fingers through my hair, and I can take the tension no longer. I turn and welcome her arms around me. "I love you, Dace." Words that sound so beautiful coming out of her mouth it is almost as if she sang them to me.

"I love you," I whisper.

We quickly let go of each other when we hear Michael coming. "Austin, Honey, we need to go. I want to be home before Sage goes to bed." She nods as he takes her hand. "Actually, could you wait for me outside? I want to talk to Dace alone."

"Okay." Austin's worried expression looks pitiful. I wonder if she is worried about leaving with Michael in a bad mood or worried for me dealing with Michael.

"What do you need, Michael?" I say, moving in between Antony and him.

"I feel like you don't trust me with my own brother?" Michael accuses.

"I'm not feeling very trusting these days."

"I don't know what has gotten into you lately, but for you not to trust me, *me*, of all people, is outrageous."

"Why did you tell Antony to leave his gun in the car?" I ask him point blank.

"Because it doesn't look very good to the press to have your supposed straight and narrow brother carrying a gun at his side. We were there to make a great impression, remember?" Michael hisses at me as if I have crossed a line. "We are trying to go legit and …"

"And get you elected. Yes, I remember."

Michael sighs, seeming to search for the right thing to say to me. "I guess that means you're not going to leave here anytime soon?" I shake my head. "Fine, then there is no reason for me to hire any guards for him then?"

"Your guards? No. We don't need them. Thanks anyway."

He looks me over for some reason before nodding and checking on Antony. "Oh, and Father will be here soon to check on Antony too. Please try to get along and not start anything with him while he is here."

"I'll try, but I can't make any promises."

"You need to trust me, Dace. Everything I have done I have done for you and Antony's best interest. That's why I am doing all of this, so you, Antony, Sage, and any other children that might come along won't have to go through what Ettore and I have had to deal with. I will not apologize for trying to protect you."

"I can protect myself now, Michael. Trust that." Michael's attitudes changes as he takes a step back from my hardened chest. It's as if he only just now realized I am no longer his 'little' brother.

"Alright, I'll let you calm down. It's been a pretty rough day for us all, but we need to get this worked out. I love you, Dace. I don't want bad blood between us like there is between me and Ettore." I don't say a word as he walks away, meeting Austin in the hallway with a kiss before taking her hand and leaving.

"You look like a lost puppy," Antony says.

"What are you doing awake? You should be resting."

"How can anyone get any sleep around here with all the drama? If I wasn't gay, I would be really annoyed by it," he laughs. "So tell me what's really going on. Who are we supposed to trust, and don't lie to me because you know I can tell when you are."

"I honestly don't know, Antony, but someone is trying to kill us, and I am pretty sure it is our own family. The problem is, I am just not sure who or why."

"Is there something I can do to help figure that out?"

"Yeah. I need you to leave town and locate some friends of mine and tell them I need their help. Otherwise, I don't think I am ever going to leave this city again, not alive."

CHAPTER 29

Dace

I spend every second I can at Antony's side until he is ready to check out. Once he does, I send him to a safe place and give him instructions on how to get a hold of my friends and tell them I need their help. It's not going to be easy for him to get a hold of them. The email I set up for them is only accessed when they are looking for their next job. If they are in the middle of one, it could be months before they check it again. In the meantime, I have to figure out who is out to get me and who isn't.

My father shows up at his usual rendezvous spot, but he looks none too happy to be here. "Thank you for coming."

"It seemed important enough," he says coolly. "So have you calmed down and realized that I'm not trying to kill you and Antony, who has suddenly disappeared. Hiding from his own father. Ridiculous."

"It's not ridiculous. Someone close to us is trying to kill us. If not you, then who? Ettore? Why would he wait until now? Why protect me all this time just to kill me? No, there is something not making sense about all this, and I have a feeling you know what's missing." He looks away from me, sighing deeply.

"Your mother. It's all your mother's fault. If she had been able to be faithful to me, then none of this would be happening."

"What are you saying? Did you have her killed?" I say, choking on the last words as if they knotted up in my throat.

"I wanted to know who he was, and she refused to tell us. I wanted to know who was my son and who wasn't."

I take a step back from him, suddenly understanding the separation between us all. "I'm not your son." He stares at me from the corner of his eyes. "When did you know?" He shakes his head. "When did you know?!" I scream at him.

"When Antony became sick and had to go to the hospital. Your mother was away at the time, and I didn't want her to worry, so I tried to handle it on my own. They were afraid he wouldn't get better, that the illness would take over his little body and destroy his kidneys. I thought it best to be prepared and had myself tested to be a donor for him, but I was not a match. I wasn't even close. After that, I had all my sons tested and discovered I only have two sons, legitimately. Your father is unknown since she refused to talk. I only wanted his name. I didn't ask for anything more to happen. I tried to have her followed and find out that way, but she must have stopped seeing him or it was one of her guards."

I stand back, looking at the monster who caused my mother's death. "You slaughtered her and would have killed us. We were only kids. If Antony had not left with me that night... you are truly ..."

"Don't say that. I loved you both, and I would have never allowed what happened. Something went wrong, and no one knows who was to blame because all the participants that we know of were either killed or killed themselves before they would tell me everything. I allowed them into my home to scare her into confessing, but they used my trust to destroy me. I loved her ..."

"Don't act like you deserve to be pitied after what you have done. And you know damn well one of them is still alive, Rowen Rodecker."

"I don't know who you are talking about. I have never heard that name before."

"Rowen Rodecker, the man with the steel toed boots? The man with the skull and cross bones engraved on the metal so he can leave it imprinted into your skin when he kicks you to death." My father looks at me as if I have lost my mind; he clearly has no idea who I am talking about.

"Dace, I promise you, I expect nothing from you, but yes, I would love to get your forgiveness. I have tried every day since to make it up to you both. I have protected you both like you were my own. No matter what you think, I fell in love with you the first moment I laid eyes on you."

"Oh, well thank you so much for not throwing the orphans out on the street after you had their mother slaughtered. How gracious you are."

"I don't expect you to forgive me, but I am telling you the truth. Someone changed the orders to have your mother, Antony, and you killed. All I know is they were going to use you both to force your mother into telling them who your father was, but they couldn't find you. So she had no reason to confess, and I'm sure she was expecting me home at any time to save her."

"I'm sure she was. Why wouldn't she expect her husband to help her rather than order her execution?"

"I gave her plenty of opportunities to confess to me, and if she had only told me who he was then she would have never been put through that. I did not want to lose her. I loved her, and I know she loved me. We ran into some rough times, and we became distant for a time." He fists his hands out in front of him. "Things were getting better, but I had to know who he was and rid him from our lives so we could move on." He looks up at me. "Don't shake your head at me. You know damn well I cared for you and your brother as I would have if you were mine."

"If you didn't order my mother's execution, then who did, Father?"

"I'm not sure, but I have a guess. I have always thought it was Ettore who changed the order. He and Michael both were well old enough to understand what was happening around them. They heard the arguments, and I'm sure they understood why there was such a gap in between Ettore and you. Michael wanted to protect you, and Ettore hated you both, well hated everyone most of the time. Michael talked me into sending you away to your aunt's because Ettore asked him to help kill you. We were sure he would find a way. What was I to do? Punish my son for his anger, when I was the one that caused it? He was only reflecting my emotions. I couldn't bring your mother back, but I could protect my sons and hers and try to bring them together one day. But it seems that's not going to happen."

"So Michael and Ettore know that we are only half-brothers?"

He nods. "And did you ever find out who my father was?" He looks away from me with a slight cringing at the corner of his eyes and I realize he does know.

"Dace, don't do anything stupid," Michael yells, running up on us from out of nowhere.

He grabs hold of me for no reason, "Let go of me." I break from him, staring at them both. "How did you know we were here, Michael?" I ask as I look over at our father who seems just as shocked as I am.

"I followed him. I have been worried about him since the attack. He hasn't been making a lot of sense lately. I'm worried about you, Father. Your mind isn't what it used to be. He has been inventing stories. I can't imagine what he has told you, Dace. I think it's time we talk about putting you in a safe, secure place for your own protection, Father," Michael says. My father suddenly retreats from us.

"Where are you going? You owe me a name!" I yell after him as he begins to run to his car. "Who is my father?!"

"Dace, get down!" Michael dives on top of me and pushes me to the ground as a car drives by and begins shooting.

"No!" I scream as I watch my father take on bullet after bullet before finally falling to the ground. Once the car is gone, I race to his side and pick up his head. "I only wanted to please you, do good so you would want me home, but you never called me home. No matter how good of grades I got, no matter how well I did in sports, none of it mattered, you never wanted me. At least tell me who my father is, you owe that much."

He stares at me and reaches out to place his bloody hand on my face. "I did already." He gasps gripping my hand until he dies.

My own body becomes limp until I see Michael lying on the ground. "Michael!"

I race to his side as he cringes. "Motherfucker, I swear this hurts like a son of a bitch." He holds his shoulder as blood gushes from it.

"Hold on. I'll call for an ambulance."

"I didn't want him to tell you, Dace."

"I should have been told a long time ago."

"Maybe. He was wrong for what he did, but he did love you Dace, and so do I. Please don't let what he did push you away. You and Antony are the only family I truly have. Damn, I told him to stop sneaking out without guards, especially after the ambush the other day."

"Just be still, Michael. We can talk later." He sits back, seeming somewhat comforted by me not leaving his side and not forcing him to let go of my hand. *How can I argue with him when he just risked his life to save mine?*

I'm back at the hospital, signing papers for my father when he isn't really my father. Michael managed to get shot in the right place and should recover easily from his wound. He asked me to stay with him, although I don't know why. His entourage showed up soon after we arrived and haven't left his side for a minute. I really don't want to be here. I'm not sure where I want to be though. I can't think of anywhere that would feel like home except with ... *sigh*.

"I want to make a statement from the hospital so I can thank them for being so helpful in my recovery. Let's also have a picture of my father available to distribute to the press. Dace, do you mind describing the events for everyone? In your own words, of course," Michael asks with his arm in a sling and apparently no loss of energy.

"I'm not really the speech giving type of person, Michael."

"It's easy. If you want, we can have something written up for you to say."

"I got to go." I walk out with my head down and run right into Austin.

"Are you okay? When they said a Colletto had been killed, I was afraid …"

"No, it was my father or, as it turns out, the man who pretended to be my father all these years."

"What?"

"Before he died, my father confessed that Antony and I are bastard children from a man my mother was having an affair with. Oh and that he was the one who gave the order to have her killed. Oh, no, I'm sorry, he actually said that he only wanted to scare her into telling who her lover was but someone changed the order to have not only my mother killed but Antony and I too. I think he was trying to tell me that one of my brothers wants me dead, only I am not entirely sure which one." Austin focuses on me with so much concern in her eyes that I begin to calm. "Don't look at me that way. I don't want to calm down. I want to stay angry."

"Why?"

"Because if I stay angry then the truth won't hurt so much," I confess.

Austin places a hand on my face. "Oh Dace, it's not fair, I know. I wish I could say something to make it better."

I look her over once and then look away. "Michael is in there, but he is busy planning his next press statement." She sighs exhaustively, and I give her a quick glance, noticing her pain nearing the surface.

"You better go tend to your husband. I need to get home anyway."

"Are you going to be okay going home by yourself?" she asks.

I actually laugh, "Yeah, I'm a big boy. I can get there all by myself."

"Dace, someone tried to kill you, not once, but twice now. Do you think they are just going to give up?"

"I'm fine, Austin. Thanks for the concern." I walk away from her, shaking my head. I can't believe she actually would suggest I would need someone to look out for me. Even if I did, who's going to do it? No sooner do I take off on my bike do I notice that I am being followed. I speed forward and edge through traffic, trying to lose them, but whoever it is takes a short cut and ends up at my place, waiting for me. Fuck this. I park my bike and get off with my gun in hand and walk towards the car, waiting to be attacked. Hell, maybe I want it. Maybe I have had enough of this fucked up world. Once I step near the fender of the car, Aaron gets out.

"You know I should arrest you for reckless driving, asshole."

"Why are you following me?" I ask him.

"I'm your protection."

"Did my brother ask for that?"

"No. My sister did. I refused at first, then she said that you're not actually a Colletto. My happy dancing feet couldn't stop me from giving you my congratulatory smile." I start to open my mouth. "No wait, here it is …" The idiot smiles wide with teeth and all before doing some type of jig in the middle of the street. "The dance was a little extra something special I threw in just for you."

He's an idiot. "Thanks, I appreciate it."

"No problem," Aaron says, erasing his smile and leaning against his car, back in work mode within an instant. "I wasn't doing much anyway but sitting with my partner. It's sad talking to him that way."

I don't know what to say to him. It's not like I know him all that well, but I don't exactly feel like being alone right now. "Do you want to come up and have a drink?" He points to himself in shock. "Yes you, you fool."

"Alright." Aaron follows me up, watching me closely as well as every corner we pass.

"Are you nervous about something?" I ask him.

"You can never be too careful, even with an ex-Colletto."

"Fair enough." I show him in and make us both a drink. Everything feels less awkward when you have a drink in your hand.

"So you're the guy my sister is in love with ... huh? How did you get her to do that? Being a Colletto and all, she would have never came near you?"

"I didn't tell her who I was, and I didn't know she was a cop."

"Ah, lying before the relationship even gets started. Haven't you ever been told that's not the way to start? It could cause some problems." He smiles.

"Funny. So how did you end up with that woman, Jamee? Don't tell me you didn't sleep with her because she was too obsessed with you and way too easy for you to have not."

He sours quickly. "It was a party for a friend and a lot of alcohol and she was my ride home."

"No kidding," I laugh.

"I know. I should not be glad that a cop was killed, but if she wasn't dead, I would kill her myself. I still can't believe she set Austin up to be killed. You know, not all cops are dirty. I'm sure you don't believe that, but I don't really care. Some of us actually believe in helping people and making a difference."

"A difference? That could mean a lot of things. My family has made a difference for years." Aaron watches me as I take a drink, and I know he wants to ask me something but, for some reason, is holding back. "What?"

"You're not like them, now I see it. Huh. I thought Austin was just hooked on your dick. That maybe you had one huge motherfucker. But no, it's that you are ... um what's the word, you know, somewhat respectable."

"Somewhat?" I ask.

"Well you still haven't rescued my sister from that dickhead she's married to."

"Michael is not that bad."

"Bullshit. I swear that fuck was the one that kidnapped me and beat the shit out of me looking for that notebook Austin had. Not to mention, it gave him a great way to get her to marry him."

"I can't imagine Michael doing that. Ettore, on the other hand, wouldn't hesitate."

"Ettore would have killed me, not release me as a wedding gift."

"You don't understand how our family works. Michael is in charge. If he tells Ettore he has to do something, then Ettore has to do it whether he wants to or not. Otherwise, our father denounces him and he has no shot at taking over."

"So Michael could also tell Ettore he has to kidnap me and help him trick my sister into marrying him and in the process make sure you're nowhere near to keep her from doing so." I look over at him, and he nods. "He's been after her ever since he saw her, and I knew it soon as I saw how he looked at her. He's all sweet and handsome and beautiful on TV, but he's nothing but a wolf in sheep's clothing. She doesn't belong with him, and you know it. So why haven't you done anything about it?"

"He's my brother, and I owe him my life, not just once but twice now. He deserves to be happy."

"And she doesn't?" he says bluntly. "Listen, I need to go. I have to get some sleep tonight." Aaron gives me a quick nod goodbye and walks out, leaving me the way he wanted—thinking about Austin.

CHAPTER 30

Austin

Michael sits up and motions for me to come to him as soon as I step in the room. "Hello, Baby. Thank you for coming, but you shouldn't have worried."

"Of course I should. When I heard that you were shot, how could I not?" I smile, kissing him with a squeeze of his hand. He instantly pulls me into bed with him and curls around me.

"Oh you two are so cute together," Monica, his assistant, says with a gasping envy. "Well let me leave the two love birds to themselves, but one thing before I go, Michael. The party is in three days. Would you like for me to make calls and have it postponed?"

"No, it's important for people to know I am okay and ..."

"And more than strong enough to handle anything anyone throws at him," I say, remembering something my father would always say.

"Exactly!" Michael laughs, kissing my cheek.

"Well alright then, I will make sure everything is still ready to go for Saturday night," Monica says and waves her goodbye before leaving us alone.

The sudden quiet makes me nervous. I am not really sure how to comfort him after his father died, but I should say something. "I'm sorry about your father, Michael."

Lying back in bed, he pulls me down with him. "Thank you, but the old man was starting to go senile anyway. It's probably best that he go out like he did, not lying on his death bed unaware of the life going around him. Let's talk about you."

"Me? You're the one with the traumatic day."

"True, so I should get what I want, and I want to concentrate on you." He sits up and leans over me with yearning. His approach is soft and slow as he leans down on top of me, taking in my lips, one after the other. "I love you, Austin," he says suddenly. He looks over my face waiting for me to say something back, but I can't say something that I don't feel. My stunned expression doesn't please him. "It's alright, I guess I can't expect you to say it so soon, but I promise, after this election, we are going to spend some quality time together, and then we can make plans to move into the governor's mansion together."

"Oh, Mr. Colletto, you are so sure of yourself."

"Of course, who would vote against me?" he says with a cute, goofy expression. I laugh which makes him happy, a little too happy. He feels over my body, kissing me here and there, pulling my hips into his, and I tell myself over and over to let it happen and maybe, just maybe, it will all be okay after. He has me half undressed when the doctor comes in and interrupts.

"Oh! I'm sorry, but actually, you should probably be taking it easy, Mr. Colletto. We don't want you ripping out your stitches. Plus, I am having the nurse give you some pain killers shortly. The local we gave you is going to wear off soon. After that, you won't be able to do much more than sleep, I'm afraid." He winks at me while I dress myself back into place.

"That is not what I want to hear, Doctor."

"It's probably best Michael. You need your sleep. I'll go and come back first thing tomorrow."

"You can't stay a little while longer? Sage doesn't need you, she is with her grandparents." He grasps my hand with pleading eyes.

I give him a good kiss on the lips and smile. "No, Honey, I think it would be too tempting for you to get into trouble. It's best I remove that option until you feel better."

"Alright be safe." Another quick kiss and a strong, cradling hug and he finally releases me.

I walk away, feeling relief. *Another day, I have made it another day.* The words I say to myself at the end of every day lately. I don't think that's a sign of a happy marriage. I swear off the guards that Michael hired for me and drive around for a couple of hours before I finally stop and find myself at his building, as I guess it is now. I try and tell myself that I'm here to see Preston. I could see if he's up, and maybe if he isn't, then I could check on Dace before I go? It should be ... oh who the hell cares? I need to see him. Life has fucked me over more than a few times lately, so I am going to fuck it right back.

My hand shakes as I reach out to knock, but he opens the door before I can reach it. "Dace ..." I manage to say before he reaches out and grasps my waist. He pulls me into his place and pushes me up against the wall. His lips are on mine instantly. I fist his shirt and hold him to me. "Don't stop." His hands roughly handle my body like a wild horse who has just been released from his restraints. Touching every part of me, he kisses down my neck and pulls out my breast, taking my nipple in his mouth and sucking on my breast with a deep fondling.

He stops long enough to grab my face and stare into my eyes. "I'm sorry ..." he says. I look into his eyes, his tearful eyes, and know ... he loves me. "I need you. Tell me you need me too. Tell me that you still want me?"

I reach out and take off his belt. "I could want nothing more than you," I say, unzipping his pants. I reach down between us and feel his erection fully. The hard flesh in my hands grows tight with my touch, becoming more powerful with every stroke. My ass welcomes his warm hands as my pants fall to the floor. I can't get enough of his mouth, the lips that sway and flow with mine. He does not need to do much more to make me crave him, but he takes control and slides his finger down against my clit and pushes into my pussy with an exhilarating touch that sends me gasping for air. He smiles as he licks his fingers, and I enjoy the happiness in his face as he lifts me up against the wall and slides me down onto his unbending cock with a slow groan of pleasure. I rip through his shirt, kissing him with desperation. "I love you. I love you, Dace."

His tears stream down his face to mine, but he doesn't stop moving. He doesn't stop fucking me, holding me, or kissing my lips with tender bites and heavy breaths. "I shouldn't be with you. I shouldn't be doing this to my brother," he says, moaning against my ear with pleasure and tears all in one. "But I love you so damn much." He lifts me up and back down again, letting me feel every part of his dick swell inside of me. Rubbing it against my clit with every stroke, he grunts as he enters me, I hold onto him even tighter. He fights his demons in front of me, wanting to be loyal to his brother but wanting to love me too. I fear I may lose, and I can't face the madness that would surely come if I do. He puts me down and steps away from me.

"Don't let go of me! Don't, Dace! It's not your fault! I remove my clothing completely and step back to him, nude and ready to enjoy him in every way.

"You understand what you are risking if you're with me, so I'm going to ask you. Do you want to be with me, Austin? If you do, I will make sure you never have cause to be with another man again." No words need to be said. He knew the answer before he asked. He only wanted to make this a united decision.

I wrap my arms around his neck. "Take me to bed, Dace. I belong with you and only you." He only needs one hand to lift me back up on him. He doesn't need the other until he lays me down in his bed and makes love to me without shedding another tear.

I love how he reaches out above my head and grabs the bed posts to get better leverage to thrust into me fully, to give me as much of him as possible. I love watching his muscles flex around me, like a protective barrier from the world. I love his heated breath on my skin and his admiring eyes, smiling at me. I love all of him, every single part. I wrap my arms around him tight as we both come. "I love you," he says, letting his naked body cover me with warmth. I have nowhere to be tonight, so I don't dare leave him, I have no desire to. We fall asleep together, and I finally rest, wrapped safely within his arms.

CHAPTER 31

Dace

My father's funeral is the blackest of black—black cars, black suits and dresses adorned with black hats and sunglasses, along with a black canopy to shield us from the black clouds over our heads. The moment is hardly one to celebrate, but I welcome seeing my brother, my true, full-blooded brother as it is now known. Antony approaches with arms out because we don't hide our feelings for each other. When you only have one person to confide in growing up, you never hide how you feel about them. No, you honor them with obvious respect and love.

"I don't understand, Dace. What happened?" Antony asks.

"I was asking him about our mother, and he admitted that he wanted to hurt her, to get back at her for cheating on him." Antony instantly focuses on me. "Yeah, we are both products of that deceit." His shoulders drop as he gazes down to his shoes. "He ran off before he would tell me much more. And then Michael showed up out of nowhere and pulled me out of the line of fire, but Dad practically ran right into it, it was as if they waited for him." Antony doesn't say much more. Instead, he hides his emotions behind his sunglasses. Dominic Colletto's known eldest sons, Michael and Ettore, walk in ahead of his casket and guide him to his final place of peace while Antony and I follow behind it to guard it against the evils of his past coming back to haunt him, or at least that it is the beliefs behind our ceremonious procedure. In other words, Antony and I will take the fall for his faults and spare the eldest sons so they can live on. It's rather telling of our lives, and without speaking with Antony, I am sure he is beginning to feel how I do— a little fed up with the bullshit. Once the casket is in place, Michael steps up and begins to talk about his father with loving memories and great respect for the man. Towards the end, Ettore is introduced, and he says some brief words of admiration before tossing a rose onto the casket and walking away. Michael follows, then me, and then Antony. We line up side by side with Austin placed behind us. Michael takes her hand and pulls her to his side, and I instantly become jealous, as ridiculous as it may seem. It's a brief moment, while I repeat to myself that we'll be together soon enough. I feel better when Ettore moves out and she slides into his place, brushing against me with a tender touch of my hand. The after gathering is somber, for Antony and me anyway. Michael, as always, is the proper politician, shaking hands and thanking each person for the prayers and concerns for our family. I watch him closely, looking for a reason to hate him, something to make it easier to be able to tell him that the woman he loves is in love with me, and I her. My perfect brother never shows any sign of cracking, except he does have a tight grip on Austin. She looks more miserable than I could have ever imagined her being as the blood from her hand is nearly squeezed out of it. *Damn, Michael! You have to know she is not in love with you. You clearly don't trust her to stay at your side?* Eventually, he lets her go and leaves with some men to talk with Ettore. I take the opportunity to track Austin down and find her shyly socializing with people she has never met before. I walk into the room and feel my heart race, my knees go weak, and there must be a smile a mile long on my face because she looks my way and smiles a very similar smile.

"Better be careful, Dace. People are noticing you both right now." Antony says.

I glance around as people whisper to each other and point at us both. "I don't give a shit about them. None of them, not a single one of them ever gave a shit about either of us, and they certainly don't now."

"So, you are going to steal Michael's wife?"

"No. No I am going to take back what was stolen from me," I say before walking away. Antony chases me down and grabs my arm to force me to look at him.

"What are you planning?"

"Just what I said, Antony. Are you going to help me or are you going to stand against me?"

"You know the answer to that. All I want to do is make sure you know what you are doing. This isn't going to go over well." I

271

don't say a word as he stares into my eyes. "Okay, brother, I'm at your side the whole way."

Michael's pre-election celebration party is an extravagant affair. We are all dressed to the nines, and my tux fits so tight I can barely breathe, or maybe it isn't the tux. Austin was going to tell Michael after the funeral that she doesn't want to be with him, and I haven't heard from her since then. As soon as Antony and I step into the house, I breathe in and don't exhale until I see her smile at me. I slowly make my way through the room until I can stand near her. "How did it go?"

"Surprisingly well. He understood and wants me to be happy, and he doesn't want to be married to someone that doesn't want to be married to him. We are going to file for separation after the election and blame it on the long hours of politics and Michael's dogged pursuit to help the people of his great state," Austin says with a hopeful exhale.

I can hardly contain my smile as I hug her and give her a quick kiss to the cheek. "I love you."

"I love you too," she says, slowly leaving me to be the proper gracious host and wife of a soon to be governor.

I am shocked to know that Michael handled it so well. I guess my fears and anxieties gave way to suspicion of the brother that has never been anything but wonderfully supportive of me. When I spot Antony, he looks so stiff I'm afraid he's going to explode any second. "Hey, are you okay?"

"No, I hate this. I hate being his token gay man, and I hate sitting here feeling I am waiting for something to go wrong."

"I think maybe things are going to be okay," I say to him.

"Oh yeah?" I nod, although he doesn't look the least bit relieved. "Excuse me if I hold off my excitement until we leave here alive?"

"A couple more days. Austin and Aaron have gotten a lead on the man that killed out mothers. Once we have him, we will all get the fuck out of here."

"It can't be soon enough. I hate to say it, but you were right, I should have never come back here."

I guess I shouldn't be surprised. I have pounded into him time and time again not to trust anyone around him and trust his gut the most. "You would have always wondered, and so would have I. Now we know and we can move on to better things." I remind him of our long talk about our new destination and new life waiting for us. We talked about it at length, about what we both want and how we can do it together, and now we are sure how we can. I pat him on the back and stay at his side most of the night until I see Austin take off towards a bathroom. My inability to be patient gets the best of me, and I follow her in, locking the door behind us. "You know this dress is incredibly revealing," I say, admiring the sides of her breasts in the low cut piece. I slip my hand down and grasp her breast fully, enjoying her gasp.

"Why, Mr. Colletto, I don't believe that is yours."

"It's not? I could have sworn you said it was."

"No, I said you could earn it," she says, welcoming my lips on her neck and my hands up her dress.

"I've missed you so much."

"I can tell," she laughs, rubbing my rapidly growing erection. A kiss and a slip of the hand, and before I know it, we are wrapped around each other and forgetting the rest of the world. Laughing, kissing, and holding each other as we talk about what we will do when we are both free from the Colletto family. I could hold her in my arms forever and never want for anything else. It's the most amazing feeling, loving someone so much that you don't want to let them go. I suddenly get a terrible feeling in the pit of my stomach as she tries to leave me to get back to Michael and the party. I hold onto her tighter.

"What's wrong?" she asks, caressing my face. "What's wrong,

Dace?"

I look down into her eyes and hold her face. "Leave with me tonight. Don't leave with him."

"Why? I told you Michael is agreeable, and although sad, he doesn't seem revengeful."

"I don't care what he says or what he seems. Leave with me. I'll take you to your brother's or father's, if you prefer, but don't go home with him. In fact, let's go now," I say with pleading eyes.

"Dace, that's not what we agreed to. I have to get my mother's killer. We almost have him, and you know it. As soon as we find that storage unit that the Martins were keeping, we could have so much more and even a reason to stay."

"Stay?! Austin you said you were happy to go, happy to try something new. Have you changed your mind already?"

"No, I want to be with you, wherever that is, but I will miss being here," she says, making me realize that as much as this city has been my enemy, it has been her home. Running away isn't going to be good enough. We have to leave free and able to return.

"Alright, then I need to figure out which one of my brothers wants me dead and which one is willing to let me live, if there is one. We need to find that storage unit and fast." I sigh and she wraps her arms around me excitedly. Life was so much easier when I only had to please myself. We slip back out to the ballroom where Michael takes the stage and begins making a speech to thank everyone. Austin takes his side, and the crowd applauds while I dream of better days to come.

Searching for something that may not even exist, is exhausting, but when I notice something odd about Mr. Martin's transactions, I dig a little deeper and find my first real lead. "Antony, let's go."

"Where?"

"To the mall."

"What?! But I hate the mall," Antony whines. I shake my head and point the way out for him to lead off to.

When we arrive, he looks at me and rolls his eyes. "This is even worse than I thought. There isn't even a cookie stand in this one," he says as I laugh.

"I'll get you an oatmeal raisin later, freak. Who doesn't prefer chocolate chip?"

"I like to be different, Dace. I'm an individual, and I like oatmeal raisin," he complains, following me into the mall as I search for the place Martin continuously bought a soda.

We walk nearly to the opposite end where there is little, if anything, but a few stores and one, little, sundries stand. "That's it."

"That's what?" I move forward as Antony continues to bug me for information.

I walk up on the guy working the stand who is seemingly more interested in the young girl working the nearby clothing store than any customers that might come by. "Hey!" I say, snapping him to my attention.

"Yeah, what do you want?" The dumbass teenager says with an attitude.

I look at Antony who is instantly as annoyed as I am.

"What do we want? You little shit. Do your fucking job and stop staring at that girl's ass. She doesn't want your raggedy clothes, infected nose ring, backwards hat wearing, scrawny, minimum wage earning ass," Antony says with little humor, but it makes me laugh all the same.

"Says you motherfucker!" he says back to Antony. Antony grabs him and pulls him over the counter. "Hey! What the fuck dude!?"

"I swear I want to hurt you bad."

275

"Antony, okay, I am sure the idiot can help us, so don't kill him yet."

"Kill me?" the kid says as Antony smiles wide and lets his gun flash from underneath his jacket. The kid suddenly finds a more respectful attitude. "What do you guys want? I don't have much cash here, just some nuts and Gatorade. We haven't gotten a new shipment in over a week."

"We don't need any of that. I was wondering about a man that would come here once a week and buy a soda."

The kid starts to say something smart ass when Antony knocks him upside the head. "Owe!"

"Think before you speak fool," Antony says.

I pull out my phone and show him a picture I have of the Martins. "Have you seen this guy?"

"Him? Yeah, he would come here all the time with his luggage, buy a soda, do a zigzag through my girl's store there, walk out, and then walk out that door. Weird guy."

"What's through that door?" I ask him.

"I don't know," he says, earning another smack to the head. "Damn man, what the fuck?"

"Would there happen to be a storage facility near here?"

The kid stares at Antony, watching for another hand smack before turning back to me with bright eyes. "Oh yeah, there is this place you can get to ... and actually you could walk there from here, the closest door would be that door. You would have to walk through the small amount of wooded area there, but I am sure if you really wanted to, you could do it with no problem."

I smile at Antony as he suddenly realizes. "You did well," I say.

"I did?"

"Yeah, you did great," Antony says, taking out some money and handing it to the kid. "Now, go buy yourself some real clothes and take that girl out somewhere decent."

"Oh fuck! Thanks!"

I grab him and pull him back to me. "We were never here, and if anyone else comes here asking about the same man, you don't remember anything. Tell them you smoke a lot of weed."

"I can't smoke weed. I got asthma," he says. I roll my eyes and squeeze his little dumbass a little tighter. "But I get your point."

"Good." Antony and I walk away to go to the storage facility. It's somewhat rundown and hidden back here. I have never even heard of this company. It must be a family owned place. No matter, it's easy to sneak in and get a hold of their records and narrow down the units to a few possibilities before we break in and start looking through them. It's one of three, or maybe all three. We use a few tricks to work through the locks and open them all up. There are boxes and boxes of stuff everywhere, except for in one, which is completely empty. "I think they got here before us."

"I hope they didn't take everything."

"There's only one way to find out." We dig through the other two units, both which prove to be the Martins, but most of it is crap.

"This is going to take forever to go through!" Antony yells.

"We need some help, and I think I know who to call." Aaron shows up with interest but still cautious as he approaches us.

"I don't like meeting you guys alone. What's this about?"

"I told you we found the units that match the key Austin has. One was cleaned out, and the other two are full of …"

"Shit," Antony says.

"What looks to be shit, but maybe within the shit, there is something we can use."

"Alright," Aaron sighs and agrees to help us go through it. He settles in and takes off his coat, which causes Antony to smile too big. I eye him mouthing words I can't say out loud.

"He's so hot," Antony whispers to me.

I dig in and ignore the drooling next to me. We spend hours before Aaron suddenly pops up. "I think I found something." He quickly looks through the rest of the box before grabbing the whole thing and bringing it to the table for us all to look through. "Look at this. It's an arrest report for Michael."

"Michael?" Antony says, grabbing it to look at. "He was caught joyriding with some other kids. This is nothing."

"Look closer. He was arrested with Victor Towns, the man arrested for the murder of my mother and ... the eldest with them was a man named Rowen Rodecker." I grab the report from Antony and look it over.

It all starts to make sense, horrible twisted sense. "There's no way Michael would have had anything to do with that man, or any of this. He's a little high strung, but kill someone's mother or his own mother?"

"No, it makes sense. Michael was the only one that could have changed Father's order. He was old enough and surely knew what was going on. It was him that talked Father into sending us away."

"For our own good, Dace!"

"For our own good? He sent us to the worst place possible, Antony, to be beaten whenever the witch needed an outlet. We were too afraid to say anything because she said no one wanted us and we would be killed otherwise. You don't remember how bad it was because you wanted so bad to believe it was done for our own good, and hell maybe I did too. It wasn't for our own good; it was to torture us, to make our lives as miserable as possible. No one came to visit us but Michael. He had to have seen the bruises on us, but he never said a word to Father. He wanted to make sure we were dejected."

"He brought us toys and played with us and made us feel loved," Antony says.

"And then he left us behind. He's the one that said Ettore had threatened to kill us. No one else heard him say that."

"Are you saying our own brother killed our mother and ..." I nod towards Antony as Aaron steps back and puts and arm around

Antony.

"He's a sick, twisted fuck. I'm telling you. He was the one that took me and he forced Austin to marry him so he could get more control of her and you," Aaron says to me.

"He thinks Billy was her lover, not me," I blurt out without thinking.

Aaron looks me over. "He tried to kill Billy because he thought Austin was in love with him?" *Not even Antony knew that, fuck.* They both stare at me with a million questions look.

"Jamee told Michael about Austin and me, but Father doctored up some pictures and some evidence that proved it wasn't me, that it was Billy instead. He had already suspected Billy, so it was easy to convince him."

"Oh my God, Dace!" Antony yells, fisting his hair and walking around the room. "He's going to fucking kill you. He's going to torture you to death and then kill you. There's no way he is going to let Austin go." We all look at each other realizing the same thing.

"Well, now we know two things: Rowen works for Michael and we have to kill them both if we want to live," Aaron says.

I don't know who else to go to other than Ettore. I have never approached him before for help, and it feels odd to do so now, but what choice do I have? Besides, I need to know who all is against me. I am hoping I don't have enemies coming from both sides.

Ettore sits down, looking me over, clearly searching for some understanding for why I am there. "I know about our mother and that Michael changed the order to have her killed," I say bluntly. He leans back with his eyebrows raised. "How much did you know, Ettore?"

"I knew how angry he was. He believed in perfection, even then. Of course, Father only encouraged it. Michael could do no wrong. Michael would knock the shit out of me, and it would be my fault." Ettore raises his sleeve to show me a terrible scar. "The fuck had his friends hold me down while he burned me."

"Why?"

"To force me to tell Father it was my fault that the order was changed. I didn't but I didn't deny either. I have built up as much as I can to try and prevent him from getting the upper hand on me again. Yet, he still finds a way to be one step ahead of me. He killed Father, you know?" I nod, realizing it the more I find out about my brother. "I'm surprised he let you two live as long as you have. You should have seen how angry he was when Father was bragging about all your abilities. It made me want to protect you just to piss him off. Then the fuck blew up my guy. I had to scramble hard to try and find a new way to launder my money. It nearly cost me everything!" Ettore slams his fist on the desk in front of him. "I'm not sure why you are here, but I can't help you much."

"Much?"

Ettore roll his eyes. "If you want to get out of town quick, then let me know. Outside of that …"

"What if I can help you get Michael?" He looks me over with doubt. "You don't have to make any promises. All I want to know is that you won't come after me while I get him." Ettore looks away, considering. "Remember, I'll know if you lie to me."

He laughs, "I will promise not to come after you while Michael is still in power if you promise the same?" He clearly chose his words carefully, but I will take it for now. One brother at a time is better than worrying about them both at the same time. "Deal?" Ettore holds out his hand to me, and I take it.

"Deal. But don't think I didn't notice that you agreed for only while Michael is in power."

"It's a tough world, Dace, I have to keep up the pace just like everyone else, so stay out of my way, and we won't have a problem, ever."

CHAPTER 32

Dace

I wake up unsure of the time but quickly realize the woman in my arms. Feeling down her bare back and over her ass, I wrap my arms around her and pull her in close. I know I need to say goodbye. Michael will be looking for her soon, and she can't be found here. "Austin, you have to get back to Michael," I whisper.

"No, just a few minutes longer," she says, burying herself into my chest.

"We are so close. With the information we have on Michael now, all we have to do is let it leak to the media and make sure he doesn't win the election. Then, we can start bringing him down for good. Antony has already mailed a package to one of the most obnoxious reporters in the city."

"Justin Lohan? Really, I can't stand him. He has always been in the middle of things and trying to make the police out to be idiots."

"He's also not afraid to say shit about anyone, including my brother. He is all about his own fame. He is even more self-centered than Michael."

Austin sighs. "It's becoming harder and harder to get away from Michael; I think he is having me followed."

"I wouldn't doubt it. Please be careful. I would really prefer you move out of there and stay anywhere else."

"Ah, Baby, don't worry about me. You know I can handle myself. I only need a few more things. I am getting a lot of information out of the staff without them realizing. They will talk endlessly if they don't think it means anything, and you know I'm good at asking questions." She smiles, and I laugh at the nutcase.

I kiss her with a soft touch. "Okay, you do what you need to, but I can't stand the thought of you two even pretending to be intimate. I can only imagine he isn't making it easy on you." She looks back up at me with a painful expression. "I'm sorry. I'm sorry about it all, but I promise it will all be over soon, as soon as he loses the election, there will be no reason to continue the charade any longer. I would prefer you out of there before then though."

"Okay, Baby. I will pack tonight and move in with my father. I will tell Michael he is sick and needs to be cared for. If my father doesn't look sick enough, I will feed him rat poison until he does," she says with a smile.

"You're scary."

"I was only kidding, but I have thought about it once or twice."

"And what would you do to me if I made you mad?"

She bites her bottom lip with a moan. "Oh the things I would do to you. I would tie you up, strip you naked, and beat you until you surrendered, and then I would fuck you so hard you would be too exhausted to get out of bed for days."

"Oh, then what can I do to make you mad?" I laugh. Her laugh lightens my mood and brings out my playfulness. Nuzzling through her hair, I kiss her face and wander down to her bountiful breasts, enjoying myself immensely.

She giggles, rubbing the back of my head. "Alright handsome...," she says, pulling my head up from her breasts, "I don't think you're supposed to be convincing me to stay."

I groan, looking her over and wanting to do so much more. "But you have something I need, and I can't get through the day without it. I neeeeeed it ..." I dive underneath the sheets and find her sweet spot. "Mmmm." I stop when one of my alarms go off. Jumping out of bed, I check my monitors and scramble. "Fuck!" I quickly call Antony, tell him to get the hell out of town and to step up his efforts to find my friends and quick. We are going to need them sooner than expected. After sending a quick, secure message to Aaron, I grab some clothes for us both to get dressed. "Austin, come with me." I grab her arm and pull her into my secret room with me. I shut the door and lock down the rest of the space so no one can get in. The rest of my things will just have to be vulnerable. Typing away on my computer, I make it as difficult as possible for them to get in, but it only deters them for a little while. They blow through my front door and instantly begin looking for me, turning the whole place upside down. I manage to save one camera from being destroyed and see the man we have been looking for. Austin looks over my shoulder with wide eyes. I motion for her to be quiet. We sit quietly with each other as they continue to search through my things and wait for me to return home. Aaron somehow manages to clear them out with a fire alarm that sends half the fire stations in the city in and searching through the building thoroughly. We sneak out with the crowd, and I send Austin away with Aaron. "They want me, not you. So go with your brother. Don't you dare go back to that house," I say to her.

"Dace, where are you going to go?"

"I need to go turn in a favor from Ettore. Once I get that done, I will come and find you, and we need to leave for a while. Only for a while, okay?" She nods. I kiss her and send her away with her brother. I check in with Antony and make sure he has moved out of his current location to another we talked about. My place is clearly being watched, so I have to somehow get to Ettore and hope he will still let me use his plane to escape this city.

Walking up to Ettore's gate, I nervously ask to be let in. After some frustrated sighs, I am permitted inside. Everything is quiet, and as soon as the door shuts behind me, I know I have made a mistake. Ettore walks through the room and sighs at me but doesn't say a word. Then Michael rounds the corner.

"Hello, Dace. I have been looking for you."

Justin Lohan walks out with a smile and looks me over. "This is your brother? I would have thought he would have looked a lot more like you."

"Well, he is only a half-brother. My good friend Justin said he got a package about me and it had all kinds of terrible accusations in it."

"It had the truth—you're a monster."

"Ahhh, don't be like that. I was hoping we could end on better terms."

"Fuck you!" I say to him, and he simply smiles and walks away.

The door behind him shuts, and I look up and see three men coming in from another direction, ready with weapons and fierce intentions. I slip my jacket off quickly and steady myself. I dodge a bat aimed at my head and grab it, breaking it over another guy's back. I knock another into a wall and break his jaw and his knee. With one left, they send in three more. I handle one and run out of the way of the others. I begin to plan my way out of the house as I fight one off and then another two. I feel pretty good about my chances when I get out the door with car keys in my hand until the door opens and Michael walks out with his arm around Austin's neck. "Look, Honey. Look how tough my little brother is?" Austin looks dazed and a little beat up. "Believe it or not, all we had to do was have one of our police friends send out a call that a man, of your height and build, was being beat to death, and she came running. When she arrived, my sweet, loving wife put up quite a fight, which was fun for me to watch for a little while, but then I grew tired, so I had her shot." I step forward. "Don't worry, she's not hurt. My men shot her with a tranquilizer. I be damn if it didn't take two in order to get her to stop fighting us."

"Let her go, Michael. This is between you and me, no one else."

"Oh, I disagree. Considering you have been fucking my wife, I would say it has everything to do with you both." Michael waves his men down, but I stay on guard. "After everything I did for you, you want to steal the woman I love, you fucking bastard?"

"Don't fuck with me, Michael. You were the one that changed that order Father gave. You ordered our mother to be killed along with me and Antony," I say, trying to get him to admit it while watching Ettore from his balcony listening in.

He laughs. "Of course, I did. She was a fucking whore with two bastard children that we were supposed to welcome into our home as our own? No, I wasn't going to stand for it. He shouldn't have stood for it, but he didn't have the balls to kill her. He said he still loved her. How can you love a woman that does that? She's nothing but trash at that point." Austin tenses. "Easy Honey, I have a special deal for you and my brother that will keep you both alive for a while. Now, clearly, my brother could easily take my men with no problem and most likely escape with ease; however, you can't sweetheart. Hell, you can barely stand, so if Dace here wants to surrender himself to my men, then I'm willing to make a deal for your life to be spared." My brother looks like the monster only nightmares form. His demonic smile and wild eyes are nothing of the brother I admired and loved.

I shake my head. "Why would I believe you? Why would you keep her alive knowing she would turn on you the first chance she gets?"

"Oh, well that's the beauty of my plan. You see, you surrender to save her life and she surrenders to spare yours." Michael kisses her cheek. "Yeah… see I want more kids, and she is going to give them to me, willingly …" I stare at him in horror as Austin groans. "…eventually. For now, all I want is the perfect wife at my side when I win the election and attend the celebratory events. I assume children will come when she finally comes around and gives up on you." I shake my head in disbelief. "Let's see if this Stockholm syndrome is a real thing," Michael says to Rowen who steps out of the house, chewing gum and kicking his steel toed boots against the stone façade.

"They both look like their mothers," Rowen says.

"They do actually, especially Austin here. Her mother was a good fuck too." I watch her cringe as Michael admits something we didn't even know. He was the attacker that got away, or rather was let go by someone on the payroll. "She fought like hell too. I love that about a woman. I have wanted to find out about this one ever since I saw her. Can't wait actually, and I am more than happy to let you go Dace and enjoy my girl here for a little while before handing her over to my friends, to fuck her to death."

"No, Michael, how could you hate this much? What about Sage?" I ask him, hoping Austin can get enough control of her body again to get away from the men holding her.

"Don't talk about my daughter, you lying bastard! You are nothing but trash and will never be anything more than that. Still, I have a heart, so here's the deal. You surrender, Dace, and Austin will live, and if Austin here agrees to be my loving wife, then you will live too, not well, but you will live."

I stare at Austin as she stares at me, shaking her head. She suddenly breaks free and slams her knee into one man and fights with another as I move into help her. I get her hand and try to run, but she exerted every ounce of energy she had fighting and falls to the ground. "Austin!" I yell, diving to the ground for her.

"Run, Dace, run!" she yells at me.

"I'm not leaving you, not ever," I say taking her in my arms as Michael watches on.

Michael's men surround us as he walks up. "Well, that was fun. Now what's it going to be? Because, frankly, I am getting hungry, and it's way past my dinner time."

Austin holds my hand, still begging me to run, but I can't. "I'll surrender, Michael. Just let her go. She won't say a word, who would believe her over you anyway? Let her go. You don't want someone that doesn't want you." I release Austin from my arms.

"Dace no, please no," Austin cries to me.

I step forward, dropping my weapon and the car keys, and close my eyes. I don't have to see Michael enjoy the moment that is coming. I can hear his excitement in his eager gasp. "Argh!" I scream out as Michael's men take turns striking me with their fists and hitting me with whatever they can find. They find their own enjoyment in the payback. My ribs crack, my jaw twists, and I begin to choke on my own blood, waiting to die.

"Dace!" Austin screams for me. "Stop, Michael!" They drop me at her side. Austin takes hold of my head and cradles me. "Stop please! Please!" I can barely see her through my swollen eyes, but her tender touch is comforting enough as I believe these are my last minutes of life.

"Strike him again," Michael orders as Austin is pulled away from me. I scream out again as my leg is broken in two.

"*Stop!*" Austin cries out. "I'll do whatever you want. Please just stop. Don't hurt him anymore."

I twist the best I can to search for her and try to argue, but all I can see is Michael's smiling face. "Now isn't this a great moment. He surrenders himself for her, and she surrenders herself for him, now that's love. I wouldn't have believed that you two loved each other so much. I thought you were just fucking. I tried everything with you Austin. I was as nice and as sweet as I could be, yet you still fucked him. I even considered cutting off his dick, but now I know that probably wouldn't have worked either because you two are actually in love. How sweet and yet very useful to me. Say goodbye, Sweetheart. We have a life to build or, maybe, we can consummate the marriage finally? Oh that might be fun. Do you want to watch, Dace?" He leans over me and grabs me by the hair. "What do you say?"

"Fuck you," I breathe hard.

"That's a no then? Oh well, this isn't exactly the nicest of places to fuck anyway. Don't worry, I'll make sure you are aware when it happens."

"You son of a bitch!" I try to crawl to her as she tries to get away from the men surrounding her. "No," I groan. Austin's cries become louder. "Austin!"

I feel her hand briefly before I hear her dragged away and shoved into a car. The harder I try to move, the more pain I am subjected to. My only relief from this hell is when the pain becomes too much and I pass out. I wake up briefly as they put me in a truck and drive me away from Ettore who can barely look at me.

CHAPTER 33

Antony

I waited for Dace to call, hoping for the best, but the call never came. I knew Michael had him, and I had to do something. It's been a really bad week, but then I finally got the call I had been waiting for. Dace's friends come through and fly into the States to meet me. I give them the information I know and hope they can help me find out the rest.

"His own brother is holding him hostage? What kind of fucked up family is this? No wonder he was running away from them. Why in the hell did he even come back?" Peter asks. I instantly assume the guilty stance. "Oh, you're the brother that called." Peter steps to my side and puts an arm around my shoulders. "Well don't worry, Heartbreak, we will get him out."

"How?"

"You worry about giving us as much information as you can on your brother Michael, and we will handle the rest. What we need right now is to know where Dace was staying?"

"Oh I'm sure they have taken over his place already and cleaned it out of anything of value," I say, but Peter laughs.

"Knowing Dace, I doubt that. I am sure they have tried, but they have given up finding what we are needing."

"Alright, I can take you there, but I can't guarantee my brother won't have people there waiting for me."

"If there are, do you mind distracting them while we access Dace's computer?" I stare at him with wide eyes. He laughs hard with everyone following him. He slaps me on the back. "I'm just kidding. You need to loosen up. Everything is going to be okay. You can only do what you can do, no reason to stress about what is out of your control."

They somehow gain access to Dace's place and his system with no problem; there is apparently a secret code between them. It is all very impressive, but it will be even more so if they get Dace back safely.

"So who is this woman?" Leandra asks, pointing out a picture of Dace and Austin together at the cabin.

"She's the police chief's daughter."

"Then why can't he get his own daughter?"

"Because Michael owns him too, so much so that he would probably kill his own daughter for him. He is not exactly above sacrificing his daughter for his own skin. His son he might sacrifice for, but not his daughter."

"What a dead motherfucker he is going to be," she says, only I am not sure who she is talking about—Michael or Austin's father. "She's really kind of scary," I mumble as a man comes at my side laughing.

"Yeah, she is, but that didn't stop Dace from fucking her." He laughs when I look back at her in shock.

"Antony, come here. I want you to look at these plans," Peter says, motioning me over to him. I walk over and only to see Michael's house plans. I'm impressed that they managed to get them so fast. "We think Dace is being held in the basement over here? Do you know anything about this area?"

"How do you know he's there?"

"We tapped into some secret military … anyway you don't want to know things that could be held against you later, just know we heard him with some really cool technical shit."

"So he's still alive?" I ask, suddenly having hope of seeing him again.

"Yes, he is alive for sure. Not doing well, but alive," Peter says, patting me on the back.

"I don't know much about Michael's security or his house except that he has twenty-four, seven security on that place. There are cameras everywhere; however, there is a servant's entrance at the kitchen. They deliver food and things at that entrance all the time."

"Good," he says happily.

I have never been more nervous in my life; however, none of Peter's crew seem the least bit on edge. It's somewhat comforting, yet I'm concerned that they may not understand the severity of what they are about to face. Fidgeting with my hands and pacing from one spot to the other, I wait for them to get all they need in order and tell me what my role is in all of this, all the while having one of their men check for me to see if Dace is still alive, and he is. I know Michael has no reason to leave him alive so why is he? Unless, he is trying to draw me in to come get him. He must know that I would never leave my brother. Maybe Ettore is helping him after all, which is even scarier. What does he have to gain by ever helping Dace and me, except problems?

"Are you ready?" Peter asks, causing me to jump when he pats me on the back. "Easy there, Heartbreak. Everything is going to be okay. We know what we are doing."

"I hope you understand that my brothers are very used to handling attacks; they are well-prepared for anything that might come at them," I say to him, waiting for him to reassure me somehow.

Peter smiles wide and puts his arm around my shoulders. "You see all these people, Antony? They have encountered every possible situation there is; they have been to every country in every fucked up situation you can imagine, and yet, we still come out of it with our goal achieved and ready to move on to the next task. We know what our enemy is going to do before they even consider doing it. Trust me, we got this." I nod, and he begins nudging me with a smile until I smile back. "Now you are going with Thomas over there. You are going to lead him through the house while we communicate with him through an earpiece about the comings and goings of the guards."

"Don't I get an earpiece? Maybe I should be told of the plan or have some kind of idea of what we are doing?"

"No, we will communicate with you and let you know what to do through Thomas, so don't lose him." I am suddenly feeling more nervous about things. "Now you know how to take on bullets, don't you? How many do you think you can take before you can't move any longer?" I look at him with wide eyes. "I'm just kidding," he laughs with a roar.

"Ha ha, that's so funny. So I will be taking my gun for sure." I load up my weapon before piling into the car with Thomas.

Our driver stops and lets us out near a warehouse where food trucks are driving in and out. Thomas presses a small computer to a fence lock that then opens and allows us onto the company grounds. He leads me into the building and grabs a hat for me and places one on his head as well. We keep moving and never bother to stop, even as employees pass us. I continue following him right, left, and down a hall and then left down another until we come to a loading dock where trucks are lined up and parked. Thomas grabs a clip board on our way in and reads it quickly as we keep moving. He then tosses it into a nearby trashcan before moving even faster. "Take this," he says, handing me a box. I take it and continue following him as he picks up a box himself and shows me a truck to load onto. We blend in and continue help loading a particular truck until they are nearly ready to go. Thomas looks around briefly and pushes me back into the truck and shuts the door. "Get in that cooler there." I look at the container and look back at him as if he is crazy. "Don't worry. You can do it, and it won't be for long. Our stop is the first one." He helps me in and shuts the container around me. I hope that he isn't outside laughing at the gullible idiot in the box. Thankfully, Thomas was right. I don't have to stay in long before he is helping me out of it again. We step out of the truck, and I find us right at Michael's service entrance. We wait for a signal and then move inside to an out of the way corner. It is late at night, and I am wondering if we can find our way around in the dark. Damn Michael and his issues with seeing service people. Thomas grabs me and pushes me ahead. "Lead the way." I walk through from one room to the next until we come to a sitting room where Michael is still up and talking to someone.

"I am about ready for bed, I called in someone to relieve my stress unless you want to take care of it for me?"

"I would rather you just shoot me," Austin says.

"Oh, Darling, I can't possibly do that. I am having way too much fun." There is a long silence of groans and nervous tension, when I hear a kiss. "Goodnight, be sure to get plenty of sleep. I need you looking especially bright and lovely tomorrow for a press event." Michael leaves the room and goes upstairs.

Austin walks out soon after and right past us. Thomas reaches out and takes hold of her arm, covering her mouth at the same time as she begins to struggle. I step in front of her to quickly get her to settle down before we all get caught. I press my finger to my lips, and she calms down instantly. I motion for her to come with us, and she does, but when we begin to take one set of stairs, she stops us and shakes her head. She points to a blinking light and Thomas follows the wire from underneath the first step.

"It's every other one and dead center, so step to the right side of all; just to be sure they stay consistent," he whispers. We both nod and go ahead of him down the stairs. Austin seems to know where to go, so we follow her, slowly. She stops and pats the door in front of us that is obviously locked. Thomas listens for a second to his earpiece and then takes out a small box and begins working the heavy door with some equipment I have only seen Dace carry. I suddenly begin to wonder what all he has gotten into since he left college. When the door opens, Austin starts to run in, but Thomas stops her and feels around the inside edge of the doorframe. He smiles wide and jerks out a wire before having us move in. Austin runs in and hovers over a blanketed pile on the floor or what I thought was a pile of blankets. It is actually Dace, badly beaten and barely conscious.

"They beat him every day. They stop just short of killing him," she says, pulling him into her arms.

I lean down and look at his bruised face and am surprised that he opens his eyes.

"Hey Antony, nice of you to visit. I would offer you a drink, but I feel like shit. You didn't happen to bring a bottle of something did you?"

I laugh, but Thomas pulls one out and hands it to Austin to help him drink. "Alright, Antony, I need you to be a decoy and run out of the house to a car waiting for us on the other side of the gate."

"Ummm... that doesn't sound good for me."

"Don't worry, we've got it handled. You go out the front door running, and whatever happens, don't stop and don't look back. We are going to go out the side and hide in the food truck that's leaving." I nod and look at the stairs considering when he pulls me back. "Make sure you run fast though." He smiles and shoves me ahead. I step outside the door, take a deep breath, and ... run. I run through the house and out the front door, triggering every alarm there is, exciting every dog, and setting off every motion light as I become the highlighted idiot running down the front lawn. *Damn it! I should have taken a drink before I went. This would be so much better drunk.* I look out and see the car waiting for me and get excited until the guns start firing. "Motherfucker! I hate this! I hate this! I fucking hate this! Oh how I fucking hate this!" I sing all the way out the slowly closing gate and into the waiting car. I slide in and breathe.

"That went well, don't you think?" Peter says with a nod.

"No, I don't. If I had known I was going to be a guinea pig, then I would have suggested another plan."

"That's exactly why we didn't tell you."

As we sit, Peter stares out at the house. I poke my head out and watch as Michael comes out with Sage in his arms and a crew of men surrounding him. The alarms are turned off, and I step out of the car and make eye contact with Michael as he smiles wide. *He's up to something.* "Peter, he's up to something. Where is Dace? I don't see the food truck, where is it?"

"Don't worry. They'll make it—I know it."

Michael hands Sage off to a woman who takes her and puts her in a car. He walks slowly towards me and stops short as his men keep him from coming too close to us. "Nice to see you again, Antony. I'm sorry to hear about your loss," he says with an emerging sinister smile. He raises his phone up, "Now," he says, and instantly, half the house explodes while the other is rapidly engulfed in flames.

"Dace!" I scream. Peter and two of his men take hold of me and push me back into the car. Michael points at me and fires his fake gun as if to say I'm next. They hold me down in the car as we drive off to some place I don't know about. It seems like we are in the car forever. The silence is killing me. When a rush of adrenaline comes over me, I sit up in a rage. "Take me back and let me kill that fuck!" No one pays attention to me. "Take me back! Take me back!"

"There is no need, Antony," Peter says calmly.

I stare at him, remembering my brother, and slowly breathing in and out, and in, and out, and in … what do I do now?

EPILOGUE

Antony

You worry so much about the thorn that keeps stabbing you and drawing the trickles of blood from your body that you never pay attention to the cancer that grows inside, slowly creeping through your veins and into your head until it controls not only your body, but your mind as well. The cancer feeds off of you until there is nothing left, and it has no use for you any longer ... then you're dead. The only way to prevent death is to trick the cancer and make it think you're already dead.

Michael stands at a podium, thanking everyone for electing him before taking a moment to shed a tear, "I am honored to be your Governor, and I promise to serve you well. I have experienced great sadness in my life, losing my mother in a home invasion, losing my first wife and son in a car accident, my father in a drive by, and now my wife and brother in a horrible fire, but I won't let tragedy defeat me. I will overcome my sadness with the help of my existing family and friends and with all the love that has been showered upon me by all of you," he announces with applause. "You are my strength, and I will be yours!" I shake my head in disgust.

"Mr. Colletto, he is waiting for you," Phillip says from behind me.

"Thank you," I say, turning the TV off. I approach his door and come face to face with Peter as he is walking out. "How is he today?"

"Pissed off and horny as hell, so I wouldn't stay in there too long. You might see some things you don't want to," Peter says, sliding a cigar into his mouth with a smile.

"So, I take it she is with him already this morning?"

"She never left him." He nods, walking away.

I take hold of the doorknob and take a deep breath. I walk in and smile wide when I see them in bed kissing and holding each other as a couple should. "You look much better these days," I say.

He sits up and opens up his arms wide to me and shows me love as he always has, with respect. "You should have run and left me, but I am damn glad you came back to get me. Although, my getaway could have been a little less bumpy."

"Don't blame me. I didn't make the plan. Hell, I didn't even know the plan until it was all over, which sucked by the way. I was ready to go back and kill him with my bare hands. If I had known they already knew he was going to blow the fucking place up and had planned to sabotage the cameras so they thought you were still down there struggling to be carried out instead of exiting out the opposite side of the estate dressed as one of his guards, then I would have felt a little better about things."

"Trust me, it wasn't easy on me either. Being tied to her and Thomas so I could stand was not exactly a pleasure, no matter how much alcohol they fed me." Dace flinches a little when he laughs.

"Oh shut up, you big baby. You would have thought your whole body was broken. You were only a bit bruised, is all." Austin kisses him and he smiles. "Maybe a few broken bones, but none that couldn't be fixed," she says as he shakes his head.

"So how are you now?" I ask him.

"I'm good. Bones are healing, I have my girl back, and we both have new identities. We can live how we want to now," Dace says, gripping Austin's hand.

"I have a new one as well. Michael thinks I am long gone in a drunken stupor on a tropical island somewhere. He's just waiting for me to die of an overdose, I'm sure." I look down and back up at him. "He has officially won by the way. They have recounted the votes for the last time. Not all of the people believe in him, but enough did. He has made his acceptance speech and thanked everyone for helping him get through this tough time. He stood up there with all his admirers cheering him on like he's their chosen King." I stand back with a sigh. "So, now what? Are we going to run away or are we going to fight?" I ask as if I don't know his answer already.

Dace lies back with Austin at his side, his eyes wander the room before they land back at mine. "Running would be easy, and fighting is what fools do right?" I nod. "Do we still have a friend on the force?"

"Two actually now. Billy has recovered and is anxious to get back to work. Aaron is keeping his distance from Michael for now; he is acting the heartbroken brother perfectly. He's the only one that knows about you two."

"Good, so what do you want to do?" Dace asks me.

"We haven't accomplished what we set out to do when we first came back here yet. Our mother's killer is still alive and free to kill again."

Dace looks at Austin. "I still want that boot wearing fuck, and his king." Austin says.

"It's up to you, Dace. Whatever you decide, we are with you," I say, taking my brother's hand and gripping it tight.

"Okay then, I would say now, now it's time for us to create a new plan—a plan for *Dethroning a King*."

ABOUT THE AUTHOR

 @JenniferLorenDE

 https://www.jenniferloren.com

 https://www.facebook.com/JenniferLoren.Author

 http://www.youtube.com/user/LorenJennifer